Matt McGuire was born in Belfast and taught at the University of Glasgow before becoming an English lecturer at the University of Western Sydney, Australia. He has published widely on various aspects of contemporary literature and is currently writing a book on Scottish crime fiction. *Dark Dawn* is his debut novel.

DARK DAWN

Matt McGuire

corsair

Constable & Robinson Ltd
55–56 Russell Square
London WC1B 4HP
www.constablerobinson.com

First published in the UK by Corsair,
an imprint of Constable & Robinson, 2012

This paperback edition published in the UK by Corsair,
an imprint of Constable & Robinson, 2013

A copy of the British Library Cataloguing in Publication
Data is available from the British Library

ISBN 978-1-78033-870-5 (paperback)
ISBN 978-1-78033-226-0 (ebook)

Printed and bound in the UK

1 3 5 7 9 10 8 6 4 2

For Maree

ONE

Belfast, 2005

It was January. It was raining. The kid was dead.

DS O'Neill pulled on his cigarette as rain drummed on the makeshift roof of Laganview Apartments. They were only a shell: steel girders, concrete foundations. The latest luxury in waterfront living. The new Northern Ireland. Least that's what the billboard said.

Thirty yards away a couple of uniforms stood behind a band of yellow police tape. They were in a hurry. They always were. Coming off a nightshift, the last thing you wanted was to end up babysitting a stiff. It was solid peeler logic. Protect and serve, so long as you're not freezing your balls off in the rain for six hours.

O'Neill looked at the body. The arched back, the pale face, the empty eyes that stared down the river and out to sea. He took a drag of his cigarette. Yeah. There was no rush. The kid was dead. He was dead when they arrived. He'd still be dead in ten minutes.

It was eight o'clock, Monday morning. Half an hour earlier the call had come into Musgrave Street – suspicious death. A low buzz went round the station. You couldn't say it, but CID liked a body. Burglary, robbery, theft – sure, they had their moments. But a body? A body was the real deal. Sharpened the mind. Put an inch to your step. You spent weeks, months, wading through the same bullshit. The same bag-snatching, same robbery, same aggravated assault. A body though, a body was a headline-grabber. Even in the North. There was something about a body, something that couldn't be denied. In a world of 'no comment', of 'where's my lawyer', of half-truths and outright lies, a body was irrefutable. It was a fact. It couldn't be ignored.

O'Neill looked at the wall of grey cloud that pressed down upon Belfast. It was January, almost February. Christmas was a distant memory. There was still no sign of spring. A line of police tape sealed off the entrance to the building site. CRIME SCENE DO NOT CROSS. Behind it the two uniforms swayed from foot to foot. They wore black boots, dark trousers and high-vis jackets. Fluorescent yellow was cut in two by a belt holding a pair of bracelets and the standard issue Glock 19. At the gates to Laganview two armoured Land Rovers stood guard like a couple of bouncers. They were dirty white with heavy grilles across the windscreen. One of them was scarred down the side – charred from some 'community relations' work in the Ardoyne the previous week.

The apartments overlooked the River Lagan as it gathered pace before spilling its guts into Belfast Lough. Across the water, the morning rush-hour crawled along Oxford Street. People huddled in their cars listening to Radio Ulster, oblivious to the contorted figure that lay on the far side of the river.

Detective Sergeant John O'Neill was anything but oblivious. He was thirty-four, but looked closer to forty. Six years of shift-work would do that to you. Beneath the suit O'Neill wore a medal, the size of a twenty-pence piece. St Michael, the patron saint of peelers. He didn't believe in saints. Didn't believe in God either. Catherine had given it to him when he joined up and he thought, What the hell, might as well have someone watching your back. O'Neill was six foot with black hair, going grey at the side. Catherine, his wife, used to joke about George Clooney. He told her: 'Keep dreaming, love. It's as close to him as you're likely to get.'

That was a couple of years ago. When there were still jokes. Now there were lawyers – or at least, it was heading that way. Every smart-arse comment might end up costing O'Neill another couple of grand. They were 'on a break'. Catherine's words. It had been six months and still no one in the station knew. O'Neill was in a flat on the Stranmillis Road. Catherine had stayed in the house with Sarah, their five-year-old daughter. O'Neill had asked Jack Ward, the DI, what he knew about lawyers.

Expensive.

That's what he figured.

It might not come to that though. There was hope. There was Sarah to think about. She'd just started primary school at St Therese's. O'Neill saw her on weekends, when his shifts allowed. Divorced at thirty-six. Christ, O'Neill thought, you fairly fucked that up in a hurry.

He looked at the body next to the river. Six years with the Police Service of Northern Ireland. It wasn't the first time O'Neill had seen death. He'd seen it ooze out of people, a dark sickly red, as the lights slowly went out behind their eyes. He'd smelled it rotting, an old man on his sofa, six weeks before neighbours noticed the stink. He'd heard it gurgle and choke – a teenage joyrider who left a stolen car, doing seventy, via the front windscreen. At Laganview though it was the stillness. The perfect stillness. The river ran on, the rain poured down, the cars rolled by. The body, however – the body lay completely still. O'Neill kept waiting for the kid to blink, to get up and start rubbing his head. He'd look round, dazed, confused, and wonder what had happened. What was all the fuss about? O'Neill knew better though. The kid wouldn't sit up. Wouldn't rub his head. Wouldn't look round him. He'd lie there. Dead still. At least until someone did something about it.

Six years. O'Neill had seen things. You couldn't not see things, that was the job. When he signed up, he thought that's what he wanted. To see things. To be the guy that got the call. The guy that didn't walk away, that didn't look away, like everyone else. He looked at the body of the twisted teenager and thought to himself: Be careful what you wish for.

O'Neill took his time, working his way down a second cigarette. You never rushed a crime scene. He knew this. Knew it deep down, like a form of muscle memory. When he'd first stepped out of the car, his stride automatically slowed and his gestures had become deliberate, more measured. His eyes changed. He stopped looking at things and started to stare. He stared at objects. He stared at sightlines. He stared at people. Bystanders, witnesses, onlookers. O'Neill knew the nightmare stories. A detective not controlling his scene. Some uniform, three weeks out of Police College, picks up a knife – 'I've got something here.' Yes, you do, mate. It's

4

a 'Get Out of Jail Free Card' for some lucky bastard. Plus a month's paperwork and a ball-chewing for me. And Uniform wondered why CID didn't always like them.

O'Neill remembered a conversation with the DI, Jack Ward, three weeks after he first came over to CID. The shift was asking itself the usual question: was O'Neill just another monkey out of uniform, better suited to wrestling drunks and handing out parking tickets? Ward was ex-RUC. He was in his fifties and had earned his stripes during the Troubles: 25 years, 300 dead peelers. The numbers didn't lie.

A robbery had come in and O'Neill grabbed his coat. He needed to prove himself, show he was a worker, that he had what it took. He hadn't popped his cherry and was still chasing his first collar. Ward stood in the doorway, smiling.

'Detective O'Neill. A question for you. But only if you have time…'

'Sir?'

'Why don't they put blue lights on the cars in CID?'

O'Neill paused. The other DCs had been taking the piss since he arrived and it sounded like more of the same.

'Sir?'

'Why don't CID have blue lights, like everyone else?'

O'Neill didn't answer.

'I'll tell you,' Ward continued. 'Because … by the time *we* get the call, the emergency's over.'

The other DCs in the room, Kearney and Reid, laughed. The Charge of the Blue Light Brigade. That was what Ward called it.

'Chasing guys down streets. Rugby tackles. Rolling in the dirt. Jesus. You guys watch too much TV.' He looked round the room. 'We're the clean-up crew. We walk. We don't run. By the time they send for us, the party's always over. Our job's to find out who made the mess.'

Three weeks later, O'Neill was up to his elbows. He'd ten jobs open. Five assaults, three thefts and two robberies. Ward asked: 'What do you think'll happen as soon as you clear one of those?'

'I get another?'

'Bingo. Sisyphus, son. That's who you are.'

'Sissy who?'

Ward laughed as he walked away. 'Never worry. You just keep rolling that boulder. Shit. We might even make a detective out of you one of these days.'

O'Neill looked down at the lifeless body. Six years on and somewhere along the way, somewhere amid the sights and the smells, the interviews and the bullshit, the paperwork and the procedure, they *had* made a detective out of him. Of that much O'Neill was sure.

As he waited for DI Ward, O'Neill drew an aerial sketch of Laganview on his notepad. The site was a rectangle, 40 by 100 yards or so, hugging the bank of the river. Three apartment blocks filled what used to be the old Sirocco steelworks. Late to the party, Belfast was getting the same makeover that Glasgow, Newcastle and Liverpool got in the 1990s. Old factories were becoming apartment blocks. Disused dockyards were transformed into high-end lofts. It was a building epidemic. The Belfast skyline was dotted with cranes, swinging their arms over the city in a mass benediction. Progress meant property. The Cathedral

Quarter. The Titanic Quarter. The Gasworks. The Troubles were over. There was money to be made.

Laganview looked across the river towards the 50-foot high curves of the Waterfront Hall. Next door stood the Hilton Hotel and the white limestone of Belfast City Court House. The apartments rubbed shoulders with the Short Strand and the Markets, working-class areas, where rows of terrace houses formed a maze of side-streets and alleyways. During the Troubles they were a no-go area for police, a breeding ground for militant Republicans. Kerbstones were still painted green, white and gold. Gable ends featured 20-foot murals. Slogans in Irish. O'Neill imagined buyers walking round Laganview, looking down on the streets below. The salesman would tell them to focus on the view. Keep their eyes on the horizon. There was a lot of that going on these days.

O'Neill put his notebook away and stood under the corrugated iron roof. He pulled smoke into his lungs, the nicotine peeling back the lack of sleep from the night before. Jack Ward arrived and picked his way across the rubble. Ward was fifty-six, stocky, and wore a black trenchcoat. He was a good boss and trusted his troops to get on with things. Ward spoke slowly and was quiet and watchful. He gave the impression he'd seen it all before, that nothing would surprise him. The DI was eighteen months away from retirement, one of the few senior CID officers who had stayed on after the Peace Process. It was the release of all the prisoners that sparked the mass exodus. Ward remembered standing in Musgrave Street canteen, watching the TV. Men walked out of prison. A quick pump of the fist before ducking into waiting cars. Ward knew half of them by name. They'd spent years murdering peelers. He'd spent his career trying to put them behind bars. Now *they* were out. All of them. In the corner of the room Jackie Robinson, a DC of ten years, puked in a bin. Tony Callaghan, one of the other DIs, summed it up rather eloquently.

'Fuck this.'

Callaghan was gone within six months. It seemed like half the force had the same idea. Guys with fifteen, twenty years on them. All gone. Ward had stayed on though, holding his ground, keeping his counsel. Something in him couldn't walk. At least not yet.

Six years on, standing next to O'Neill, he pulled a packet of B&H from his jacket and lit one. Ward looked at the ground by their feet.

'Two fags? Christ. You're really drinking this one in.'

Ward was relaxed with his troops. Occasionally he sounded like an old schoolteacher; everyone still 'sir-ed' him, out of respect more than anything. The two detectives stared at the scene. Their eyes moved over objects, holding them for a moment, committing them to memory. O'Neill looked at the rain, then up at the dark, threatening sky.

'Reckon someone up there doesn't like us, sir?'

Ward laughed quietly. 'You only figuring that out now?'

Ward looked at the body in the grey tracksuit. He nodded, pointing his cigarette.

'You see? That's why I never go jogging.'

O'Neill smiled. Nothing came between a peeler and his attitude. He had learned that during his first week in CID. He glanced at the billboard where powerful up-lights illuminated a finished version of Laganview Apartments. The building was a glistening silver cube, all glass and mirrors.

'I don't know, sir. I could see you in one of these yuppie flats.'

Ward glanced sideways. 'On my salary, son? I wouldn't believe everything you heard in Police College.'

It had rained all morning and looked like it was on for the day. O'Neill imagined the waters rising over Belfast. A second Great Flood. Christ knew, the place could do with it.

'Take your time here,' Ward announced. 'I'm putting you up front on this one.'

O'Neill swallowed hard. He'd worked Suspicious Death before but only in a support role, never as Principal Investigator. PI meant calling the shots. Bodies were a big deal, even in Northern Ireland. There would be SOCOs, Forensics, the pathologist, not to mention the press and top brass, all breathing down his neck. When a body turned up, people wanted to know.

On the drive from Musgrave Street Ward had thought through his options before deciding to give O'Neill the case. O'Neill had been an Acting Sergeant for nine months and it would be his first major case as PI. It was a big call. Bob Townsend, the regular DS, was on secondment and due back next month. The Review Boards were coming up and Ward knew the Chief Inspector, Charles Wilson, wanted O'Neill out of CID and back in uniform. If the truth be told, Wilson wanted O'Neill gone altogether. Uniform would do though, for the time being. Wilson didn't like O'Neill. As a DC he'd made the fatal mistake of disagreeing with the Chief Inspector in front of people. It was two years ago and something pretty minor, but the Chief Inspector didn't forget. He reckoned O'Neill wasn't cut out for CID. He was wrong – Ward knew it. He'd watched O'Neill for three years. Sure, he was a bit rough round the edges and he made mistakes, but once he bit on to something, he didn't let go. O'Neill was the real thing. He was just enough of a stubborn arsehole to be a really good detective.

None of that mattered though. Not to Wilson. The Review Boards were next month and the Chief Inspector would make his move there. Being sent back to uniform would mark O'Neill out. He'd be damaged goods. Everyone would know it. His only hope was to have a big case under his belt, and they didn't come much bigger than a murder. If O'Neill could wrap Laganview up before the Review Boards, Wilson wouldn't be able to touch him.

The Chief Inspector was a new breed. Twenty-first-century police. A company man. An accountant. Happier in meetings, reading reports, compiling budgets. Flying off across the water to drink cups of coffee with other number-crunchers from the Met, Greater Manchester Police, Lothian and Borders. Don't ask him to solve a crime though. The last place you wanted Wilson was on a job, knocking on a door, interviewing a suspect.

Ward had watched over the last ten years as a slew of Wilsons came in and slowly took over the force. He knew one thing: they might wear a uniform, but they weren't peelers. They thought crime could be solved with spreadsheets and graphs, with statistics and pie charts. And when they opened their mouths they sounded more like politicians than cops.

They played the angles and made the right friends. They were never happier than when they were getting their mugs on TV. He'd seen a generation of Wilsons rise up the rank – at the same time as he was passed over.

'Next time, Jack. There's always next time.'

It was bullshit and Ward knew it. He was too old. His face didn't fit. He didn't speak the lingo. He would retire next year anyway, leave the force to Wilson and the rest of the bean-counters.

There was still O'Neill though. O'Neill was a peeler. A real peeler. On the drive over to Laganview, Ward had come up with an idea. What if he left O'Neill behind him. Make him the stone in Wilson's shoe. Always there. Niggling away. Ward had smiled at the thought. He knew it wasn't just about Wilson though. It wasn't just some personal vendetta. It was bigger than that. The North needed peelers like O'Neill. Now more than ever. It needed guys to get out there, to get involved, to get their hands dirty. Hiding in meetings, ducking behind spreadsheets... what did that ever get done?

Standing beside Ward, O'Neill studied the area round the body. The SOCOs were on their way with a tent. *Protect the integrity of the scene*. He remembered his Locard from Police College: the first rule of forensic science, every contact leaves a trace. O'Neill looked at the rain. Most of the forensics would have washed into the river and be halfway to Scotland by now. Maybe the rules didn't apply in Belfast.

O'Neill still hadn't gone near the body. When the SOCOs arrived they'd begin from the perimeter and work their way in, in ever-decreasing circles. They'd go slowly, patiently, following the golden rule which says there may be only one crime scene, but there are many ways to fuck it up.

The body was an IC1 male. Late teens, pale and skinny, with hollow cheeks and a shaved head. The most important question was, who was he? Ninety per cent of homicides were committed by someone who knew the victim. A neighbour, a friend, a relative. That was right. In a detective's litany of cynical thoughts, the nearest and dearest were never excluded from the list. Random attacks? Stranger danger? Ward was right. People watched too much TV. Start with his mates, call them killers, see who blinks. Find out who the victim was, you were halfway to finding out who killed him.

The kid's grey tracksuit was wet through. A 3-foot pool of red spread out from his head, mixing with a puddle of rainwater. They would wait for the pathologist, but it looked like a fatal head wound that finally turned the lights out.

O'Neill ran his eyes the length of the body. The legs were wrong. Twisted out of shape, like an Action Man tossed away by a child. Was he a jumper? O'Neill looked at the roof of the apartment block, 30 feet away. Not unless he was Jesse Owens.

No. This thing had 'punishment beating' written all over it. Sure, they'd been a bit over-enthusiastic with the bats, but it was a punishment beating nonetheless.

O'Neill rolled his eyes. Punishment beatings were a Grade-A nightmare. They were a paramilitary thing, a hangover from the Troubles, when Catholics and Protestants policed their own areas and handed out vigilante justice to drug dealers and joy-riders. A bullet through the knees. A couple of rounds with a baseball bat. One thing was sure, you didn't forget in a hurry. O'Neill thought about the ASBOs the PSNI gave out for the same thing. A curfew? In bed by ten? No wonder the kids laughed in their faces.

With a punishment beating the victim never pressed charges. There were never any witnesses. Victim dragged from a crowded bar? Folk were always in the toilet. Peelers joked that Belfast pubs had some of the largest toilets in the world. Entire bars had been known to all go for a piss at exactly the same time. What were the odds of that?

No one pressed charges and after a while, a punishment beating went away. A few forms, a few questions, that was it. A murder inquiry though, a murder inquiry had legs. It always went the distance.

If all men were created equal, all victims certainly weren't. You'd hear people:

'He deserved what he got.'

'Fucking wee hood.'

'He had it coming to him.'

O'Neill peered into the black river as it flowed under Queen's Bridge and out into Belfast Lough. Anything tossed in – a bat, say – would be long gone. He knew the stats. PSNI solved three out of four murders. Northern Ireland hospitals had treated over 300 punishment beatings last year. The cops hadn't made an arrest for a single one.

O'Neill felt Ward standing beside him.

Up front on *this* one?

He looked at the rain, pulling out another cigarette. There was no doubt about it: someone up there *didn't* like him. At least it was one thing he could be sure of.

TWO

Marty and Petesy were hoods.

Hoods because they wore tracksuits. Because they stood on street corners and stared down traffic. Because they hung outside off licences, drinking Buckfast and White Lightning. Because they were fifteen and hadn't been to school for two years. They liked it that way. So did the school. Hoods because security guards followed them round shops. Because every second word was 'fuck' or 'cunt'. Because they loved getting off their faces. Because they liked happy hardcore. Because they stole cars. Because they were joy-riders. Because they were drug dealers. Because they had shaved heads, black eyes and baseball caps. Because they didn't give a fuck, because what the fuck are you looking at, because I'll knock your fucking ballicks in. They were hoods.

It was half ten on Monday morning. The boys had been busy. They hunkered behind a large bin in an entry off High Street. The alley smelled of piss and rotting food. Marty and Petesy sucked in air, trying to get their breath back.

'You're a mad bastard,' Petesy said. Marty raised his eyebrows, taking the compliment and smiling.

'The guard was a fat cunt. He couldn't catch a fucking cold. Mind you, he fairly got a hold of you. Fuck me, Petesy. My ma's quicker than you are.'

'Fuck away off,' Petesy said. 'You were running before we were even in the door.'

Marty had always been quick. When he was selected for the Belfast U-12s the coach said he was greased lightning, one of the quickest things he'd even seen on a football pitch.

'No flies on you, Martin Toner.'

Marty was kicked off the team three weeks later. Fighting. He'd skinned the full-back, some brick shithouse from Ballymacarrett, who'd brought him down. Marty got up and whacked him. It was only training, but so fuck, what were you going to do. There were no flies on Marty.

That morning the security guard had grabbed Petesy, and Marty had had to go back for him. Now he pulled off his old jersey and put on the white Kappa top, courtesy of the morning's outing. Marty adopted a mock melodic voice, like he was announcing the football results.

'Martin Toner one – JJB Sports nil.'

JJBs was one of the only shops in Belfast that didn't have foreigners working as security guards. Lithuanians. Poles. You didn't fuck with *them*.

'Hard to make a living these days,' Marty had said after his first and last encounter with the latest addition to the Northern Irish workforce.

Before they showed up, it was a piece of piss. The security men were all locals. Guys that didn't give a shit. They stood round all day, chatting up sixteen-year-old shop assistants. They'd chase you round the corner and give up. The Polish guys, the Lithuanians, they were different. Chase you for miles. Like it was personal. Like it was their shop or something.

15

'It's fucked up,' Marty said, after his one experience with a Lithuanian security guard. He'd run full pelt the whole way down Donegal Place, past the *Belfast Telegraph*, all the way down York Street.

'I was near in Carrickfergus before he stopped. I mean, what the fuck does he care?'

'No flies on those Poles,' Petesy joked.

In the entry off High Street, Marty stroked the sleeve of his new top. He leaned off the wall, not wanting to get it dirty. Petesy laughed.

'I thought I was fucked when your man had me. Next thing, I turn round and he's got the fucking Tasmanian Devil on his back.'

Marty held up his fists, kissing the right then the left.

'Told you. I taught Muhammad Ali everything he knew.'

'That's what your ma said.'

'Away and fuck yourself. You'd be in the back of a peeler wagon right now if it wasn't for me. Who's the one with a new top? Meanwhile you're walking round looking like Stig of the Dump.'

'Up your hole. You bolted before we were even inside the shop.'

Marty peeked round the bin and down the entry. There was no sign of anyone. He pulled out a packet of Regal and lit one. He took a drag and exhaled, clicking out three neat smoke-rings. He then passed the cigarette to Petesy.

'Here. Have a smoke and dry your eyes.'

Petesy took the cigarette between his thumb and forefinger. His cheeks hollowed as he took a draw. One of his cousins had taught him how to smoke when he was eleven but he could never blow smoke-rings like Marty.

Marty looked at his new top. 'That Cara's definitely going to let me ride her when she sees this.'

'Wise up to yourself. You've no chance.'

'That not what your ma said.'

Petesy went quiet. He'd lived with his granny for three years since his mother moved to Derry with a guy she'd met one Saturday night at the GAA club in Andy Town. He was about to hand the fag back but hesitated and took another long drag. Marty received the butt, his voice going up an octave.

'What the fuck am I supposed to do with this?'

Petesy smiled, pleased to get his own back. Marty took the last drag and flicked the butt off the wall. A shower of red ash cascaded to the wet ground.

Petesy remembered him doing the same thing to Brendy McIlroy. 'Mackers', everyone called him. He was two years older than them and had three big brothers. He had been picking on Petesy, slagging him off, saying his ma had run off with the first bit of dick she got her hands on. After a minute of ignoring him, Petesy told him to go fuck himself. It was what Mackers wanted. He announced, John Wayne-style, he was going to finish his can of Harp, then come over and beat the fuck out of Petesy. Marty sat there, not saying anything. Then he took the final drag from his cigarette and flicked it in Mackers' face. They went for each other and Petesy piled on. Some old boy pulled them apart, threatening to call the peelers. That was Marty though. He didn't give a fuck.

Hiding in the entry of High Street, Marty stroked his new top and thought about Cara. She was a wee ride. He was going to take her somewhere with the money they'd made from dealing the week before.

'Has your cousin come through with more gear yet?' he asked.

'He said to come up to the Ardoyne and see him tomorrow.'

'Nice one,' Marty said.

THREE

Joe Lynch sat on the black leather sofa and waited.

The receptionist was slim, early thirties. She had looked at him over the top of her glasses, saying Dr Burton would be right with him. Lynch asked how long the appointment was. She told him half an hour.

Nothing about the plush reception suggested a psychologist's office. Lynch had imagined *One Flew Over the Cuckoo's Nest*. Formica floors, sudden outbursts, occasional drooling. Instead it was burgundy carpets, dark mahogany and abstract painting.

He chided himself. This was a mistake. This was what you got for going to the doctor's – an appointment with a shrink. All he'd wanted were a few pills, just to help him sleep. He didn't need his head examined. A few nights' kip, he'd be right as rain. Instead he got a week's worth of tablets and an appointment with Sigmund Freud here.

Lynch was fine, when he'd just come out of prison. He'd gone to London. Needed to get away from Belfast. All the old contacts, the familiar faces, the knowing looks. He'd stayed almost two years, trying to make a life for himself, working in bars, doing shift-work in kitchens. One day, he just woke up and realized, enough was enough. He couldn't do it any more. The constant lying, making things up, taking shit from middle managers, baby Hitlers he could have dropped in half a second. There was nothing else to do. He had to go back.

It was coming home when the sleep problem started. Lynch tried to laugh it off at first, joking about the Northern Irish air – too frigging fresh. He told himself to harden up. He'd done interrogations, solitary confinement, twenty-four-hour lock-down. He could do a few all-nighters. After three months he realized why they used sleep deprivation as a torture technique. He felt like a ghost, as if he only partially existed. Dr MacSorley had suggested the psychologist. It might help to talk. Lynch didn't think so, but made a deal. It seemed to be all the rage these days: negotiation, compromise, agreements. He'd see the psychologist, in return for a prescription. MacSorley was in his sixties, an old-school doctor. He gave him a week's worth of tablets.

'Come back after the appointment and I'll give you next week's.' He smiled. 'Just to keep you honest Joe.'

MacSorley had been around the block a few times and it was only this that made Lynch agree to the deal.

Dr Burton's office was on the fifteenth floor of a glass tower-block on Bedford Street. Out the window Lynch saw the green copper dome of Belfast City Hall. After ninety years, the shining white limestone had faded to grey. Daily life had taken its toll and the architect's allusions to civic virtue were now no more than a vague memory. In the gardens, the Belfast wheel arced upwards, lifting spectators above the roofline of the City Hall. From its height, tourists gazed out at the hills that surrounded Belfast. The mountains themselves, looking down on the city, like disapproving adults on their recalcitrant offspring. Lynch looked towards the waters of Belfast Lough and the dark green slopes of the Cavehill in the distance. The colours were muted, depressed by the dark grey sky and the low January light.

As he waited, Lynch reminded himself he wasn't a fruitcake. It was simple. He just couldn't sleep.

A door opened and Dr Burton walked into reception. He wore a brown suit and had a swarthy complexion. He was in his fifties and spoke in a low, confident voice.

'Joe Lynch? Come on in.'

The room continued the theme of comfortable opulence that had begun in the reception area. A wide oak desk and a high-backed chair sat in front of a row of large windows. Along the wall a beige sofa and two chairs huddled round a rectangular coffee-table. Burton motioned to the chairs.

'So. What have you come to see me about?'

'I'm not sleeping.'

'Why aren't you sleeping?'

Joe paused. He hadn't thought they'd get right into it. He'd imagined some chit-chat. A warm-up or something. He looked round the room, raising his eyebrows.

'Must be some money in this psychology business.'

'I do all right.'

'How come you aren't in a hospital?'

'Private clients.'

'What does a man charge for that these days?'

'One hundred pounds an hour.'

Lynch hadn't thought Burton would tell him.

'I must be in the wrong line of work.'

'What line of work *are* you in, Joe?'

Silence.

Fifteen floors up. The traffic was quiet on the road below. Cars hummed past, providing a low background music. Joe knew what was going on. The short, staccato answers. They were to encourage him to speak. Make the patient do the running.

'Why can't you sleep, Joe?'

'You tell me, Doc.'

'That's not how it works.'

Silence.

Burton stopped speaking. He wasn't going to chase Lynch. If someone wouldn't meet you halfway, he knew there was no point.

The silence hung in the air for ten seconds, then twenty. It was a stand-off, neither man wishing to blink. After a minute Lynch spoke.

'So what do you know about me, Doc?'

'Nothing.'

'MacSorley must have sent a file.'

'No.'

'How come?'

'Works better this way.'

'So you're telling me you have nothing?'

'Joe Lynch. Monday. Eleven o'clock.'

For a moment Lynch imagined himself as a blank page. No marks. No scars. Free to be whatever he wanted. Free to …

In the Maze they had tried to use psychologists. Rumour had it the room was bugged and there was someone from Special Branch taking notes next door.

Burton continued. 'Why are you here, Joe?'

'MacSorley made me come.'

22

'*Made* you come? What are you, six years old?'

'I'm not sleeping.'

'You're not sleeping.'

'I wanted a prescription. It came with strings.'

'You could have gotten sleeping pills from anywhere. They're not exactly hard to come by.'

Lynch looked at the dark wooden bookcase along the wall. *The Effect of Trauma. The Invisible Injury. The Psychology of Conflict.*

'I haven't suffered a trauma.'

'I never said you had.'

'That's what you do though. Isn't it?'

'Among other things.'

'Do you see peelers?'

'None of your business.'

'Soldiers?'

Silence.

'Not much of a talker, Doc. I thought that is what this was all about. Talking. Feelings.'

Burton turned it back on him.

'How *do* you feel, Joe?'

Lynch paused, turning his gaze inwards. He groped around, trying to get hold of something. He rummaged in the dark. He was tired. No, exhausted. More than that though, he had no idea how he felt. There was a kind of emptiness. A hunger. It was as if he had lost something, but he couldn't remember what it was.

Burton waited, watching Lynch's eyes search the empty space in front of him.

Lynch snapped back to the room, remembering where he was. He stood up and walked to the window, looking down on the street. A woman rushed through the rain. A couple huddled under an umbrella. A homeless man sheltered in the doorway of the Ulster Hall. The fifteenth floor was high. It gave a sense of perspective, made things seem smaller, less difficult somehow. Lynch looked out over Belfast, as it sprawled into the distance.

'Why are you—'

'Where do you live, Doc?'

Burton raised his eyebrows.

'OK then. What car do you drive?'

'Audi.'

'That's my point.'

'That's your point,' Burton repeated sarcastically.

'The car. The house. The suburbs. Stranmillis. Dunmurray. The leafy streets, the grammar schools, the university degrees. You took the tests, passed the exams. Dinner parties, drinks with friends. The wife. The kids.' Lynch was gathering momentum. 'The books, the office, the view. My point is: what the fuck could you possibly know about me? About where I come from. About what I've seen. About what I've done.'

Lynch took a breath, letting his words hang in the air between them.

'A hundred pounds an hour. Listening to a bunch of rich pricks. Their colleagues don't respect them, their kids won't talk to them, their wives won't fuck them. And when you get bored with that, you go for a bit of Troubles tourism, a wee holiday in someone else's misery. A bit of gritty realism, like reading a book about it. And all from the safety of the fifteenth floor. It's cosy cushions and pretentious paintings by cunts that can't draw to save themselves.'

Lynch stared at Burton. The doctor held his gaze, allowing the silence to hang between them. Burton waited. He wasn't intimidated.

'Impressive, Joe.' His voice was calm, almost monotone. Lynch had become more animated the more he tried to dismiss Burton and everything he stood for.

'Were you practising that on the way over? The self-righteous indignation. Gives you an edge, I'll bet. A bit of purchase. I've known you for twenty minutes and you're right. What the fuck could I possibly know? About you. About where you've been. What you've seen. What you've done.'

The doctor paused.

'I'll tell you what though, Joe. It still doesn't answer the question: why can't you sleep?'

Lynch paused, knowing he hadn't thrown Burton off and that they were back where they started.

'Thousands of people don't sleep.'

'We're not talking about thousands. We're talking about you.'

Joe glanced at the clock on the wall. 11.25. Burton saw the look and knew they were coming to the end of the session.

'OK. Since you don't want to tell me anything, Joe, I'll try to tell you something. What could I know? What could I possibly know about you? About your world? Let me give it a shot.'

Lynch held the psychologist's eyes.

'You're a Catholic. Working-class. Did well at school. Didn't get on with the teachers though. Authority, you see. Bit too much to say for himself, our Joe. Left school early. Tried to get work. Late seventies. Not a lot of that going. Even less for a Catholic in Belfast. The dice were stacked. The courts. The police. Housing. Jobs. It pissed you off. But you could take it. Discipline, you see. Not easily got to. Sure there was the harassment, the taunting, the abuse. The stop and search. Where you from? Where you going? The Brits. The RUC. Not a bother. Sure, they're cunts. But you're Joe Lynch. It doesn't go away though. Day after day, week after week, month after month. Drip ... drip ... drip ... Then it happens. Or rather *something* happens. You take a hiding. The police kick your door in. They intern your brother. Your da. Your uncle maybe. Some off-duty soldiers have a go, want to fuck up a Fenian. They put you against a wall, put a gun in your mouth ...'

Lynch's gaze sharpened and began boring into Burton.

'... was that it, Joe? They put you against a wall? Put a gun in your mouth?'

Burton paused, letting the memory come washing back up from wherever Lynch had buried it.

'You can probably feel it now – as if it was yesterday. The metal against your teeth. The oily taste in your mouth. Your palms are sweating, just thinking about it.'

Lynch's heart thundered in his chest. His hand was still though. It had always been that way. He stared at the man opposite.

'You've read the books, Joe. Religion, history, politics. All the talk. All the theories. Theories are all well and good, until they kick in your front door one night. Until they put you up

26

against a wall. Going to blow your fucking Fenian head off. None of the theories mention the taste though, right? That cold steel. The metal. The oil.'

Burton stopped and took a breath.

'They backed you into a corner. What were you going to do? Sit there and take it? No, not you. Not our Joe. People round here have been sitting taking it for years. Look where that's got them.'

Lynch stared at Burton, wondering where he was going to go next. Burton stopped talking, letting the atmosphere cool for a few seconds. He looked away, breaking eye-contact, defusing the tension. Slowly, Lynch's pulse began to calm.

'That was then, Joe. This is now. Things have changed – or so they tell us. Agreements have been signed. The war is over. Decommissioning? Decommission a gun, sure. But how do you decommission someone's head? You see, you're out there, Joe. You're still out there. You want to know if it's possible to get back. You're not even sure what getting back would look like.'

Dr Burton stopped talking. The two men sat in silence. Lynch looked out the window. The drizzle was thickening, turning to proper rain. He'd get wet on the way home.

'Break Free,' Joe said.

'Sorry?'

'The taste. I looked it up. Break Free oil. It's gun cleaner.'

Lynch looked past Burton and out over the grey skyline of Belfast. The room was quiet. Burton waited for the other man to speak.

Lynch looked up at the clock. 'Eleven-thirty. Time's up.'

He stood up and walked out of the office, leaving Burton on his own, staring out over the rooftops of the city.

FOUR

By one o'clock O'Neill and Ward were in the car and about to head back to Musgrave Street. The site foreman and the Polish worker who had discovered the body were already there, waiting to be interviewed.

O'Neill thought about Laganview. With a murder, the scene was everything. You wanted to know why the body was there. How it got there. Was this the crime scene or the deposition site? If there was a league-table of crime scenes, Laganview would languish somewhere near the bottom. It was an enclosed piece of ground. There were no passers-by, no witnesses. You wanted a house on some leafy street. A house was top of the table. An enclosed space with tons of forensics. Nosy neighbours, a few curtain-twitchers. A house did half the job for you. It asked its own questions. Did the murderer know the victim? Did he force entry? What did he touch?

It had been four hours and O'Neill still didn't have a positive ID on the body. Already though, it had become 'his' body. The kid's pockets were empty. No wallet, no keys, no money. O'Neill imagined a robbery gone wrong. Some hood, doing a bit of dealing, gets jumped by a couple of junkies.

There were two CCTV cameras at Laganview, both outside the fence and well away from the body. Both had been vandalized the week before and hadn't been fixed. It was convenient.

Four Scenes of Crime Officers were present, combing over things at a snail's pace. The white overalls, facemasks and gloves gave Laganview a surreal air – part moon landing, part nuclear clean-up. O'Neill wanted soil samples, footprint casts, cigarette ends. On his sketch of the site he'd marked out the position of the body, possible entrance points and sightlines to all the buildings across the river.

With Ward in the passenger seat he steered the unmarked Mondeo past a billboard advertising Spender Properties. They were the development company on Laganview. In four hours neither of the armoured Land Rovers had moved. At the back of one stood a female uniform, her hat pulled low over her eyes.

The officer turned her head and looked at the car. O'Neill did a double take. The cheekbones, the blue eyes, the short ponytail. It was Sam Jennings. They'd been at Police College together. They had got on well. He had only been seeing Catherine for two months. After passing out, Sam was sent to Dungannon. O'Neill went to North Belfast and hadn't seen her since.

The jury was still out on female peelers. Some reckoned they were a liability. Good in the office. Good at typing, consoling victims, that kind of stuff. The famous Musgrave Street story was Carol Smith. She was a female uniform attending a call off the Cregagh Road, in East Belfast. Her partner ended up inside the house getting the shit beaten out of him by two guys. Back-up arrived to find her standing outside, pointing at the door, shouting: 'He's in there!' Since then new recruits, men and women, were all Carols, at least until they proved themselves otherwise.

The last O'Neill heard, Sam had got into a fight in Dungannon one Saturday night. Two of her shift were arresting a guy for Drunk and Disorderly when his three mates piled in to try and liberate him. Sam waded in, getting a black eye and a fractured cheekbone for her trouble. They kept hold of the guy and got his mates a couple of days later from the CCTV. They were all sent down.

From the back of the Land Rover Sam locked eyes on O'Neill in the Mondeo. She'd heard he had gone to the dark side and ditched his uniform. Jennings had her street face on – mouth set, eyes fixed. She gave nothing away. O'Neill remembered from Police College, Sam had her stare down long before she ever put on a uniform. Almost unnoticeably she flicked her head back, acknowledging O'Neill with the slightest of gestures. O'Neill nodded back, edging the Mondeo between the Land Rovers.

His mind snapped back to the kid. It was his first body. He'd heard about detectives who had ended up with bodies hanging over them for years. People spoke about being followed. Every dead end in every case became an accusation, like someone picking open an old wound. Cops told themselves it was only a job, that you couldn't take it personally. That was the theory anyway.

Outside the car, the rain showed no signs of letting up. Two white vans, *UTV Live* and *BBC Northern Ireland*, were parked along the road. Presenters stood under umbrellas, speaking into cameras. 'Reporting live from the scene ...' O'Neill wondered what they were saying. If the peelers knew nothing, what could the TV know? Still, it never seemed to stop them.

The Mondeo waited for a break in the traffic.

'You're pretty quiet there, Detective,' Ward said.

O'Neill sighed. 'I've got a bad feeling about this one, sir.'

'You're just hungry,' Ward said, deadpan.

'I'm serious, sir.'

'You've got bad feelings about everything.'

'Have you seen the cases I've been pulling lately? I mean, whatever happened to karma?'

'Don't know her. She sounds nice though.'

'You've seen the job. You know what I'm talking about, sir.'

'Listen, Boy George, just keep your eyes on the road. I've seen a hell of a lot worse in my time.'

Ward didn't let on, but he knew what the younger detective meant. The more time he'd been at Laganview the more he saw its potential to bury O'Neill. Walking round the site, he had begun to wonder if he hadn't saved Wilson the hassle and written O'Neill's ticket back to uniform himself.

Across the road, a 20-foot mural loomed over the car. The red hand of Ulster hung in front of them like a giant stop sign. It was two storeys high and filled the gable end of a council house.

O'Neill squinted at the blood-red hand, thinking about his da and the story he always told when he was half-cut. The red hand was on the coat-of-arms for the O'Neills, who'd been the ancient Kings of Ulster.

'Let me tell you something, son. We are the descendants ... (hiccup) ... the red hand. That's us. That's ours. At least it was, before these bastards stole it.'

31

Apparently there'd been a contest for the kingship of Ulster. A boat race. The first man to touch Irish soil would claim the place. When they were all 20 yards from shore, one of the O'Neills cut off his right hand and threw it on to land to claim the kingship of Ulster.

It was a family cliché, rolled out every time his da was blitzed and got sentimental. As a boy O'Neill had thought about the story. Cutting off your hand. It was clever, but also desperate, reeking of something fanatical. 'Remember that, son,' his da would slur. 'We mean something. Do you know what I'm talking about? Are you listening to me?' By the time he was ten O'Neill felt like he'd heard it a million times.

'Hey. Sleeping beauty,' Ward interrupted. There was a break in the traffic. 'Let's go then.'

O'Neill slipped it into first and pulled out on to the road, turning towards the station.

Musgrave Street was more military barracks than police station. Nestled in the city centre, its perimeter wall was three feet thick, made of reinforced concrete, and topped with a high fence of corrugated iron. Bomb-proof. Mortar-proof. You could drive a tank at it and the place wouldn't flinch.

The station stood 500 yards from High Street, which covered the old River Farset as it rumbled, unnoticed, below the feet of Belfast shoppers. A 113-foot gothic tower pierced the dark grey sky. Built on slob land, the Albert clock had a four-degree lean, like the ghost of a drunken sailor, looking for one of the hoors who used to ply their trade in the shadow of the clock.

At Musgrave Street O'Neill and Ward sat in the navy Mondeo, waiting for the gates to open. Inside they parked alongside a white Land Rover. It was adorned with a blue and yellow check band and the Crimestoppers phone number. The side of the Land Rover had several dents and a splash of red paint.

Doris was on reception as the detectives entered the main building. She was in her fifties, with short blonde hair. Civilian support staff, Doris had been at the station longer than anyone, including the Chief Inspector. Her husband was RUC, a Reservist who'd been shot in the late seventies. He'd survived the bullet, only to go down with cancer a few years later. There was something very Irish about it. Ward had introduced O'Neill to Doris when he first joined CID.

'Most important person in the station. Piss off the Chief Inspector, but you'd better not piss off this woman. There's nothing goes on round here that she doesn't know about.'

Doris told O'Neill not to believe everything he heard. And especially not if it came out of the DI's mouth.

Doris spoke up as the two men walked past. 'DS O'Neill. The Chief Inspector called down.'

O'Neill and Ward stopped.

'Wanted me to send you up as soon as you came in.'

O'Neill looked at the DI who shrugged his shoulders. Wilson had called Ward that morning, wanting a report on the scene and to know who the PI was. The DI had cursed as he hung up, harking after the days when you were left to do your job in peace.

'How'd he sound?' O'Neill asked.

'The usual.'

O'Neill wasn't convinced. He knew Wilson didn't like him and would want to ride him hard over the body. Try and catch him out. The Review Boards were coming up next month and he didn't want to have to answer questions about why he still didn't have anyone in custody for Laganview.

The Chief Inspector's office was on the third floor, nestled among the rest of Senior Management of B Division. The general consensus was, the less folk on the third floor knew about you, the better. There was an invisible divide running through Musgrave Street. First floor was uniform. The second was CID. The third was management. Each floor thought they were God's own and harboured suspicions about the ability and integrity of the other two. The third was the worst though. Politicians dressed as peelers. When the shit hits the fan, you made sure you weren't in the room. The third floor would hang you out to dry as soon as look at you.

The Chief Inspector was writing behind his large oak desk when O'Neill knocked and was summoned. Wilson's office was the same size as CID, which housed six desks. The Chief Inspector was slim and neatly dressed. He wore a shirt and tie, his shoulder-boards showing three silver diamonds denoting his rank. He didn't look up when O'Neill entered, but continued writing. O'Neill made to speak, only for Wilson to hold up a finger and cut him off.

O'Neill did a sweep of the room. There were pictures on the walls. Pencil sketches of Belfast: two giant cranes from the shipyard, an old-fashioned cinema, a tram at Carlisle Circus. Wilson's office was neat and well-ordered. If it wasn't for the uniform, you'd have no idea you were in a police station. The view from the third floor, O'Neill mused to himself. Peace and quiet. Law and order.

Wilson signed his name and looked up.

'DS O'Neill. Take a seat.' He gestured to a chair in front of his desk. 'How's CID?'

'Fine, sir.'

'So I've heard.'

O'Neill didn't flinch, but his mind instinctively sped up. What had Wilson heard? Who'd he heard it from? He started going through the guys on his shift.

'Ward tells me you are the PI on Laganview. It's a big job. You'd better be up to it.'

O'Neill knew he was being simultaneously challenged and doubted.

'So fill me in then, *Detective*.' Wilson offered the last word like an accusation.

O'Neill couldn't believe he wanted a progress report. The case wasn't four hours old. He wanted to tell Wilson to go fuck himself but he knew the game, knew he needed to put on a show, let Wilson see he had a handle on things. He spoke quickly, breaking down the facts – the scene, the state of the victim, the lack of ID, lack of weapon, lack of witnesses …

'There's a lot lacking here,' Wilson said, implying these circumstances were somehow a personal reflection on O'Neill.

O'Neill ignored it, continuing with the facts. Wilson interrupted him when he mentioned a possible punishment beating.

'Hold on. You need to calm yourself down there, Detective. We need to tread very carefully here.'

'Sir?'

'Punishment beating? We don't need the press getting hold of that kind of language. And we don't need them getting it from us.'

'With respect, that's what it looks like. Sir.'

'Punishment beatings mean paramilitaries. We're supposed to be past all that. It's too political. We need to catch who did this, but there are things here that don't need to be said out loud.'

That was Wilson. The consummate politician. O'Neill knew what he was getting at but it didn't mean he had to like it. Instinctively he pushed back.

'It looks like a punishment beating. *Sir.*' The mark of deference came out like a swear word.

'I don't care what it looks like, O'Neill. The Peace Agreement was signed eight years ago. We're trying to return this country to a state of normality. Punishment beatings, paramilitaries. They're a thing of the past. They're gone.'

'Well, someone forgot to tell that kid down at Laganview.'

Wilson's face reddened.

'This is not about Laganview. It's more than that. It's about money, investment. America. The European Union. The less we hear about punishment beatings, the better. What do you think would happen if people start getting cold feet? Investors pull the plug. Then we're all in the shit.'

O'Neill wondered when exactly it was that a dead body ceased to be important in its own right. It was Belfast though. Nothing was ever simply what it was.

Wilson pulled back, realizing he had strayed from the topic.

'Don't get me wrong – we need to catch whoever did this. We just need to go about it in the right way.'

O'Neill knew he should let it go. But ...

'On hospital numbers we had almost three hundred punishment beatings last year. Two-fifty the year before that. It doesn't sound as if everything's over, as if it's all behind us.'

'I don't need a statistics lesson from you, Detective.' Wilson glared at O'Neill. 'But if you like though, we can start drilling down into your own stats. Maybe begin with your clearance rate, eh?'

O'Neill knew he'd gone too far. Wilson had made his threat. It was subtle, but there nonetheless.

'This is *not* just another body, whether we want it to be or not. And we're not just a police force. There's history to consider.'

History again, O'Neill thought. For years history had been kicking in doors, shitting on people, giving folk reasons, putting guns in their hands. The North had had too much history. O'Neill remembered the TV when Tony Blair had flown in for the peace talks. He met the press, grinning: 'I can feel the hand of history on our shoulders…' O'Neill wondered who had been grinning the night before, as they stood over the body of a dead teenager on the bank of the River Lagan.

DI Ward waited for O'Neill in CID. Paul Kearney, one of the other DCs, sat typing at his desk. It was O'Neill's case, but Ward wanted to help out with the interviews.

Kearney spoke when O'Neill entered.

'What did the big cheese want?'

'Wants to fast-track me. Make me a DI. He says the current one isn't up to much.'

Ward smiled in the corner of the room. He knew O'Neill was giving Kearney the brush-off.

'*Detective Inspector* John O'Neill,' Ward piped back. 'God help us all.'

O'Neill sat at his desk and switched on his computer.

'Your wife called while you were upstairs,' Kearney said.

'Oh yeah?' he replied casually. 'What did she want?'

'Said she wants a real man. Someone who can get the job done in the bedroom.'

Ward watched O'Neill who refused to take the bait. Kearney kept running.

'If you need some help there, mate, just let me know.'

O'Neill didn't look up from the computer screen.

'Some smelly culchie from Ballymena? A gut like yours? A bit too *much* of a real man, I'd say. Still, I'll put a word in for you. See if she feels like doing some charity work.'

O'Neill's mind started racing. Why was Catherine calling? Was something wrong with Sarah? Had she had an accident at school? No, there'd be a message if something had happened. It had been six months and no one at Musgrave Street knew. Maybe this was her coming round. Asking him back. He'd get to see Sarah every day. She would be six in April. He was supposed to see her at weekends but with the shifts it was more like every second one. Even then, he was often coming off nights and ended up falling asleep on the sofa. Sarah watched cartoons and didn't bother him. She was happy, just hanging out with her daddy.

While O'Neill had been upstairs, Ward had got Kearney to run background checks on the site foreman and the Polish worker. He looked at the print-out again.

'These guys are in rooms three and four. The foreman is Tony Burke. Fifty-two. Lives off the Ravenhill Road. He had some connections back in the late eighties. Brother did ten years for membership of a terrorist organization, possession of a firearm, intimidation.'

'Was Burke involved?' O'Neill asked, using the local word that covered a multitude of sins.

'Don't know. He might have only drunk in a few bars, whispered in a few ears. Could be more. He didn't do any time though. Two arrests for assault. Drunken brawls by the looks of it. In both cases the charges were dropped. One of them was outside the Crown in 1988. Fella suffered a broken nose, broken jaw and three cracked ribs. The victim told the police he slipped and bumped himself on the kerb.'

'Sounds like a nice guy,' O'Neill said.

'Yeah. Proper choirboy. I'll tell you better than that. Burke's son?' Ward never forgot a name.

'Who?'

'Remember the break-ins on the Ravenhill last year?'

'The two junkies?'

'That's right. Jerome Burke was one of them. It's his son.'

'Whatever happened to Jerome?'

'He's in Maghaberry, doing three years.'

O'Neill and Ward agreed to start with the labourer, before having a shot at Burke.

Victor Puslawski was in his thirties, but looked older. His face was like a piece of leather. Fifteen winters on a building site would do that to you. In the last four years he had lived in Birmingham, Hull and now Belfast. There were thousands of Eastern Europeans in Northern Ireland working as builders, cleaners, security men. Anything they could turn a bit of money at. O'Neill had read a story in the paper the week before about a fight in Craigavon. Some local lads had jumped this Lithuanian as he was walking home from work. They gave him a hiding. An hour later Ivan came back with one of his mates and put the four of them in hospital.

Puslawski was nonplussed, matter of fact. You wouldn't think he had come across a body that morning. It was the same attitude you saw from the State Pathologist standing over a corpse. Another day, another dollar. O'Neill figured this wasn't the first body Puslawski had seen.

It was true.

'I see my grandmother, my grandfather, my father. People die. You want me be sad for some boy I never know? How long you keep me here?'

O'Neill stared at him. 'You're here until we say so. Have you got that?'

A silence fell as the two men glared at each other.

'Now tell us what happened this morning.'

'Nothing. I see body. I tell foreman. I go back to work.'

'You didn't think he might still be alive?'

'No. He is dead. I know. Look, how long you keep me here? I get paid to build apartment. Not answer question.'

O'Neill told him the site had been closed. There would be no work for anyone that day.

'Great. No one work, no one get paid.'

They questioned Burke afterwards. The foreman leaned back in his chair. Smug, self-assured. He'd played the game before, several times, by the looks of it. O'Neill kept it light, getting Burke to walk him through the morning.

40

He'd arrived at seven to open up the site. The workers dribbled in to start at seven-thirty. Just before eight one of the Poles came back to the office, told him someone was dead. Burke thought it was someone from the site. He went to have a look. Then called 999. By the time he'd got there, a crowd of workers had gathered – mostly local lads. The Poles had taken a quick look and gone back to work. That was what they were like.

'Tell me about Puslawski.'

'Not much to tell. Never misses a day – but then none of them do. He's never late. None of them are. Doesn't say much.'

'How many Poles do you have on the site?'

'Forty. We're about half and half, local lads and foreigners. I'll tell you what though. If we had more of them, we'd get the thing finished in half the time.'

'What about CCTV?'

'The cameras? Kids broke them a couple of weeks ago. We're still waiting on Securitas coming out to replace them.'

'Convenient.'

'They were reported two weeks ago.'

So far Ward hadn't spoken in either interview. He interrupted O'Neill now though.

'How's your Michael these days, Charlie?'

Burke went silent, his face hardening at his brother's name. He had seen the kid's body, the state of the legs. He knew what they were thinking, that Michael knew one end of a baseball bat from another.

During the Troubles, once volunteers had been convicted they couldn't resume active duty. If they were known to the

41

police they might jeopardise operations. A lot of them spent their time running their communities, securing safe houses, gathering intelligence, dealing with complaints.

Once Michael was mentioned, Burke clammed up. He hadn't seen him in six months. He was living in Newry, sixty miles from Belfast. It corroborated what Kearney had taken from the Police National Computer.

Later O'Neill and Ward sat in CID. It was after four. The three DCs, Kearney, Reid and Larkin, had all gone home.

'So what do we know?' Ward asked.

O'Neill thought for a moment.

'Burke's dodgy, sir. He has previous himself and knows more than a few boys who could do something like this. The brother might be an in as well.'

'The pathology lab called,' Ward announced. 'They've scheduled the post-mortem for seven. Just in time to put you off your dinner.'

As Principal Investigator, O'Neill would go to the mortuary.

'And we still haven't got a positive ID on the body?' Ward asked. It had never taken this long to put an ID on a body before. He couldn't believe the victim didn't have some kind of previous.

'We're going to make an appeal for information, sir,' O'Neill said. 'Oh – and don't expect to hear too much about punishment beatings. Apparently there's no such thing any more.'

'Said who?'

'The Chief Inspector, sir.'

'Well, if he said it,' Ward said sarcastically, 'it must be true.'

***

The reinforced steel door thundered shut behind Burke. He stood outside Musgrave Street and looked at his watch. It was just after four.

The rain was coming down but had eased off from the morning. It was already dark. Burke put his hands in his pockets and walked towards the shops and the city centre.

Four streets from Musgrave Street he stopped at a phone box. Inside he took out his mobile and scrolled through the numbers. He dropped a pound into the phone box and dialled.

Two miles away in The George a man sat at the bar reading the *Irish News*. He was working his way down a pint of Guinness. It was late afternoon and the bar was half-empty. His mobile rang, flashing 'Number Withheld'. Michael Burke put the phone to his ear.

'Yeah?'

'It's me. They took me to Musgrave Street. They were asking about you – nothing they didn't just pull out of a file … It was Ward and some new guy. Think you need to get out of Dodge for a few days. Aye … OK.'

Burke hung up the receiver. He put his hand in his pocket and pulled out another pound. He slotted it in before scrolling through his mobile again. When he got to 'Spender' he stopped. He punched the number into the call box and waited as it rang on the other end.

A businesslike voice answered at the other end. 'Hello?'

'It's me.'

O'Neill went to the autopsy. He watched the boy, laid out on the cold steel slab. The table had a slight tilt, to allow fluids to drain away. He watched Rob Leonard, the State Pathologist, slice open the teenager. He removed his organs, examining each one carefully, taking samples for the toxicology report before putting them in a plastic bag and back into the empty chest cavity.

O'Neill was embarrassed to be there, watching such a private thing. He was embarrassed for the boy. Embarrassed he'd been laid out like this, that he'd been stripped bare, that there was no one there for him. No one to give a shit. No one to claim him, to say he was theirs.

He returned to Musgrave Street and spent three hours filling out paperwork. At eleven o'clock he drove to the flat in Stranmillis and showered. He still had the smell on him. Decomposition mixed with disinfectant. You couldn't wash it off. He'd wear fresh clothes the next day and it would still be on him. It would be there for several days. Only after the steady accumulation of other smells, the grime of everyday life – sweat, cigarettes, petrol – might it finally start to become less noticeable.

FIVE

Petesy's cousin lived in the Ardoyne. He was in his twenties and had been dealing for a few years. Marty and Petesy had been at it for six months, starting off for Johnny Tierney and Sean Molloy who ran the lower Ormeau Road.

Tierney gave them dope. Ten quarters. Told them to get rid of it and come back with the money. They hung around outside the Spar for six hours, speaking to people they knew and anyone that looked as if they might smoke. It was cold and afterwards Tierney paid them by giving them each a quarter. He told them to come back when they wanted to earn some more.

Two weeks later Marty had had enough.

'This is shite. Even in McDonald's they don't pay you in fucking hamburgers.'

They decided they would get their own gear. Go into business. Sell it for themselves.

'Entrepreneurs, Petesy. That's us. Fucking *Dragon's Den*. Here we go.'

They started with a nine bar from Petesy's cousin. He had scales and cut it into ounces, then quarters. Petesy and Marty wrapped them in clingfilm. They knew the drill. You kept a few on you at a time, left the rest stashed away somewhere. You kept them in your keks, tucked behind your balls – that way if the peelers searched you they wouldn't find them. And even if they did, they'd only get a couple of quarters and would probably just take them off you.

Getting the gear was Marty's idea. Petesy made the mistake of mentioning his cousin and Marty practically marched him up the Ardoyne.

'A nine bar at six hundred quid. Thirty-six quarters at twenty pounds a go. Seven hundred and twenty quid. That's over a hundred for us.'

'You're forgetting one thing,' Petesy said. 'What about Johnny Tierney? And Sean Molloy? They'll have our fucking knees if they find out. Remember Jackie Magennis.'

Everyone remembered Jackie. Tierney caught him skimming and had beaten the fuck out of him at half one in the afternoon in the middle of Cromac Street. He put him in hospital. Fractured skull, two broken ribs and a punctured lung. Tierney was twenty-four, Jackie fourteen. He'd lain there, completely motionless, until the ambulance came and took him away.

'You know where Jackie went wrong though?' Marty said, looking at Petesy's eyes. 'He got caught. There's two of us. We can look out for each other. Batman and Robin. Butch and Sundance.'

'Who the frig are Butch and Sundance?' Petesy asked.

'Never mind. Listen, the boys working for Tierney and Molloy are slaves. Do you want to be skint your whole fucking life? No? Well then. You have to use your initiative. He who dares, Petesy, he who dares.'

They shifted the nine bar in a week, selling it round the Markets and in the Holy Lands where the students from

Queen's University lived. Cairo Street. Damascus Street. Jerusalem Street. Marty and Petesy's own Promised Land.

They came out with over a hundred quid. Petesy'd bought his granny a box of chocolates but she wouldn't take them as she thought they were nicked. They blew the rest on a two-day bender. White Lightning and a load of Es. Steako and Micky came round and they all got fucked. Marty and Petesy were like kings, doling out the goods. It was brilliant.

After a few weeks the students started asking if they could get them other things. Speed. Coke. The first time they took coke into the Holy Lands they doubled their takings.

Marty bought a mobile phone. He used it to text birds to try and get his hole. *Hey drln. Cnt stp thnkng abt u. Wt u up to later. MTxxx* He would scroll through and send the same message to six different girls.

'You gotta be in it to win it, Petesy.'

Round the back of the twenty-four-hour Maxol was where they counted their takings. Petesy stood up and started trying to do keepy-ups with an empty can of Club Orange.

'We need to calm ourselves, Marty. Locksy was telling me that Tierney and Molloy are out looking for us. Someone said they were the ones that done that boy down at the river.'

'Nobody knows who the fuck that guy is.'

'It doesn't matter. He's dead, isn't he?'

'That's his fucking problem. Grow a dick, will you, Petesy. Sometimes I feel like I'm out here working with a wee girl.'

'I'm just saying, I don't want to end up limping round on a pair of walking sticks.'

Petesy managed two keepy-ups before the can clattered to the ground.

'Aye.' Marty nodded. 'It would ruin your chances with Man United and all.'

Marty stood up and started walking. He shouted back, over his shoulder, 'Come on, Beckham. Let's go and find that Cara one. Apparently Sean McAteer got a go at her tits at a party last Saturday.'

SIX

The sleeping tablets only half-worked. Lynch looked at the clock. 3.42 a.m.

He lay in bed, his thoughts going back to what the psychologist had said. As much as he hated the plush furniture and the rooftop views, Burton had been right. He could have gotten sleeping pills from anywhere. He was right about the memory as well – the taste, the smell, the metal. Lynch began to wonder what else Burton might know.

After the appointment he'd walked round the town for two hours. He'd tried to go for a pint in the Kitchen but it wasn't there any more. It had been knocked down and was a building site for a new shopping centre that would stretch half the length of Victoria Street. At home Lynch lay in front of the TV, flicking between programmes. The choice was between cooking and DIY. Some chef ran round a kitchen telling people to fuck off every ten seconds. On the other channel people were renovating some house they'd bought, plotting how to make their millions on the property market. At half ten Lynch had had enough. He popped two pills and went to bed.

Awake at four in the morning, Lynch went downstairs to make a cup of tea. There was no milk. He thought about taking it black, before dismissing the idea. On the small table lay a job application, staring up at him accusingly. The work was on a building site that needed labourers. Lynch had filled in his name and address. For a moment he'd felt lifted, like he was getting somewhere, even just putting pen to paper. It wasn't long before he came unstuck. There were large blank boxes: *Previous Experience, Employment History, References*. He wondered what he was supposed to do with them.

Lynch went through to the lounge and lay down on the sofa. There was an old black-and-white war film on TV. American GIs were trying to capture an island from the Japs. The soldiers were cleanshaven and wore neatly pressed uniforms. It was war as it was supposed to be. Well ordered. Us and them. When guys got shot they threw their arms in the air and fell over. There was no blood, no screaming, no pleading for their lives. There was no one begging to be let off, telling you to wise up, that they had a wife, that they had kids, please ... Television had a lot to answer for, thought Lynch. He turned the volume low in the hope that he might doze off.

At 8.15 he awoke and put his jacket on to go out for milk. As Lynch stuck his head out of the door he noticed there had been a break in the rain. The next shower didn't seem far away though. Across the street a young girl was struggling to squeeze a buggy out of her front door. When Lynch couldn't sleep he had watched her silhouette, pacing the floor at all hours of the morning. She was slim with bobbed blonde hair. The make-up did a good job of covering the shadows under her eyes. Lynch hadn't seen any sign of the father in the two months he'd been in the Markets. He jogged over and held the gate open for her as she steered the pram through.

'Thanks. It's like driving a frigging tank, this thing.'

'How old is the wee one?'

'Five months.'

'He's cute.'

'He's a she.'

'Oh. Sorry.' Lynch raised his eyebrows. 'What's her name?'

'Ciara.'

The two of them walked in silence for a few yards. She was on her way to the Health Centre. Lynch knew her routine. He knew the routine of almost everyone on the street. He couldn't help it. Memorizing people, their habits, their movements. The girl went to the Health Centre every Thursday. On Mondays and Fridays her mother came, just after nine, to clean the house and help with the child. There was no father, at least none that had been anywhere near the house. Lynch feigned ignorance.

'So where yous off to now then?'

'Health Visitor. Nosy cow. It's like being under surveillance. If you don't go and see them, they think you're killing your own child.'

'Still,' Lynch said. 'It can't be easy.'

'Tell me about it.'

'Is her da not around to help out?'

'Her da's an arsehole. Frigged off when he found out I was pregnant. Wanted an abortion. And before you start, I'm not like the rest of those wee girls, getting pregnant to get myself a house and all that. I was working before I had her.'

Lynch didn't reply.

'Anyway. It's just as well he frigged off. Couldn't have handled the lack of sleep. I'm up half the night.'

'Don't start me off,' Lynch said, rolling his eyes. 'Who would have thought getting a bit of kip could be so difficult?'

'You tried gin? Works for me every time.'

Lynch laughed. The girl smiled at him sidewards, enjoying a bit of adult company.

'A right pair of zombies, we must look,' he joked.

'Hey, speak for yourself, mate.'

Lynch smiled. It was good to be out walking, talking to someone, doing something normal. He introduced himself. Her name was Marie-Therese. He wondered about asking her if she fancied a cup of tea or something. A café somewhere. After she got done with the Health Visitor.

At the end of the street two men leaned against a parked car. As Lynch and the girl approached they got up and stood shoulder-to-shoulder, blocking the pavement. Lynch had never spoken to either of them, but he knew Tierney and Molloy by sight and reputation. The girl started to speak.

'So what are you—'

'Listen, love, you head on there. I'll catch you later.'

The girl looked up and recognized the two men. She immediately stopped talking and put her head down, pushing the buggy onwards. The men parted to let her pass, looking her up and down, like she was something they might eat. Molloy spoke.

'A bit young for an old fucker like you, don't you think? Now a good-looking guy like me...'

Lynch didn't respond. He kept his hands in his pockets, sizing up Molloy and Tierney. Molloy was the bigger of the two of them. He knew he could put Tierney down pretty quickly, then concentrate on the other one. He couldn't tell yet if they were holding. If they were it was a different story altogether.

'Mr McCann has sent for you.' Molloy gestured at a grey Ford, parked at the kerb. 'Get in the car.'

'I don't think so,' Lynch said.

He didn't move. He stared at Molloy, seeing that he was calling the shots.

'Listen, Clint Eastwood.' Tierney chipped in. 'We're not asking you. Get in the fucking car.'

'I've nothing to say to McCann.'

'We don't give a fuck what you've got to say.' Tierney had a mouth on him. Molloy was more deliberate, weighing things up.

Lynch didn't move. They weren't holding. If they were, they'd have shown something by now.

'You might have moved into the Markets with Hughesy,' Tierney continued, 'and you might have done your time together. The big heroes. Up in the Maze. The Cause and all that.'

Lynch half-listened to Tierney, keeping his eyes fixed on Molloy.

'You see, Hughesy's gone, he's not here any more. And when *he* goes, so does your pass for the Markets.'

Lynch had known this was coming. Tierney was doing all the talking, but it was Molloy that counted. He was the one to worry about.

'You need to come and see Mr McCann,' Molloy said. 'Need to have a chat with him. There are no freeloaders here. Everyone has to earn their keep.'

'I'm retired.'

'Retired!' Tierney exclaimed. 'Away and fuck yourself. Retired? Don't make me laugh.'

Tierney was a slabber all right, but Lynch had heard the stories and knew he could back it up. Meanwhile, Molloy was trying to do the same thing Lynch had done earlier: figure out if he was carrying.

Lynch took his hands out of his pockets. With his right hand he reached round into the belt at the small of his back. There was nothing there, but Lynch kept his hand hidden, holding on to the leather.

Molloy saw it and his eyes narrowed. He knew the stories, knew that Lynch had several bodies on him. The Lynch Man. The Lyncher. Molloy knew he wouldn't hesitate, wouldn't shirk at putting a bullet into either of them. Lynch found himself sliding into character. The passive face, the eyes taking on an empty, hollow stare. Molloy looked at him. He thought he was bluffing, but he couldn't be sure.

'Come on, Tierney,' Molloy said, putting his hand on his partner's shoulder. 'This one'll keep.'

The two men turned and went towards their car. Tierney was still slabbering.

'I'd go out and buy a lottery ticket if I was you, Lynch. 'Cause I'll tell you, this must be your lucky day or something.'

The two men got into the car and drove off, leaving Lynch standing by the kerb.

After weeks of anticipation, weeks of waiting, weeks of wondering, it had begun. Lynch sighed, feeling some of the tension flow out of him. It had started. At least he knew that now.

SEVEN

O'Neill sat at his desk in Musgrave Street, hunched over the Laganview file. He flicked through the pages. Paperwork. The holy commandment of police work. Thou shalt not shit without filling out a form. Paperwork covered the cracks. It meant you followed procedure. It was management's way of keeping an eye on you. Their way of staying in the loop. O'Neill wondered what the world looked like from the third floor. Dunking biscuits into cups of tea, flicking through pages of neatly typed reports.

It had been three days since the body turned up and there was a thick file on Laganview. There were interviews, canvassing reports, a list of site workers, criminal records, known drug dealers, SOCO reports, evidence slips, statements, photographs, lab tests. There was nothing like a body for generating a paper trail. The tree huggers would have a field day, O'Neill thought. He imagined the headline: *Murder Bad For Environment*.

For all the paperwork though, they still didn't have a name.

The appeal for information had been repeated on TV throughout Tuesday and Wednesday. The *Belfast Telegraph* led with the story on Monday night. It had fronted radio bulletins throughout the week. Still they had nothing. It made no sense. Absolutely none.

At the press conference Wilson had looked the part. Reassuring the public. 'No stone unturned ... most horrific crime ... perpetrators to justice.' All the usual. Tell them what they want to hear. There was no talk of a punishment beating. The press had been kept well away from the scene and the state of the body hadn't been disclosed.

For two days Musgrave Street flexed its muscle. Uniform stopped kids on street corners. CID lifted anyone with half a history of drug involvement. Jackie McManus, Micky Moran, Johnny Tierney, Stevie Davie, Sean Molloy. All the local celebrities.

They sat in interview rooms. Bored, inconvenienced and mildly amused, watching the police flounder.

'Where were you last Sunday night?'

Silence.

'Who were you with?'

Silence.

'What time did you get home?'

Silence.

These guys didn't even bother to 'no comment'. They knew what was going on, knew the peelers were stirring the pot. It was what you did when a body showed up. The cops kicked the hornets' nest. McManus, Moran, Tierney ... they'd been questioned often enough to know that this time, the police really did have fuck all.

O'Neill had called the Royal Victoria Hospital on the Grosvenor Road. The hospital boasted the best knee surgeons in the world. In thirty years they'd had plenty of practice. He spoke to the head of orthopaedics and got the files sent over of every punishment beating in Belfast in the last eight years. There were 308. Where did you begin? O'Neill asked the hospital to keep him informed if any new victims came in, particularly if they were local.

He frowned at the open pages of the Laganview folder. How could the kid still not have a name? There was no Missing Person report. His prints were nowhere on the Police National Computer, which meant he didn't have a record.

'How many wee hoods are there,' O'Neill muttered to himself, 'that have never been arrested, not even once?' He stared at the six digits on the manila folder. 880614. That's what the kid was. A number. At this stage, it was all he was.

In the next room DI Ward looked into the empty space in front of his desk. He was thinking about his retirement. What the hell was he going to do? He had no family any more, except for a brother in Scotland. He and Maureen had planned to have kids but it just had never happened for them. He didn't know why. Maureen blamed herself. She turned to him one night, told him that if he wanted to leave her, she would understand. Ward couldn't believe what he heard. Couldn't believe it had affected her so much, that she was that down about it. He tried to make it a joke.

'You trying to get rid of me? Have you got a wee thing with the milkman that you're not telling me about?'

Maureen smiled and a solitary tear ran down her cheek. That night in bed Ward held her. He told her to wise up, that she was the best thing that had ever happened to him. Maureen squeezed his hand. He told her he was going to have words with the milkman and all.

When the breast cancer came, Ward knew what she was thinking. She'd got what she deserved. She'd let him down and this was God's way of punishing her. She did three rounds of chemo but it was too late. Ward had been on his own now for fifteen years.

His mind went back to O'Neill next door in CID. He was having a tough time of it. If the kid was in the drug scene there was no way he wouldn't have some kind of previous. These kids didn't have records, they had rap sheets. O'Neill had sent the prints down to the *Garda* in Dublin, in case the boy was from the South and had been dumped in Belfast. Again, it came back a blank.

Ward wondered if this was the perfect crime. He snorted, reminding himself that you only read about such things in dodgy crime books. And anyway, everyone knew the perfect crime was, by definition, the one that no one ever knew about.

Ward tried to think what the play was. O'Neill had done everything right and he was still drowning. It wasn't his fault though. He'd been sent into choppy waters with a lead weight tied round his ankle.

Ward looked up to see the Chief Inspector stride past his door, a man happy in his work. Wilson rarely came to the second floor, but he'd made the trip on Tuesday, Wednesday and now, again, on Thursday. He was riding the shit out of O'Neill. Keeping the pressure on. Ward thought he might be trying to get O'Neill to take himself off Laganview. To throw in the towel. It would make the Review Boards a walk in the park, a mere formality. It would prove O'Neill couldn't hack it in plain clothes.

He heard Wilson from along the corridor, interrogating O'Neill.

'Detective, we've given you every resource this station has to offer and you're telling me you still don't even have a name for the victim?'

O'Neill didn't answer.

'What's your investigative strategy?'

O'Neill outlined what they'd done so far.

'Well, that hasn't worked, so what will you do next? And what are you going to do after that? And what will you do *then*?'

You. You. You. He was putting the whole thing on O'Neill, cranking up the heat, making it *his* job and his job alone.

Ward thought about going in, but crossing the Chief Inspector wasn't going to help anyone. He remembered when Wilson had first come over to Musgrave Street. Within six months he had the Chief Constable visiting the station. Wilson chaperoned him round, talking about crime rates, how they were down 5 per cent across the whole of B Division.

Wilson might be Chief Inspector, but he wasn't half the peeler that O'Neill was. Or could be, given half a chance. DC Kearney had told him a story about being out with O'Neill, back when he'd first come over to CID.

It was assault and robbery. A guy had mugged some old dear in the town and uniform had a suspect, Janty Morgan, whom they wanted to bring in for questioning. O'Neill and Kearney were on their way back from another job when they heard the details over the radio.

'I know him,' O'Neill said. 'We're two minutes away. Let's swing by and bring him in. I fancy a chat. Catch up on old times.'

O'Neill knew Morgan from his uniform days in Antrim Road. He explained it to the uniform who handed him over.

'Let's play a game, Janty,' O'Neill said, steering the unmarked Mondeo into the Belfast traffic. 'I feel like a game. What about you?'

Silence.

'Kearney?'

'Sure,' Kearney answered, playing along, though he'd no idea where O'Neill was going with it.

In the back, the eighteen year old stared out the window. He was giving nothing away, playing it cool. Not easy with your hands cuffed behind your back. Janty had been on the PSNI radar since he was thirteen. He had what they called pedigree – a scumbag from a long line of scumbags. The da was a scumbag, the brother was a scumbag. Now it was Janty's turn.

O'Neill shouted over his shoulder, 'Hey, Janty. You like games. Don't you, big lad?'

In the back Janty mouthed to himself, 'Fucking peelers.'

'OK. It's *I spy* today. Janty, you ready in the back there?'

No reaction.

'I spy,' O'Neill began, 'with my little eye, something beginning with P.'

Kearney roused some fake enthusiasm. 'Police?'

'No.'

'A prick?' The other detective laughed, thumbing towards Morgan in the back.

'No.'

Kearney paused. 'I give up.'

'Prison,' O'Neill announced triumphantly, forcing a laugh.

60

'Shit. I should have got that,' Kearney said, faking disappointment.

'That's right, Janty.' O'Neill knew he was talking to himself, but he kept up the performance. 'You can call me Mystic Meg from now on. HMP. Her Majesty's Prison. On its way for you, son. We might as well take you to Maghaberry right now. Save us all a load of paperwork. How many years do you fancy? I'll make you a deal right now.'

Janty Morgan slouched further into the back seat, his eyes narrowing.

'That's right, Detective,' O'Neill continued. 'Swipe a lady's handbag. Not too bad. But you better hope she doesn't grab you. You may have to smack her a few times, just to get away. I mean, hey, *she* grabbed *you*. Judges tend to not really go for that though. Help me with the maths here, Kearney. What does theft plus assault equal? Two years? Four? Hey Janty, you any good at maths?'

Silence.

'No. I didn't think so. 'Cause if you were, you'd have known better. And you know what else, Detective, whenever I am going to smack some auld doll I like to make sure she's not the sister of anyone important – like, say, the frigging Lord Mayor.'

Janty mumbled to himself in the back, 'Fuck sake.'

'Oh. You didn't know? That's right, Janty. The Lord Mayor's sister.' O'Neill laughed out loud. 'You definitely didn't do your homework on this one, son.'

The lady had had her bag snatched in the Clifton Street car park. Truth was she only saw a blur of white tracksuit and the car park didn't have CCTV. The attendant's description matched Morgan. They could charge him but it wouldn't get a conviction. Half the hoods in Belfast were wearing a white tracksuit that day. Janty had been two streets away when he saw a PSNI Land Rover and bolted. Uniform caught him but he was clean so unless they could get something out of him now, they wouldn't sniff a charge. The PPS would take one look at it and tell them to wise up.

O'Neill kept on at Morgan. 'Snatching a bag in broad daylight – you must be one dopey fucker. This is the twenty-first century, Janty. There's CCTV everywhere. Did you want to be famous? Was that it? Couldn't get on *X Factor*, so thought you'd go for *World's Dumbest Criminals*. Obviously you don't watch *CSI* either though, eh Janty?'

Silence.

'That handbag will have left traces all over you. There's all that technology now. We take you to the station, shine the blue light on you, you're going to light up like a Christmas tree. A regular old Papa Smurf.'

O'Neill was bullshitting, trying to sow some doubt, to get beneath Morgan's street persona.

'By the time we get to the station though, Janty, it's going to be all over. We'll have you then and nothing you say then will make a bit of difference. You need to start talking, Janty. And I mean now.'

'No comment.' A mumble from the back.

'*Buuuurrrragh!*' O'Neill shouted, like a game-show buzzer. 'Wrong answer.'

Janty was sticking to the golden rule. The one that stretched across the city, crossing every Peace Wall and all the old divides. From the Ballysillan to Ballymacarrett, from the New Lodge to the Short Strand – you didn't talk to peelers.

'Try again, Janty.'

Silence.

'The strong silent type. That's what I thought.'

O'Neill turned right off Millfield and steered the car up the Shankill Road. The Shankill was the heart of Protestant Belfast and had been a stronghold for Loyalist paramilitaries during the Troubles. It wasn't the best place for a young Catholic from the New Lodge to be hanging out. O'Neill knew it, so did Janty. Almost instantly the playful atmosphere in the car started to darken. The eighteen year old got more nervous as the red, white and blue kerbstones rolled by and they got deeper into the Shankill.

'Where the fuck are yous taking me?'

O'Neill ignored the question and continued his monologue.

'*No comment.* Do you hear this, Kearney? This one thinks he's some kind of criminal mastermind. Are you some kind of criminal mastermind, Janty? Is that what it is? 'Cause that's who *no comment* is for. Wee hoods from the New Lodge? *No comment* is not for you. Right now, commenting is the *only* thing you need to be doing. Commenting's the only thing that'll stop us turfing your arse out of this car in the middle of the Shankill.'

O'Neill paused, letting the situation sink in.

'Wait a minute, Detective. I've got it! Janty *is* a criminal mastermind. He knows even if he gets done for this, it'll only be another stretch in Young Offenders. He's only seventeen, after all.' O'Neill paused, looking in the rearview mirror. 'You're still only seventeen, aren't you, Janty?'

Silence.

'Shit. You're eighteen? They grow up so fast these days, Ward. You're in with the big boys now, Janty. Forget Young Offenders – all that playground stuff. This is the real McCoy. Guys from Sandy Row. Tiger's Bay. Bet they can't wait to get their hands on a fresh wee Fenian like you.'

Morgan's eyes darted from side to side as they drove further into the Shankill. Union Jacks saluted from lamp-posts. The car pulled up at a set of traffic-lights beneath a large mural. A 20-foot masked gunman stared into the car. During the seventies this was the home of the Shankill Butchers, a loyalist gang that used a black taxi to abduct Catholics. They drove them outside the city and decapitated them with a meat cleaver. There was a certain mythical edge to the Shankill.

'You stole that purse, didn't you, Janty?'

Hesitation. 'No comment.'

O'Neill was getting close. He could feel it.

He sighed in mock resignation. He slowed the car and pulled over. On the opposite side of the street the Regal Bar stood between a Sean Graham bookmakers and an off-licence. Black paint flaked off the walls. Four men stood outside smoking. Half-drunk pints sat along the window-ledge. They clocked the car as soon as it pulled up and started glaring across. Janty could feel their eyes boring into the car.

'OK, Janty. If you don't want to talk we'll just have to let you go.' O'Neill reached back and opened the rear door of the Mondeo.

'I'm not fucking going anywhere.' His voice was almost a yelp.

'Come on, Janty. Wise up. Sure you'll be halfway down the road before they get near you.'

The group outside the pub saw the door open and became more agitated. One man ducked back inside. The Troubles weren't so long gone that three men in an unknown car didn't reek of something.

'You see, Janty, it's like that Van Morrison song. Things have changed. We don't beat people up any more. We just talk to you and if you don't want to talk, we let you go.' O'Neill sang to himself, laughing. 'Did your mama not tell you, there'd be days like this?'

The gang outside the pub had been joined by two more men, both of whom had tattooed forearms. The drinkers were gesturing towards the car, explaining the situation.

O'Neill leaned back and shouted out of Janty's door: 'Orange bastards!'

'What the fuck are you doing?' Morgan said. High-pitched. Desperate.

The gang of men started making their way across the street towards the car.

'Ah, don't worry about us, Janty. They might drag you out of the back, but we'll get away OK.'

The men picked their way through the traffic, stopping cars, getting nearer the Mondeo. Janty had backed up across the seat, as far from the open door as possible. A tattooed arm reached into the car, trying to grab hold of his feet.

'All right! All right! It was me. I done her,' he screamed, kicking out at the hands.

O'Neill lifted the clutch, peeling rubber as the Mondeo shot off down the road. The car left an empty space that the rest of the men seemed to tumble into.

Two years later, thumbing through the file, O'Neill wished Laganview was that easy. There was no one he could lean on. No one to apply a bit of pressure to. Hell, he didn't even have a name.

He walked into the coffee room and poured himself the third cup of the day. It was still only 8.30 a.m.

In the office next door DI Ward hunted through the bottom drawer of a steel filing cabinet. He pulled out a series of black notebooks, the ones he'd used in the eighties, back when he was in uniform.

He was looking for William Spender, the developer at Laganview. He knew he was in there somewhere. It was a complaint; although nothing ever came of it. Ward had been sent to interview him over allegations that he had threatened one of his neighbours. Something to do with an extension.

The investigation had been dropped. Out of nowhere, the neighbour retracted the complaint. Ward sat at his desk, thumbing through old notebooks, trying not to get sidetracked by the names and memories that leered out of the pages.

Next door, O'Neill continued to circle Laganview. The more he looked at the file, the less he believed it was a straight-up punishment beating. Punishment beatings were a warning, a signal that drug dealing wasn't tolerated. A dead body was one way. Better though was a living, breathing victim. A daily testimony, in 3-D Technicolor. If the young ones saw their mate hobbling round on a pair of walking sticks, taking painkillers for the rest of his life, they would know what was coming to them. A punishment beating was about control. A way of making sure the hoods knew who was in charge. If you were dealing for someone and thought about ripping him off, there were going to be consequences. It wasn't a crime of passion. Things didn't get out of hand. O'Neill heard of incidents where they even called the ambulance, waiting until they heard the sirens before doing the guy's knees.

He thought about Wilson's warning. About not calling this a punishment beating. The political ramifications. The need to be careful. The Chief Inspector might get his wish, after all.

O'Neill sighed and prised himself up from his desk. He went outside to the car park. Two white Land Rovers sat in the shadow of the station wall. He lit a cigarette. Three uniforms stood by the back of one of the Land Rovers, sharing a story.

The door from the lock-up opened and Sam Jennings walked out. She had her hat pulled down, her short blonde ponytail peeking out the back.

'Hey, John,' she said. 'Or should I say, Detective Sergeant O'Neill?'

'That's right.' O'Neill lifted three fingers, tapping imaginary stripes on his shoulder. 'You need to stand up when I walk in the room.'

'Hah. You forget I knew you when you didn't know your radio from your pepper spray.'

'Fair point.'

Jennings glanced over at the three male uniforms at the back of the wagon. She saw her shift stretching out in front of her. Stuck in the Land Rover, taking a ribbing for chatting up CID. From what she could tell, Musgrave Street was a boys' club. She felt as if she was being watched, that the guys on her shift were still waiting to see if she could cut it when things turned rough. It had been the same in Dungannon. A load of lads waiting to see if she wasn't another empty uniform. The PSNI playing politics, filling another bullshit equality quota.

'So how's Musgrave Street working out?' O'Neill asked. 'You got a good shift?'

Jennings raised her eyebrows sceptically. 'I'll let you know. There are a few cowboys round here, I'll tell you that for nothing. Guys who think they're hard lads, that they can do whatever they want.'

'Yeah? Just keep your head down. And anyway, what was wrong with Dungannon? Last I heard, you were entering boxing competitions.'

'Listen. It's official. Dungannon's been pacified. I thought I'd come to the big smoke. Show you boys how it's done.'

'And how are the Belfast streets treating you?'

'Yeah. They're lovely. Spent most of yesterday being told to fuck off by twelve year olds.'

Uniform had been ordered to stop and question any young ones within a three-mile radius of Laganview.

'Yeah, that was my fault,' O'Neill answered. 'The Belfast hood though – there's a lot of spirit there.'

'Is that what they're calling it these days?'

O'Neill felt the memories coming back from Police College. Sam was quick. She had an answer for everything and plenty of street smarts. She glanced over again at the Land Rover.

'And what about you? How is ...' Sam hung over the name, not quite able to remember.

'Catherine?' O'Neill hesitated for a second. 'Bit of choppy water there.'

'Sorry to hear that. You have a wee girl, don't you?'

A loud whistle came from the Land Rover across the car park.

'I've got to go, John. Listen, we should catch up though ...'

She was off before O'Neill had time to answer.

He watched as they piled into the back of the Land Rover, swinging the doors shut behind them. The engine fired to life and the wagon reversed out of its space. Inside, Jennings looked out from behind a small rectangle of blacked-out glass. She watched as O'Neill took a final drag from his cigarette, tossed it aside and walked back into the station.

EIGHT

Marty stared at the blonde in her underwear. She looked straight into his eyes and pouted invitingly. He reached out towards her.

Suddenly Petesy grabbed him and yanked him down, behind the magazine rack.

'Petesy, what the fuck?'

'Shut up,' Petesy whispered. 'Fucking Johnny Tierney just walked past.'

In front of the Spar, Tierney stopped and took out twenty Regal Kingsize. He lit one and walked on. Marty and Petesy crept up to the display of birthday cards. They peered out over pictures of cats, dogs and orang-utans, in various states of confusion. Tierney was across the street, outside Tony Loughrin's house. He had his hands cupped against the window, trying to see inside.

'What does he want at Locksy's?' Petesy asked.

'How the fuck should I know?'

Locksy had been in the same year as them at school. He had been obsessed with Man United, and when they had a kick-about he would provide a running commentary. 'Giggsy to Keane, Keane to Cantona, Cantona *shoots*!' He'd been dealing for Tierney for three months now.

Marty pulled Petesy outside and they made a run for it, going down an entry beside the Spar and along a back street.

Ten seconds later Tierney had Locksy by a combination of earring and ear. The fifteen year old groaned. His nose was broken and a red patch of blood was spreading down the front of his coveted Man United away strip. Tierney twisted the earring. Locksy screamed. He had opened the door, half-asleep, and been greeted by a punch in the face. The teenager had been in bed, recovering from the weekend. He knew not to answer the door, but he'd been dead to the world, and thought it was only Micky.

'Where's my money, you wee cunt?'

Locksy couldn't speak, only yelp. His ear was on fire and felt as if it was being ripped from the side of his head.

'Aaaah, Tierney! Wise up. My fucking ear.'

'Your ear is the least of your fucking worries. Where's my two hundred quid, you wee cunt? And don't have me to ask twice.'

Tierney towered over the scrawny teenager trembling in his boxer shorts and white T-shirt. He picked Locksy up by the ear and marched him upstairs. Tierney knew what he was doing. Two hundred quid or not, he knew whatever happened to Locksy would make the rounds of the estate. People had short memories: they needed to keep being reminded that he wasn't to be fucked with. It was about the two hundred quid, but it was about more than that. Cunts talk. At the moment they were talking about how Locksy'd taken the piss out of him, sold his gear and spent his money. That would change. It was one thing he was sure of.

In the bedroom Locksy grabbed a pair of tracksuit bottoms from the foot of his bed. He had no idea how much was left. He had been on his way to see Tierney when he bumped into Micky. It was Friday night and they had meant to check in once they'd taken the pills, but the Es had kicked in and they'd ended up forgetting.

Locksy pulled a roll of crumpled notes out of the pocket, wincing at the size of it. He was well short and he knew it. Tierney held the money and counted it silently. As he flipped the last note, he punched Locksy round the head.

'A hundred and thirty quid? What do I look like? The fucking Northern Bank?'

He then punched Locksy in the stomach, sending the teenager to the floor.

'Please, Tierney,' Locksy groaned. 'I'll pay you back. I swear.' Locksy had seen what Tierney had done to Jackie Magennis and knew he could be a real nasty fucker. There were no two ways about it.

Tierney kicked the fifteen year old in the ribs, then again, and again. Locksy curled up on his knees, gasping for air. The older man knelt down and grabbed the small hoop earring, ripping it from the teenager's ear. The boy screamed, clutching the side of his head. He hunkered into an even smaller ball, fearful about what might come next.

'This is your last chance, Locksy. Do you hear me? Otherwise you'll end up like that cunt down by the river. You owe me, son. And don't have me to come looking for you again.'

There was a party at Micky's on Saturday night. He'd been spreading the word and everyone was going to be there.

Marty was flush from his trip to the Holy Lands with Petesy the night before and still had a load of Es. It would be mental. Earlier in the day three different people, folk he hardly knew, had asked if he was going to the party. Word had started to spread. Marty Toner was somebody to know.

That morning Marty had gone into the city centre to get himself a new jersey. He'd heard that Cara was going to be at Micky's. He was after a black Ralph Lauren number. A hundred and twenty quid's worth. He hung around outside Debenhams, waiting until the security guard was talking to the girl on the make-up counter before slipping in. As he strode behind them he heard the sleazy bastard introducing himself. She must have been half his age and leaned over the counter, enjoying the attention.

In the menswear section Marty marched straight to the labels and, without breaking stride, took a Ralph Lauren from the shelf. The guards were always on the lookout in that part of the shop and he kept walking to the back, where they kept the underwear and dressing gowns. It was pensioners' stuff and there wasn't too much nicking went on back there. He bent down, pretending to tie his shoe and snapped the electronic tag off with his Stanley knife. Marty put the jumper on and zipped his tracksuit over the top. He strolled out casually, smiling at the guard as he passed.

'All right Paul, big lad? Ever get those crabs sorted out?'

The guard frowned. The girl looked at her admirer, her face curling downward in disgust.

Marty felt invincible. Security guards? Dozy fuckers.

Outside he took off his tracksuit top, catching sight of himself in the mirrored windows of Castlecourt. He put his hand in his jeans pocket and felt the two hundred pounds he had made with Petesy the night before. Happy days, he thought.

On Thursday they had made their usual trip into the Holy Lands, a grid of fifteen streets, made up of three-storey terrace houses. It was Belfast's student village, a five-minute walk from Queen's University and the pubs round Shaftesbury Square. Landlords packed as many twenty year olds into damp, mouldy houses as they could legally get away with.

Marty and Petesy had been dealing there for three months. They'd grown bored with hanging out at the bottom of the Ormeau Road, waiting for folk they knew to walk by.

'Those students are loaded,' Marty told Petesy.

They started walking round the Holy Lands, approaching anyone who looked a bit scruffy, asking if they wanted to score. An hour later they'd sold their last six quarters.

They knew Johnny Tierney was also on the lookout for them so the Holy Lands were a safer bet as well. They'd be on the move, not standing round like a couple of sitting ducks. The Holy Lands put a bit of distance between them and the lower Ormeau. You weren't constantly looking over your shoulder, waiting to get jumped.

After a few weeks Marty and Petesy had regulars. Nine or ten addresses. Marty called it their paper round. He walked out of the Holy Lands shouting, 'Tele-eeagh!' imitating the newspaper vendors that sold the *Belfast Telegraph* in the town. They had made over two hundred quid in less than three hours.

The students were mostly culchies, guys from Fermanagh, Tyrone and Derry. Gaelic football flags hung on the walls in living rooms. Petesy kept watch outside while Marty went in. After a couple of weeks people knew him and were pleased to see him.

'Marty mate, what about you?'

In a house on Fitzroy Avenue two guys were buying coke. Marty looked at the thick books piled up on the desk. He wondered why anyone would want to read something like that.

'What are all the books for then?' he asked.

'Law,' one of the students replied.

Marty laughed. 'I'll remember that. You might be a useful guy to know some day.'

The guy didn't get it. Or didn't think it was funny. For a split second Marty felt like some kind of servant. As if, despite the fake enthusiasm, he wasn't really wanted. Like he was making the place dirty. Like he was some form of necessary evil. The student pulled out his wallet and handed over the money. Marty took it without saying anything. He gave him the gram of coke and left.

NINE

The George was the nearest pub to the Markets. A cold breeze came off the river, whipping into two men who stood smoking outside. Joe Lynch walked past, hearing them mutter about the weather and the fucking smoking ban.

Inside, a dark oak counter stretched the length of the bar. Black and white tiles covered the floor and a row of optics glistened with amber vials of whiskey – Black Bush, Paddy's, Dunhill's.

Lynch ordered a pint of Guinness and took it to a booth along the wall. From there he could sit quietly, inconspicuous. He could also look out across the whole room, an old habit, but one he never felt like changing, and especially not now.

He had hoped that a bit of normality, a few pints, might help reset the body clock. Failing that, it would at least give the sleeping pills a hand. He remembered Marie-Therese from a couple of mornings back: 'Try gin.' He smiled, thinking about her attitude, a two fingers to life and whatever it threw at you. She was just right. On the way to The George he'd walked past her house and considered asking her out for a drink. It was too blatant though. It needed to be something casual, to look spontaneous. During the day, that was the way to go. A cup of coffee. Just talking. No obvious subtext.

Every few minutes the snug at the back of the bar erupted in shouting and roars of laughter. There was a group of men and by the sound of it they were well on their way. Lynch looked round the bar, recognizing a number of faces from the Markets. The old man with the Jack Russell had nodded as he had walked in. Lynch liked seeing him, liked the thought of him and his dog, doing everything together. That was loyalty. Real loyalty. The dog never left his side. Right then it was curled up at the foot of his bar stool.

At the back of the pub the snug let out another roar. Lynch looked round. The group were hidden by the glass partition that topped the seats. He couldn't make out any faces. He couldn't make out Sean Molloy, busy holding court. He couldn't make out Johnny Tierney, banging his empty glass down, ordering someone to get a round in. The rest of the pub were oblivious, or were acting that way. See no evil, hear no evil. Lynch could tell from the fake indifference that whoever was back there had carte blanche to do whatever they wanted. No one was going to say boo to them.

He was about to get up and leave when a half-drunk pint appeared beside him. It was the dog man. The wee Jack Russell trotted over after him.

'Mind if I join you?'

'Work away.'

The old man groaned as he shifted into the seat. He introduced himself with a wheezing, raspy voice. Arthur McNally. He was five foot nothing and well into his seventies. He motioned to the dog.

'Sit down there, Sammy.' He turned to Lynch. 'Has me run ragged, this boy. It's like he gets younger, every year I get older.'

Wee Arthur was a talker, which suited Lynch fine. He was more than happy listening. It was good to sit there, soaking up someone else's thoughts instead of suffocating in your own. The old man ranged round, talking about the football, how Cliftonville were rubbish, again, and all the building work that was going on round the town. He hardly recognized Belfast any more. Lynch asked him when the pub round the corner, The Kitchen, had disappeared. For ten minutes they added to the rumble of conversation rolling round the pub. Lynch went to buy himself another pint and got one in for his new friend, making a joke about Care in the Community.

As the barman put the drinks in front of him, a glass shattered inside the snug. In unison the bar turned its head, expecting fireworks. A burst of laughter erupted from the corner. It was only a spilled drink. The bar settled again and Lynch returned to his seat. Arthur lowered his voice and nodded towards the back of the pub.

'Hallions. The lot of them.'

When he finished his drink Lynch made his excuses and got up to leave. As he backed out of the snug he bumped into someone.

'Sorry there ...'

He turned to see six foot two inches of Sean Molloy staring down at him. Molloy stood with four men at his back, on their way out of the bar. He looked at Lynch, backing him up against the table. The room was silent, glasses hung in the air, halfway towards gaping mouths. Molloy spoke with menacing quiet.

'If it isn't Joe Lynch. The big hero. Out walking amongst us.' He pushed Lynch in the shoulder with his finger. 'If I was you, Lynch, I'd take a bit more care where I was stepping. These aren't the good old days any more.'

Lynch knew about Molloy's reputation. He was one of Gerry McCann's boys and could handle himself. That wasn't the worry. It was the four others that stood behind him. One more Lynch could handle, probably not two, and definitely not four. It didn't matter who you were, four to one were pretty lousy odds.

No one in the bar moved.

Lynch looked at Molloy. It would be one punch and a run for the door. You would make it or you wouldn't. The rest would look after itself. Lynch braced himself, ready to throw. At the same moment Johnny Tierney stepped forward and jostled Molloy along.

'Come on, big lad,' he said, slapping his mate on the back. 'The birds are waiting. This one'll keep. He's not going anywhere.'

Molloy stepped back from the edge. The five men made their way out of the bar, Tierney smirking back at Lynch. Conversations resumed as the doors swung shut behind them. Lynch took his seat, making sure he could see the door, just in case. He looked at his empty pint. At his side, Arthur petted his dog and muttered to himself, under his breath.

'Hallions, the lot of them.'

TEN

Ward gave it a poke down the middle with a three wood. Two hundred yards away the ball skipped over a ridge and disappeared out of sight. He'd always thought the first wasn't the same, after they had filled in the bunker on the right-hand side of the fairway.

It was 7 a.m. and Fortwilliam golf course was deserted. Ward's navy Mondeo sat alone in the car park. The fairways sloped along the side of Cavehill and down to Belfast Lough. The grass runway of the first shimmered silver with early-morning dew. This was Ward's ritual. Nine holes of golf, early doors, while the world was still in its bed. He used an old, rusty set of clubs that had belonged to his father, and always played alone.

The day before, he had sat for three hours in a divisional meeting. Wilson gave a presentation on the last quarter's crime stats for East and South Belfast. Slide after slide, he broke down call rates, arrest figures, charges brought. Each column totalled to a nice neat percentage. Policing by numbers. Round the table, the senior management of Musgrave Street nodded in agreement. You couldn't blame them, Ward thought. The measurement, the neatness, the accountability. If he worked on the third floor and never left the station, he'd probably like to see something so neat and tidy.

Ward had sat in the meeting, staring at graphs and tables, wondering when policing had become a form of accountancy. Digging out his old notebooks, looking for Spender, had brought back memories from when he'd first joined up. He found himself reading over various incidents he'd attended. Detail after detail rose up within him – faces, names, charges; injuries, victims, suspects; blood spatters, registration plates, street addresses. Ward remembered his first ever Sergeant, Stanley Hannah. Hannah was in his late fifties, six two and built like a bear. He had been at Dunkirk and Normandy. It was an unwritten rule at Musgrave Street, every new man got six weeks with the Sarge. You rode together, twelve hours a day, Hannah conducting lessons on the art of policework. They would sit in the car, or walk the street. The Sergeant would ask – What do you see? What's he doing over there? What kind of car's behind you? How long has it been there? Hannah taught Ward – you watch, you listen, you remember. *That* was the job. You didn't police with your fists and your boot. At least not when you could help it. In the early eighties things started to heat up and Hannah warned him, 'This thing's going to get a whole lot worse, before it gets any better.'

Ward took a five iron and knocked the ball towards the first green. He couldn't get up in two any more. In fact, he hadn't been able to manage it for a few years. There was no need to worry though. That was golf. It had a habit of telling you things you didn't always want to admit to yourself.

Hannah had died in the early nineties. It was a big funeral. Guys came in from everywhere. From across the water. The church was dotted with CID from the Met, from GMP, from

81

Strathclyde. Ward wondered what the Sarge would have said about the likes of Wilson, the careerism, the way the numbers-men now owned the force.

He pulled a wedge from his bag, thinning his third which skipped through the green and buried itself in a hedge that ran along the boundary of the course. After a quick hoke Ward walked to the second. An hour and a half later he was done. A par, a couple of bogeys and two lost balls. It would do. Coming down the eighth he had stopped and looked back up the fairway behind him. A pair of solitary footprints weaved their way down the wet grass. It was a quiet morning. There wasn't a breath of wind and Ward felt as if the whole world was there, just for him.

Afterwards he lifted his clubs into the boot of his car. Ward looked round and saw that the car park was empty. He reached into the pocket of his golf bag and took out his personal protection firearm, a Glock 19. He put it in the door of the car, started the engine and headed for Musgrave Street.

Catherine sat in the coffee shop, her bag on her knee, thumbing the brown envelope. John was late. He was always late. It was half eleven and the lunchtime rush would be starting soon. She didn't want an audience. Didn't want to hear someone gossiping about their workmates while she handed her husband, the father of her child, a set of the divorce papers. She tried not to think about it, about what he would say. If only she could just hand them over – that was enough. It would start and she knew things would take on a momentum of their own.

The solicitor had told her he would post them to her husband. It was easier that way. She didn't agree. No, she'd do it herself. It may only be your job, she thought, but it's my life. And anyway, things aren't always supposed to be easy.

As she waited, Catherine went over it in her head. It wasn't a discussion. They weren't going to argue. She would be calm. Tell him what was happening. Hand him the envelope. Simple.

A waiter dressed in black swept up to the table and asked for her order. She said she was waiting and looked at her watch. Her line manager at Anderson & James was a total clock-watcher. She'd have to be back no later than twelve.

O'Neill hurried into the coffee shop, his black coat fanning out as he turned the corner. His suit needed cleaning, his shirt could do with an iron and he hadn't shaved. He leaned down to kiss her and she offered him her cheek. His smell lingered near her face, that familiar mix of tobacco and aftershave. Catherine felt some vague memory of desire stirring up inside her. She pushed it back down, reminding herself what she was there to do.

O'Neill liked his wife in her work-clothes. The black suit and crisp white shirt. He found he always wanted her the most when she was dressed like that. He imagined her walking round the office, issuing orders, getting things done. He loved hearing her on the phone to colleagues, the authority in her voice. It reminded him of the girl he had met seven years ago, when she was about to finish her degree at Queen's.

O'Neill's phone rang in his pocket. He looked at the number. It was Wilson. The Chief Inspector had taken to calling him on a daily basis. He wanted updates. Wanted to know what progress was being made with the case. O'Neill imagined Wilson taking notes at the other end of the phone, compiling a dossier against him. He swore under his breath and rejected the call, putting the phone back in his pocket.

The waiter swept in again with his pen poised, a mix of pomp and self-importance. O'Neill picked up the menu, his eyebrow creased at the two-page list of drinks. Cappuccinos, lattes, americanos, all in Italian sounding sizes.

'Tall skinny latte,' Catherine said.

The waiter wrote her order down with a contrived flourish.

'Do you have coffee?' O'Neill asked sarcastically.

'Sir?'

'Black coffee?'

The waiter picked up the vibe and held back on his offer of muffins and pastries. He went back to the bar to place their order.

Catherine was embarrassed. Embarrassment became annoyance, which then became resentment and finally anger.

'I see charm school's really paying off?'

O'Neill had been hoping she was going to ask him back, to move in again with her and Sarah. He'd hoped the 'break' was over, that she'd had some space, that Sarah's constant questions about when her daddy was coming home had finally brought her round. Looking at Catherine's face, he knew he hadn't helped his cause.

'Wise up, love. It's a cup of coffee.'

'It's not a cup of coffee, it's you.'

'What's that supposed to mean?'

'Why do you have to be so dismissive? You don't care about anything that's not chasing round Belfast, trying to lock up the latest arsehole who's broken the law.'

'All I did was ask if they had coffee.'

'You know exactly what you did.'

Catherine broke off as the waiter returned with their drinks. He placed them on the table and went back to the counter. O'Neill lifted the cup and took a drink.

'Mmmm. Good coffee,' he said with mock enthusiasm. 'How's yours?'

'F-off, John,' Catherine replied, smiling a little, despite herself.

She felt herself start to soften, being won over by O'Neill's sense of humour. He always did this to her. But no, she reminded herself, not today. She had to remember what she was there for. She went back and tried to find the resentment. It was easier that way.

'It's always the same. It was the same when we went out for dinner that time.'

'That again? Is this a history lesson? Is that what you asked me to meet you for? To talk about some dinner we went to last year?'

'There you go. If it's not important to you it's not important to anyone.'

Catherine had invited two other couples, women from work and their husbands. It was to celebrate her birthday. They'd met at half seven on the Saturday night. O'Neill had told her he'd finish his shift at five but he still wasn't home from work. She'd spoken to Jack Ward who'd said he was questioning a suspect but he'd get him out of there as soon as possible. O'Neill had been an hour late. Catherine was furious and struggled to keep a lid on things.

Her eyes bored into the menu while they all waited for him to arrive at the restaurant.

'Those criminals,' she laughed, cursing herself for repeating her husband's words. 'They don't work a nine to five like the rest of us.'

In the café, O'Neill slurped his coffee. 'It's not my fault those girls married two of the most boring men on the planet.'

'You could have been polite.'

'I was polite. I listened to rocketing house prices, to fluctuations in the stockmarket, to the sound of the new Mercedes ... you know, the S-class just wasn't going to be big enough.'

'You got drunk and called him an arsehole.'

'He was an arsehole.'

'That's not the point.'

'He asked me how my day was. I'd spent three hours interviewing a sixteen-year-old girl who had been raped by her step-father. It took an hour for her to stop hyperventilating so that she could string a sentence together. She kept saying, "It was my fault. It was my fault." And you wonder why I didn't give a shit about the fuel injection in your man's fucking car?'

'There you go again. Hiding behind the job. It's always about you, always about the job. You care more about frigging Musgrave Street than you do about your own wife and daughter.'

'What are you talking about?'

'You were like a ghost. You were never home.'

'I can't do anything about the shifts.'

'It's not the shifts, John. Even when you are home, you're not really there. You're staring into space. Running down some street in your head. In some interview, asking a different set of questions. Wondering where it went wrong, what you should have done ...'

Catherine broke off. She knew why she'd come now. She wasn't there to change him. She had been trying for six years and it hadn't worked. John wouldn't change. He couldn't.

'John, it's not all up to you, you know. You can't fix everything. The robbery, the theft, the assault, the rape. You can't stop it.' Catherine lifted her coffee. It had cooled and she took a large warm mouthful.

'So what do you want me to do then? Talk about cars? Sit in restaurants, wanking on about how fresh the mussels are?'

'No, John.'

O'Neill wondered how they ended up arguing. It was like an invisible gravity that always managed to pull them off-course. He knew he was going nowhere. He needed to get off the subject, stir up some memories. Talk about something good.

'Listen, you're right. I could have handled that one a bit better.'

Catherine stared out of the window at people walking by.

'Anyway, how's our Sarah? How's she getting on at school?'

Their daughter was halfway through her first year of primary school. Catherine tried to ignore him but acquiesced. No matter what she did, he was still the father of her child.

'A right little fixer, apparently,' she said.

'Oh yeah?' O'Neill replied, sensing a chink of light.

'I met Ms Harper at the school gate and she was telling me Sarah had volunteered to sit beside the new boy that joined the class. He had spent the morning crying because he didn't know anyone. She's a right little fixer that one, so the teacher said.'

O'Neill smiled, blue eyes shining, crow's feet gathering at the corners of his eyes. Catherine couldn't help but see her daughter sitting across the table. The eyes. The smile. The stubbornness. She tried to ignore it.

'I need to go to the toilet,' she said, picking up her bag and walking in the direction of the ladies'.

On her own in the cubicle she set about rallying the troops.

'Hand him the envelope,' she whispered to herself. 'There is nothing more to say. He won't change. He can't.'

As she said the words, another voice in her head was telling her this was why she fell for him in the first place. This was why she loved him. He didn't back down. He didn't know how.

Walking back to the table Catherine saw O'Neill, his mobile pressed to his ear. She knew he would be on the phone to the station as soon as she left the table. That was it. That decided it.

O'Neill stood up quickly as she approached.

'Listen, love, I need to run. I'm really sorry. Something's come up. I'll call you later.'

And he was gone.

Catherine stood with the brown envelope in her hand. She stared after her husband as he ran across the street, a car almost running him over.

ELEVEN

Marty heard the bass thumping when he was 30 feet from the house. It was 9.30 on Friday night. He knocked and heard a voice over the music.

'This is fucking shite. Get the other CD back on.'

'What the fuck do you know?' someone shouted back.

Micky peered through the curtains before answering the door. There was a cheer when Marty walked in the room. It was as much for the gear as it was for him, but he tried not to think about it.

Ten people sat in Micky's ma's front room. They were draped over chairs, on the arms of sofas, huddled on the floor. Marty saw Petesy in the corner talking to Tony Loughrin. Locksy had two black eyes and a white plaster taped round the bottom of his left ear.

'Cunt beat the shite out of me,' he said loudly to Petesy over the sound of the heavy bass. He took a drink from a two-litre bottle of cider. 'Still. Fuck him. You should have seen the state of us last weekend. Off-our-faces. Pure brilliant.'

Petesy smiled, pretending to buy the forced bravado. He looked away and took a drink from his can of Harp. For all his talk, Locksy looked as if he'd gone nine rounds with Mike Tyson. Across the room Marty was laughing, playing the big man, handing people pills and taking the money. He looked up and caught Petesy staring at him. Locksy was the last person he wanted Petesy talking to. Marty tipped his head and raised his eyebrows. For a moment Petesy thought about blanking him, about trying not to like his mate. He looked at Marty's Ralph Lauren sweater and remembered the crabs story. He grinned, realizing he couldn't dislike Marty if he tried.

As soon as he walked in, Marty had clocked Cara and her mate sitting on the floor in the corner. She had on a blue tracksuit top with the zip halfway down. Her hair hung across her face and she kept flicking it back with her hand. Marty decided to give it half an hour. He knew the cheer as he walked in would have done him a favour, but you didn't want to seem desperate.

Micky was supposed to be staying with his aunty while his mother was in Benidorm with his step-da. His real da had left when he was six and his mother had taken up with someone else a couple of months later. Micky hated him and spent as much time out of the house as possible. His mother had locked the place up before they left but Micky had climbed the drainpipe and got in through his bedroom like he always did.

'Peter Parker's got nothing on me.'

They all scored off Marty and were waiting for the pills to kick in, slagging him off that his gear was shite. Half an hour later and folk were chewing gum as if their lives depended on it. They nodded to the music, rubbing their faces with their hands. Micky was talking fifty miles an hour about who would win a fight between Bruce Lee and Jackie Chan. Locksy stood in the corner, jabbing his hands in front of him in time with the music.

'Fucking brilliant!' he exclaimed to no one in particular.

Upstairs, Marty was in the toilet. His head was buzzing. After he pissed he stood and stared at himself in the mirror. He rubbed his face. Warm waves rippled through his body. He smiled, trying to connect the face in the mirror with the mad thoughts whirling round his head. It was OK. It was all OK. No. It was better than that. It was mental. It was fucking mental. He tossed another pill in his mouth and took a slug of water from the tap.

Outside the bathroom Marty heard a girl's voice call him from one of the bedrooms. He walked in and saw Cara sitting on the bed. Micky still slept under the same Liverpool FC duvet he'd had when he was eleven. His da, his real da, was fanatical about Liverpool. If you got Micky started he would name every single player that had ever played for them. Positions, previous clubs, everything. The light was off in the bedroom but Marty could still make out the poster on the wall. Thirty men in red sat in three rows, their hands on their knees. They looked out into the room, smiling their encouragement.

Marty had no fear now about talking to Cara. He was going to get off with her, he knew that. He had been watching her across the living room earlier in the night, trying not to let on. She sat on the bed, chewing gum, sipping her can of Harp. He sat beside her and could smell perfume, mixed in with the odour of beer, cigarettes and the stale scent of Micky's teenage bedroom.

'Got any pills left, Marty?' Cara asked.

'Might do.'

'Go on and give us another one, would you?'

'What's it worth to you?'

'Don't know.' She smiled with fake coyness. 'I am sure I can think of something.'

Cara reached over and ran her hand up the leg of Marty's jeans. She pressed down on his fly, raising her eyebrow at his knob underneath. The warmth flowing over Marty's body rippled towards his crotch. He felt himself start to harden.

'I might have a few left in my pocket there.' He leaned back on the bed.

Cara reached into the pocket of his jeans. She moved her hand around, taking hold of his knob through the lining. She squeezed it a few times, and began working him up and down. The pills added to the pleasure and Cara's hand movements sent warm waves out over Marty's body. She felt the small bag of tablets in his pocket and took it out, handing it to Marty.

'I think I've found it.'

Marty smiled, taking a pill from the bag and handing it to her. She threw it in her mouth and washed it down with a mouthful of Harp. Marty leaned over and started kissing her. He could hear muffled voices downstairs, the bass coming up through the floorboards, the distant sound of Locksy shouting: 'Fucking yeeeeow.'

It was after four in the morning. Marty was downstairs rummaging through the cupboards of Micky's ma's kitchen. Heinz tomato soup. Jacob's crackers. An empty biscuit tin.

'Fuck me, Micky,' he said to himself, biting into a dry cracker. 'You call this a kitchen? I'm calling social services. Report your ma for neglect.'

Nobody was listening.

Marty turned round and saw Petesy sitting just through the door.

'Come on, Petesy. Twenty-four-hour garage. Let's go.'

'Ah Marty, I can't be fucked.'

There followed two minutes of cajoling, talk of crisps, chocolate bars, cans of Coke. It was the promise to tell Petesy about Cara that finally clinched it.

At the garage Marty bought twenty Regal, four bags of salt and vinegar, two Mars bars, a Drifter and two cans of Coke. They sat round the back of the garage, eating like their lives depended on it.

'I fucking love these,' Petesy said, stuffing a handful of crisps into his mouth. Half the crisps ended up on the ground near his feet. He picked up the fallen soldiers.

'It's OK. The three-second rule.'

Back at Micky's there was no talking, no drinking, no dancing. The music had stopped.

Three men stood in the middle of the living room. Black ski-masks covered their faces. They wore jeans and dark green Army jackets. Two of them held baseball bats. The other held a large flick-knife in front of him. He was turning it round as if it was some kind of foreign object that fascinated him.

In the hall Micky lay in a ball, wheezing. He'd opened the door and been hit in the stomach with the butt of a baseball bat.

Heavy footsteps came down the stairs. A fourth man, also in a ski-mask, entered. He had a deep voice.

'They're not fucking here.'

Locksy sat in one of Micky's ma's armchairs, wishing he was invisible. The man with the knife came over, his eyes bulging, staring out of the mask. He raised the knife and stroked it down the side of Locksy's already bruised face.

'Where are those two cunts?'

He didn't need to name them. Locksy's eyes were wide open as he tried to pull back from the knife.

'They were here a while ago. They must have gone out.'

The man pressed the blade harder against Locksy's cheek. A drop of blood gathered and ran along the metal of the knife. Locksy's pupils dilated and he winced.

'You tell those cunts we're looking for them.'

The man stepped back, sweeping the knife around the room. His eyes were a mixture of disdain and disgust.

'Fucking wee hoods.'

The four men turned and walked out of the house. When they were gone no one moved. No one spoke. No one put the music back on.

TWELVE

O'Neill stood in the corridor outside CID, pretending to look at the noticeboard. Inside the office he could hear two DCs, Larkin and Kearney, talking to one another.

'That Laganview has to win some sort of prize,' Larkin was saying. 'I mean, it's complete bullshit. A total waste of time.'

O'Neill heard the sound of a file being tossed down on the desk.

'Tell me about it,' Kearney answered. 'All I can say is, I'm glad we're off it.'

Wilson had pulled everyone off the case. O'Neill was now working it alone. The squad had been on it for three days, making a show of things, throwing some resources at it. No stone left unturned, Wilson had said. It was good for the TV cameras. Once *they* lost interest though ...

'I'll tell you what,' Larkin continued. 'O'Neill must have pissed someone off in a previous life to get landed with this crap. Chasing after some kneecapping, some wee hood that nobody gives a shit about. I mean, it's one wee frigger we won't have to spend ten years running around after. Arresting him every six weeks. Watching him yo-yo in and out of jail, until he can walk in here and recognize us all by name.' Larkin spoke through his nose, doing an impression of a Belfast hood. 'Fuck you, Kearney. Fuck you, Larkin.'

The other detective laughed.

'I'm telling you, whoever did this saved us all a shedload of work. You can't say it, but that's the truth. Do you remember being in uniform? Getting spat at, told to go fuck yourself, by a bunch of wee cunts that never worked a day in their lives. You just know no one downstairs is losing any sleep over it. It's one less piece of shit for them to have to deal with.'

O'Neill felt his jaw tighten. He remembered the image of the boy, lying naked on the steel slab of the morgue. Pale, skinny, his ribs protruding. Maybe it was because he didn't have on his customary uniform – tracksuit and baseball cap. Or maybe it was because he couldn't answer back, and wasn't cursing his head off. Or maybe it was because he was on his own. Lying there in the cold, in the disinfectant of the morgue, with nothing but O'Neill, the pathologist and a tray of scalpels for company.

Larkin kept going.

'It's almost a week and they still don't even have a name. Nightmare. Total nightmare. Tell you what, I'm glad I don't have Laganview hanging round *my* neck – especially with the Review Boards coming up. Talk about being thrown overboard with no life-vest. This will drag O'Neill to the bottom of the ocean. All I can say is, when it's my turn to get fucked by the third floor, I hope it's over something better than a shitty kneecapping. Wilson's going to do him over this. Mark my words.'

O'Neill's eyes bored into the noticeboard. Kearney was right. He was nowhere on the case and if it stayed that way, it wouldn't be long before Wilson came at him. It was almost the perfect crime. No ID, no witnesses, no evidence. It was perfect for Wilson at least. He'd gotten the chance to pose for the cameras, to play the big man, the all-powerful Chief Inspector. Now the spotlight had moved on and it wouldn't be back. Wilson would be able to hang O'Neill out to dry and no one would so much as notice.

O'Neill headed for the coffee room. He'd heard enough. He poured some coffee into a polystyrene cup and took it outside.

In Musgrave Street car park he leaned against the main building, he lit a cigarette and listened to the midday traffic on the other side of the wall. Larkin had only said what everyone else was thinking. All the money, all the man hours. It was true. The kid was a frigging hood. So what did he matter? He would probably mug his own granny as soon as look at her.

O'Neill had spent the morning reading through the case-files on the other kneecappings that had gone into the Royal since September. Gerard Robinson, 'Geardy', father unemployed, mother an alcoholic, kicked out of three schools. Multiple arrests – possession, affray, shoplifting. Michael MacNamee, 'Mackers', sixteen, mother with five kids to five different men. She'd been done three times for child benefit fraud. Multiple arrests – GBH, stealing, possession with intent. David MacAtackney, 'Deags', father and mother not around, lived with his granny who was disabled and housebound. Multiple arrests – possession, criminal damage, theft of a motor vehicle. They were hoods all right. That was no argument. The world told them to go fuck themselves, so they turned round and told the world to do the same. It was a pretty logical response, O'Neill thought.

In the car park he threw away his cigarette and went back inside. Up in CID, Larkin joked, 'Ah, DS O'Neill. How's our great murder investigation getting on today? Anyone in cuffs yet?'

It was standard office banter and Larkin didn't mean anything. O'Neill snapped though.

'What the fuck would you know about it?'

Larkin stood up from his chair. 'What's your fucking problem?'

Someone cleared their throat in the doorway. Both men turned. It was Ward. The two detectives backed down.

'DS O'Neill,' Ward said. 'Can I have a word with you?'

Four hours later, Ward sat in an unmarked Mondeo watching 16 Tivoli Gardens. The house was a standard piece of Belfast suburbia: three bedrooms, front garden, small garage. Down the side of the house, a five-year-old girl threw tennis balls against the wall, singing a song to herself.

Ward recognized O'Neill's daughter, despite the changes in her from a year ago. Even now he was here, sitting outside the house, he wasn't sure about talking to Catherine. He was violating an unwritten rule. Your loyalty lay with other cops. No one else. Not even their family. Ward knew it was Brothers in Arms bullshit, used to hide a multitude of sins. He'd watched peelers get their partners to cover for them, lying to their wives: 'Pat's questioning someone ... he had to go to court ... he's tied up with a suspect.' Ward wondered what made cops such prolific cheats. O'Neill wasn't messing around though, he knew that much. He also knew about the flat in Stranmillis and that he hadn't been home for six months.

Earlier that morning, Ward had stuck his head into CID. It was empty, except for O'Neill, sitting in front of his computer. He'd checked with Doris on the front desk. O'Neill had been in for two hours before his shift. It had been going on for months. First in, last to leave. Anyone else, Ward would have been pleased. Showing some initiative, getting a head start. It wasn't anyone else though.

O'Neill had done a good job of hiding his personal life from Musgrave Street. The rest of the shift hadn't noticed a thing. Ward started to wonder if he worked in a station full of blind men. He told himself they were busy, up to their eyeballs in paperwork. He knew though that half the shift couldn't find a criminal unless he walked into the station, carrying a bloody knife, saying, 'I killed the bitch.' With O'Neill it was small things he had picked up on. The same suit. Same three shirts. He looked like shit. O'Neill had even started taking stuff home, reading through police files at night. He looked as if he hadn't had a proper night's sleep for months. Ward had been waiting on a sign and the outburst with Larkin was enough to convince him.

Ward had seen it before with other peelers. There were three outcomes. O'Neill would burn out, he'd smack someone, or else he'd end up getting killed. It used to be drink was the way most peelers went. Home alone. Half a bottle of whiskey before they could close their eyes. That wouldn't be O'Neill. Smacking Larkin though ...

There was also the possibility he'd go down the third route. O'Neill had the kind of obsession that would get a peeler in trouble. When he locked in on something and put the blinkers on, he didn't care. It was what had made him a good peeler. No matter the situation, no matter the odds, O'Neill would go after it. He said what he thought and didn't care who was listening. It was also what had got him in trouble with Wilson in the first place.

Without Catherine and wee Sarah, Ward knew O'Neill would make the job everything. He was still young and it wouldn't be long before he became reckless. Ward had seen it before. Detectives who reckoned they were invincible. A guy with nothing to go home to becomes a guy with nothing to lose. They start putting themselves out there. Going it alone. Thinking they can do it all. They find themselves drinking in bars they shouldn't be drinking in. Not knowing the difference between 'off duty' and 'on duty'. Peace Process or no Peace Process, this was still the North. It wasn't hard for a peeler to disappear. To get into his car one morning, turn the key and ...

O'Neill hadn't got that far yet, but he'd started down the path. Ward could see it. There was a car crash on its way.

The door of 16 Tivoli Gardens opened and a man walked out. He was in his late thirties and wore a sharp grey suit. He was tall, handsome, the kind of man women found attractive. He paused by O'Neill's daughter, working her tennis balls against the wall. She stopped and they exchanged a joke. Sarah smiled and the man put his hand on her head, ruffling her hair. He got into a black BMW 3 series and drove off.

Ward took mental note of the licence-plate. Could Catherine have cheated on O'Neill? Had she moved on already? Ward thought back to the first time he met her. It was a Sunday. He'd been walking the dog in the grounds of Belfast Castle and come across the family.

'Ah, the O'Neills,' he'd announced in gentle mockery. 'Now isn't this a lovely sight.'

O'Neill and Catherine were with Sarah, who wobbled behind on her pink bike. Ward's dog was ex-police canine, a German Shepherd called Rex. He loved kids and licked Sarah's face, prompting bouts of, 'Mummy, Mummy, can we get a dog?' Catherine asked if Ward fancied a cup of coffee, said she wanted to meet the great DI that she'd heard so much about.

In the café opposite the Shaftsbury Inn, Ward could see that O'Neill's wife was smart. She gave as good as she got and wasn't afraid of ribbing her husband in front of his superior. Ward also liked the daughter. She was pretty and well behaved. He asked about school and let her pet the dog, promising to bring him round to visit.

Catherine had thought Ward was the kind of uncle you would wish your kids had. She left feeling reassured, knowing her husband had someone like Ward looking over his shoulder at work. She had asked O'Neill several times to invite him round for dinner but they never managed it and life seemed to take over.

On the drive home that day, Ward had looked at Rex, curled in the footwell of the passenger seat, and he felt a pang of regret, thinking about O'Neill and his young family. He thought about Maureen and her tears when they learned that they couldn't have kids of their own. He thought about her telling him that he could leave her and that she'd understand. He thought about the cancer, about the tint of her skin when the chemo started, about the vomiting, the worry and eventually, the resignation. That had been fifteen years ago. Ward had thought about remarrying but somehow it didn't seem right. Maureen would have laughed, told him to stop being so stupid. He couldn't get his head round it though and felt that he'd be betraying her. The dog had looked up at Ward from the footwell. He took his hand off the gear-stick and reached down to pet him.

Outside 16 Tivoli Gardens, Ward watched the BMW drive away. Catherine wouldn't have moved on so quickly. It wasn't in her. Too much respect. For O'Neill, for Sarah, for herself. He got out of the Mondeo and approached the house, thinking about the hand ruffling the girl's hair.

'Hi, Sarah.'

'Hey!' the girl exclaimed, recognizing Ward. 'Do you have Rex with you?'

'Not today, honey. He has been asking for you though. Wants to come over. We'll get you to take him for a walk. Would you be up for that?'

The girl nodded enthusiastically.

'Was that your uncle just leaving?'

'Yeah.'

Ward remembered hearing about Catherine's brother. A solicitor for McRoberts & James in Belfast. A pretty decent guy, O'Neill said, for a lawyer.

'Your mum in?'

'Yeah. Will I get her?'

'No. Don't worry. You just keep playing.'

Ward waited for Catherine to answer. He heard her approach, speaking as she opened the door.

'OK. So what did you forget this ti—'

She faltered as soon as she saw Ward. Her face fell. She had known this day was coming. She'd waited for it ever since

O'Neill joined up. The lone policeman, standing on your doorstep. 'Mrs O'Neill?' She thought about Sarah, hearing the tennis balls against the wall. She suddenly felt an urge to hold her daughter, to pull her close, to protect her.

Ward saw Catherine's face and put up his hand.

'Calm down. He's all right. This isn't one of *those* calls.'

It didn't register.

'Listen, Catherine. John's fine. He's alive and well. Probably getting up someone's nose at this very minute.'

Slowly Catherine's expression softened. The look of horror was replaced by one of curiosity.

'This is ...' he searched for the words, 'more of a social call.'

Ward waited. He had stood on hundreds of doorsteps and knew the territory. He needed her to invite him in, into the familiarity of the house, the cosiness. He needed it to open her up, to get her talking, and then to get her to listen.

'You'd better come in,' Catherine said as she opened the door and stood aside. She shouted round the corner: 'Sarah. Five more minutes and then your bath.'

'OK,' a distracted voice shouted back.

In the kitchen Catherine offered Ward a cup of tea. He accepted, knowing it would help with what he wanted to say. It would make it feel less like she was talking to a cop.

'So, Detective Inspector Ward?'

'Please. Jack is fine.'

'OK, Jack. So tell me, since when did the PSNI start making social calls?'

'We're a twenty-first-century police force, you know. We do everything now. Bobbies on the beat, old ladies across roads, cake sales.'

'I'll believe it when I see it,' Catherine joked.

She handed him his tea. Ward took a drink. The woman didn't speak, waiting for him to make the first move. You could tell she was married to a cop, Ward thought.

'O'Neill doesn't know I'm here.'

'That's what I thought.' Catherine gave a faint smile, realizing that Ward probably knew her husband as well as she did.

'How long's he been out of the house?' Ward asked.

'He told you?'

'He hasn't told anyone. No one at Musgrave Street knows.'

'Except you.'

'What can I say?' said Ward humbly. 'Guess us old dogs have our uses, after all.'

Catherine paused before she spoke. 'It's been six months. We've been on a break.'

'Those don't sound like O'Neill's words.'

'He was never here. It was like living with a ghost. Sarah sees him almost as much now as when he lived here.'

Ward didn't answer. He wanted to hear what she had to say, to give her a sympathetic ear, let her know he was on her side. Already he could see the crack in the dam growing and with a little prodding ...

Catherine went into the litany of problems. The shifts, the tiredness, the last-minute phone calls, the cancellations, the staring into space. Ward listened. It sounded like she'd rehearsed it hundreds of times, over and over in her mind, trying to make sense of it all. He thought this was the first time that she'd said it out loud. The first time she'd let it all out. She was a peeler's wife, after all. There weren't exactly a lot of people you could bare your soul to. It was more than that though, he thought. Catherine was a private person. There was something old-fashioned about her, a pride, not wanting to hang your dirty laundry out in public. He let her go on, sensing the tension that had built up over months. She needed to tell someone, to unload, to let it all out. Ward sat quiet, listening and nodding.

After ten minutes Catherine began to slow up and run out of steam. She lifted her tea and slurped. Ward took his time. He needed to let it settle. Let everything come to rest before trying to talk to her. The two of them drank their tea in silence. Finally Catherine spoke.

'Sorry to throw all that at you.'

'The course of true love,' Ward said, then paused. 'Sounds like it had been brewing for a while.' He looked round the kitchen, taking in its domesticity.

'He needs you, you know.'

'He needs the job. Let's not kid ourselves. That's all he needs.'

Ward slowly shook his head. 'That's not true. And I think you know it's not. He needs *you*. He needs this place. He needs Sarah. He needs those frigging tennis balls,' Ward rolled his eyes, laughing softly. 'He needs to know that there's five more minutes and then it's bath time. He needs to know there is more than chasing after some guy, trying to get a charge, a confession, something so it will all make sense.'

'*You* might know that, but *he* doesn't.'

'That's because he's young, because he's stupid, because he's trying to prove himself. Because he thinks he's the smartest guy in the room. That he knows better than everyone. You've got to understand, Catherine. It's what makes him a good peeler.' Ward took a breath. 'But it doesn't mean he doesn't need you. You and Martina Navratilova out there.'

Catherine smiled. Ward went on, telling her about his thirty years, about the other detectives he'd seen, guys like O'Neill. Stubborn. They'd bite on to something and never let go. Great cops. But they needed something else, something to come home to, something normal. Otherwise, it was them against the world. They'd go out on a limb. Start taking risks. Nothing to lose. Half the time they didn't even know they were doing it.

'Jack, it's the job he cares about. Not us. He isn't capable of both.'

'I don't think you really believe that.'

Catherine had thought about giving John an ultimatum: us or the job. But she knew her husband, knew he couldn't stand being told what to do. Not by her, not by anyone. He'd leave in a moment of anger, just to spite her.

The front door opened. 'That's me in,' Sarah shouted, pounding up the stairs.

Ward grinned at her voice and the thunder of her steps. 'She's a great kid, that one.'

Catherine sighed.

'She needs him, Catherine. And I think you need him too. But I'll tell you something else: we need him. The job needs him.'

Ward searched his thoughts, trying to get his head round it, trying to explain it to her.

'The police here have changed, you see. I'm not saying it was perfect before, far from it. But at least it was full of peelers. Nowadays the place is run by glorified secretaries and accountants. Bean-counters.'

'Careful,' Catherine joked. 'You're talking to one of those bean-counters.'

'Yeah, but you're not a cop. It's all about paperwork these days. Filling in forms. These guys wouldn't know their way round a suspect if he walked into the station and wanted to confess. John's different though. You can see it. He's got instincts. He can read people, read the street. He knows the score. You put him in a room and in five minutes he'll tell you who beats his wife, who steals from his boss and who's done two years for GBH.'

Ward took a drink of tea.

'This probably sounds like a load of rubbish to you. But Catherine, I know. I've been around – I've seen it. That is what gets the job done. This is what puts people behind bars. Muggers. Murderers. Rapists.' Ward paused. 'Paedophiles.'

Catherine nodded, acquiescing slightly. She'd been married to a peeler long enough to have heard the romance before. The thin blue line. She hadn't met a cop yet who didn't believe themselves to be the only one who knew what was going on out there. She knew what they told themselves. Half of her wanted to laugh at it, the other half believed it. She gazed out the window, thinking about what kind of a world Sarah would grow up in.

'We were on our second date, back before he joined up. He'd taken me to the pictures and we were walking down the Dublin Road. Three guys had started into some fella on the other side of the street. They had a load of drink on them. The next thing, the guy was on the ground and they were kicking lumps out of him. I'd pulled John beside me, telling him to leave it. He couldn't though. He ran over and the three of them started on him. I thought he was going to get killed. They never got him down though, and after a while they realized he wasn't going anywhere. They just gave up and ran off, jeering as they went. John just stood there, his face bleeding, standing over the guy.'

Ward could picture O'Neill, running across the road, piling in.

'A black eye, a bloody nose and four stitches,' Catherine told him. 'That's John. Never happier than when someone is beating the crap out of him. Always giving a shit, even when it's not his turn. Tell me, Jack, when is it ever someone else's turn?'

Ward didn't know the answer. Catherine paused, taking a drink of her tea.

Ward could sense the fondness for her husband starting to resurface. He could feel the story beginning to melt some of the ice from the previous six months. He stood up, saying he needed to get back, and thanked Catherine for the tea. He asked her just to think about it. That was all.

Heading back to Musgrave Street, Ward wondered if he had done enough. There was a chink of light, a glimmer of hope. It was something, at least.

THIRTEEN

He was twenty minutes late. The lift hummed up towards the fifteenth floor of the anonymous glass building on Bedford Street. Lynch wondered if Burton would still see him. He had been early, but found himself doing another lap of the block, toying with flagging it altogether. He didn't need a shrink. Lynch told himself it was the sleeping tablets. They'd helped. A few hours of broken sleep was better than nothing. So if it took another trip to Burton to get another prescription, then so be it. He could sit and listen. Tell the doc what he wanted to hear. Spin a few stories.

He was lying to himself though. He knew it. The truth was, he was curious. Curious and hopeful. It wasn't a great combination. Lynch knew you could end up in a lot of shit on the back of those two. He tried to ignore his better instincts. He wanted to know how Burton knew. About the Brits. About the gun. He'd thought all that was long gone. A distant memory. Pure history. Turned out it hadn't gone anywhere. It was there, hidden away, lodged in the back of his mind. He'd spent the week having flashbacks – the faces, the taste, the smell. Pupils dilating, palms sweating, heart racing. Lynch wondered what else Burton might know about. What else he might uncover. Could he tell him why he felt like a ghost walking round inside his own body, like a stranger in his own town?

Lynch stepped out of the lift into the plush reception area. The leather sofa was empty. To the left of the receptionist's desk, Burton's door was open. The blonde girl looked up from her computer as he approached.

'Joe Lynch ...'

She nodded at the door. 'You can go right in.'

Lynch stepped forward, pausing in the doorway to Burton's office. The room was exactly as he'd left it. Beige carpet, neat furniture and the vista, out over Belfast. The doctor sat behind his desk, writing on a piece of paper. He looked up at Lynch who was momentarily framed in the doorway.

'Come on in, Joe.' Burton's voice was businesslike. 'Grab a seat.'

Neither of them mentioned that Lynch was late. Burton himself guessed why, but knew it was a bad place to start and would guarantee he'd not get anywhere. Why slam shut what was already a pretty closed book. He'd been surprised when Dr MacSorley had phoned and requested another appointment. He could see, looking at Lynch's face, it had been touch and go whether he would actually come.

Lynch sat in the seat he'd occupied the week before. Burton closed the door and sat opposite. His chair was offset slightly, so that he didn't face his clients directly.

'So?' Burton said.

'So.'

Silence.

'*You* came to see *me*, Joe.'

'They teach you how to set these chairs up, don't they?'

Burton looked at the furniture.

Lynch continued. 'You don't face people. Too intimidating. Too much confrontation. Like an interrogation.'

'For some people, yes.'

'But that's what it is though, isn't it? You want to know what's going on with folk. What makes them tick. They sit down and you ask the questions. Examine them. Their secrets. It's like going to Confession.'

'Maybe. Except we don't offer forgiveness.'

'That's fine,' Lynch snapped back. 'No one's asking for it.'

Burton sighed. He knew Lynch would want to spar with him. To feel him out. Decide whether he was going to say anything. Still, Lynch had come back, which meant something. Burton knew that was his leverage.

'Get out, Joe.'

'What?'

'I said get out.' Burton paused. 'If you want to talk about furniture, then take yourself to MFI. I don't have time for it.' The psychologist leaned forward to stand up and go back to his desk.

'You didn't know, did you?' Lynch said, halting the other man's movement.

Burton paused before sitting back in his seat. 'Know what?'

'About the Brits. Being put against a wall. About them putting a gun in my mouth.'

Burton looked at Lynch and shook his head.

'No, I didn't. But there had to be something. I went fishing, that was all.'

'So that's it. There's some theory out there, some textbook. How people get "involved". What makes them say they've had enough of doing nothing. Makes them decide to do something about it.'

'Radicalization. It varies from person to person. It's all about Muslims these days. September Eleventh. Those planes and the Twin Towers. Iraq. Afghanistan. Ireland's yesterday's news. Nobody wants to hear about us any more. The peace deal's been done. It's time to move on.'

'Suppose there's a theory about that and all?'

Burton raised his eyebrows and nodded. If there was an A–Z of conflict resolution, he was yet to be convinced by it.

'Thing is, Doc, the guys who write these theories, that's all they do – write them. They don't fucking live them.'

The conversation had found its rhythm from the previous week. Back and forth. Lynch wanting to square up. Confrontation was where he was most comfortable. Burton wondered if he always needed to be on the offensive.

The two men stopped talking. Burton's eyes fell and he gazed at the table, deliberately ignoring the other man. Finally Lynch spoke again.

'So what are we supposed to talk about?'

'You tell me, Joe.'

'You've read the books, Doc. Surely there's a list. Seven Steps or something. Is that not how it works?'

'What do *you* think, Joe?'

'Hey, it's your patch. How am I supposed to know how it works?'

Burton's eyes fell back to the table. Lynch watched him disengage.

'So we just sit here?'

'You can leave if you want.'

Lynch looked round the room, glancing from the bookcase to the desk to the window. Beyond the green domes of City Hall the yellow arm of a crane slowly swung across the rooftops of the city centre. They were building a new shopping centre round the back of Corn Market. He'd stopped on the way over to look at the gaping hole, the size of a football pitch. A huge billboard announced: *Victoria Square*. Two women passed behind him.

'It's going to have a House of Fraser and all, so it is?'

The other woman gasped, confessing that she couldn't wait.

Lynch looked back at Burton. 'There's some changes going on round here, eh?'

'What do you mean?' Burton asked.

'Around the town. I mean, I went the other day to put a line on at a bookies I used to go to down Smithfield. I turned the corner and it's one of them frigging coffee places. It's like every time you walk round the corner, someone's building something. And shops – I mean, how many frigging shops do people need? It's getting as bad as London.'

'You lived in London?'

'Just for a while.'

Lynch remembered the stories his Aunt Annie told about the seventies. She used to come home talking about signs outside boarding houses. *No Blacks. No Irish.* As soon as they heard your accent, they treated you like something the dog dragged in.

Burton knew that Lynch was avoiding any real engagement. Still, at least he was speaking. If he kept him talking there was a chance they'd end up somewhere by the end of the session.

'Know anything about Buddhists?' he asked.

'Hari Krishnas. Enlightenment and all. You going to start chanting, Doc?'

'I wouldn't get your hopes up. Buddhists reckon everything is always changing. All the time. The thing is, we just don't see it. Living and dying. Growing and rotting. Our problem is that we don't get it. We expect things to stay the same. And they don't. They can't. Nothing can.'

'That's deep,' Lynch said dismissively. 'Pass the spliff, man, would you?'

Burton tried to mask a sigh. He knew Lynch could oscillate all day between aggressive question and cynical put-down. He was clever. Disciplined. He gave nothing away, not unless he wanted to. And he didn't let you in, not for a second. He had been involved, but Burton could tell he wasn't the kind of person who blindly followed orders. He thought about other ex-prisoners he had worked with. Ninety per cent of the time it was about ego, vanity, self-worth. Being involved gave them something to do, someone to be. They were the star in the film of their own lives. At least that was how it felt. And there was always a father figure, someone senior, someone to tell them who they were. Tell them that they were part of something. An heroic struggle. A great cause. That history would remember them.

Lynch was different. Too practical. Too deliberate. Burton couldn't imagine him buying the romance. That was for followers, for those who needed pulling along. Burton looked at the clock. Lynch had been late and the session was almost over.

The other man spoke, interrupting Burton's thoughts.

'So what about people?'

'What do you mean?'

'What do your Buddhists say about people? Do people change?'

Burton paused.

'What do *you* think, Joe?'

Lynch knew what Burton was up to, deliberately turning the question back on him.

'Maybe they do. Maybe they don't. Maybe there comes a point when it's too late. When somebody has been someone or something for so long, they've gone past the point where it's possible to change, and maybe they don't realize it. They walk round, thinking they're someone new, only they're not. All the time though, lurking below the surface, the real them is waiting. Just waiting for a chance to stick his head out of the water.'

Lynch's eyes narrowed and he went back to looking out the window. Burton wanted to let him run but he had closed down, just as quickly as he had opened up. Lynch snorted a quiet laugh to himself.

'So the other day, I'm walking round to the shop to get a pint of milk. It's eleven o'clock in the morning, and round the back of the Spar there's these two young ones, sitting among the bins. Glue sniffing. Twelve, maybe thirteen. They're passing this plastic bag between them, taking turns to put their faces into it. They have that red rash round their mouth like you see. They look up for a second, almost look through me, and go back at it. It's their eyes. Empty. The lights are on but there's nobody home. Like they're completely dead on the inside. They'd pull a knife on you as soon as look at you. They don't give a shit. Don't care about getting caught, getting a beating, getting locked up. Because nothing can happen to them that will make their lives worse than they already are. I mean, how the fuck do you hit rock bottom by the time you're twelve? So that there is nothing to be done. Except you stick your head in a bag so you can forget about everything, even if it's only for thirty seconds. What I want to know is this, Doc: if your Buddhists know so much, then are things going to start changing for these two?'

Burton paused, allowing the question to drift away.

'What are you so angry about, Joe?'

Lynch's eyes moved from side to side, weighing up whether to speak, to tell Burton what he really thought.

'It's bullshit. All of it. A new dawn. A new day. A load of fucking crap. Stormont. Politicians chuckling for the cameras. Collecting their fat salaries. Meanwhile, the guys are out there running everything. Making sure ... well, making sure things run. And what are we doing, sitting here in your plush office, looking at the nice view, talking about Buddhists ... I haven't seen too many frigging Buddhists walking the streets of Belfast.'

Lynch gestured to the window with his thumb. Burton sensed he was about to leave. He'd talked himself to the point of walking out, recovered that sense of indignation, of being wronged.

'You used to like to work alone, Joe. Didn't you?'

Lynch was taken aback by the change of subject.

'Come again?'

'It was people. People were the problem. They were a liability – even the ones on your side. They'd let you down.

Lose their bottle. Not follow through. Sure it was fine, talking about it beforehand, but when push came to shove, there was only one person you could really rely on.'

Lynch sat quietly, listening.

'And that's not really changed. We can talk about Buddhists all day, but it's not about them, Joe. It's about you. You haven't changed. You go days out there, not saying a single word to anyone. And why? Because they know you. Or at least you think they do. It's in that look you get. Fear and respect. But mostly it's fear. Yeah, they know you. So you sit in front of the TV, nothing but you and your memories, and no matter what you do, they keep coming back. You can't make them go away. They don't want to vanish.'

Lynch stared at Burton. He couldn't acknowledge how close he was. It would be like giving something away, losing some control.

'The past. It doesn't just go away on its own,' Burton said. 'The memories – you've got to replace them with different ones. New ones. Better ones. And sometimes, it still won't get rid of them altogether.'

'So what are you supposed to replace them with?'

'It's not up to me, Joe. Only you can figure that out. But it's going to involve other people. I can probably guarantee you that.'

There was a light knock on the door. The signal from the receptionist. They were five minutes beyond their time and Burton's next appointment would be waiting outside. £100 an hour. It didn't pay to keep people waiting.

FOURTEEN

It was Monday morning. Laganview was a week old. Ward drove across the Sydenham bypass and out of the city. The road skirted the coastline of Belfast Lough leading to Holywood, Cultra and eventually Bangor.

O'Neill still didn't have an ID on his body. The forensics had come back and were as weak as they both feared. Wilson had reassigned the investigating team, leaving O'Neill on his own. Ward was a DI though and could do what he wanted. He was on his way to Cultra to visit William Spender, the MD of the developers behind Laganview. It was little more than a fishing expedition but Ward had history with Spender and thought, what the hell, it wasn't as if O'Neill had a cell full of suspects.

Cultra was fifteen minutes along the south shore of Belfast Lough. Nineteenth-century mansions with large bay windows stared out to sea, turning their faces from the city up the coast. Ward imagined an Agatha Christie novel. Guilty butlers, billiard rooms, candlestick-holders. It wasn't the kind of place where the PSNI spent much time.

He had called Spender the night before. The developer didn't have time to meet him. The body was an inconvenience and had already cost a day's work on site. Ward rolled his eyes. The richer people got, the less they wanted to play the helpful citizen. He was about to make Spender come in to Musgrave Street when the developer cut him short, saying he could see him early Monday morning. Ward didn't read much into it. It confirmed what he remembered about Spender: the ego, the arrogance, the self-importance.

Spender Properties had been in the *Belfast Telegraph* a few years earlier over allegations of corruption. Nothing ever came of it though and the papers dropped the story after a few days. The North had a pretty visceral news diet. 'Business Back-Hander' *v* 'Brutal Bomb Blast'. It wasn't really a contest.

On Sunday Ward had called up one of his old contacts at the *Telegraph*. Stuart Colman was in his late fifties and had forgotten more about Belfast than most people would ever know, the police included. He was from York Street but had gone to London, 'Dick Whittington style', in the late seventies. He'd got a start with the *Evening Standard* and stayed a few years until his father died and he came home. Colman agreed to meet him in the Duke of York. When Ward asked about Spender, Colman clocked it straight away.

'You're on Laganview? I thought that was O'Neill?'

Colman was a dying breed. A real reporter. You didn't have to spell things out. He knew most of Musgrave Street by face and never forgot a name. Ward thought he would have made a good detective.

'Anything worth sharing with a humble, hard-working journalist?'

'Nothing yet. But you'll be the first to know.'

'Since when did I start doing *pro bono*?' Colman joked. 'You were always a lousy first date, Ward. Not even a wee kiss, a bit of a fumble in the back row?'

'Slowly does it now. Whatever happened to respecting a girl?'

'I never had you as the prudish type. Anyway, how can I help the Police Service of Northern Ireland?'

'Spender. You guys were looking at him a couple of years ago. It was over some fraud allegations. What do you know about him?'

'Spender? He's building the new Northern Ireland. At least, that's what they say. He probably owns half the new builds going up round here. Started as a family of builders. His father was an apprentice bricklayer and worked his way up. Died when Spender was in his twenties and left the firm to his son. At that stage Spenders were building houses, one at a time type of thing. The son was ambitious though and wanted to expand. Within a few years they were doing housing developments. Small estates. First-time buyer stuff. Three bedrooms, a patch of grass out back.'

Colman stopped talking and drained the rest of his pint.

'This is thirsty work.'

Ward took the hint and got in two more Guinness.

'Spender's ambition took the company in the right direction. Along came the Peace Process and when the price of property started soaring they were in the right place at the right time. Laganview's just part of what they have on the go. They're the main players in the redevelopment of the old gasworks at the bottom of the Ormeau Road. They did the Cathedral Quarter and are bidding to get part of the Titanic Quarter.'

'Interesting,' Ward said. 'So what was the scoop back then?'

'Bribing public officials. Someone in the Planning Office at City Hall.'

'Did you get a name?'

'Don't know. Wasn't my story.'

'Why'd the *Telegraph* get cold feet?'

'Usual story. Businessman calls lawyer. Lawyer calls paper. Paper shits itself.'

'What happened to the Fourth Estate and all that?'

'Who are you kidding? The Fourth Estate's a housing estate. Half these journalists wouldn't know a story if it jumped up and bit them on the arse. Soap stars shagging footballers – that's all people care about these days. Or who's the latest contestant on *Big* fucking *Brother*. Honestly, the place is going down the pan. And no one gives a shite about it.'

'Well,' said Ward, 'do a bit of hoking round. I might be able to get you a second bite of the cherry on this.'

'I'll see if there is anything I can come up with. Do you think Spender has some connection with the body?'

'No. But I thought I might be able to have a little fun with him though. Stir it up in Cultra. Give them something to talk about over their sherry in Royal Belfast.'

'A man after my own heart. Keep me posted. I'll be waiting here with my dress on.'

The cars became more expensive as Ward turned off the carriageway into Cultra. He passed a black BMW saloon, followed by a silver Porsche. The navy Mondeo looked out of place. Ward imagined the Victorian mansions looking down their noses as he rolled along the wide avenues.

Spender's place was guarded by a 12-foot, wrought-iron gate. Ward pressed the intercom and it slowly swung open. Up a curved driveway he came to the house. The triple garage held two Mercedes, a silver coupé and a long black saloon. There was another car. A red TVR with personalized registration: WS 1. The front lawn looked like an oversized tennis court and stretched down to the shore where a 20-foot sailboat was tied to a jetty. Ward imagined summertime – long white tables, jackets and dresses, glasses of Pimm's. He looked at the view. Belfast was a silver slither on the horizon, hidden by a row of elm trees along the western wall. It was almost as if the city wasn't even there.

Before Ward had a chance to ring the bell a petite woman opened the door. She had bobbed blonde hair and wore a black skirt and white blouse. A deep olive tan made her look several years younger than she probably was.

'Mrs Spender?'

'Please. Call me Karen.'

'DI Ward. Musgrave Street.'

'You're a long way from home, Detective.'

Ward glanced up at the house. 'You're not wrong there.'

The woman smiled. Ward looked down the garden toward the water.

'This is quite a view you have here.'

'Yes. We like it.'

'You know, there're people out there make fun of Cultra but I think I'm beginning to see the attraction.'

Ward knew he had a chance to make a friend. And friends could turn out useful further down the road.

'Believe me, Detective, there's plenty to be made fun of down here.'

The wife and Spender weren't from Cultra. They were Belfast people. New money. He imagined the local women, gossiping over their pearls and afternoon tea.

122

'Sorry to call so early.'

'Don't worry. William's been working from six. He has an office here as well as the one in Belfast.'

'Busy man. Still I guess with the property market ... making hay and all that.'

Ward followed Karen Spender down the hall. Her heels clicked loudly on the large black and white tiles. A large gilt mirror hung in the main artery of the house. On the wall was a framed family photograph – husband, wife, two teenage children, a son and daughter. Spender smiled out of the frame: smug, assured, proprietorial. Ward paused.

'Your two then?'

The woman paused before she spoke. 'Yes. Although that was a few years ago. Zara is now—'

'I am sure he doesn't need your whole life-story, Karen.'

William Spender strode out of an adjacent room. He was in his late fifties, older than his wife and not wearing so well. Spender wore a shirt and tie, his wrists flashing a pair of gold cufflinks, bearing the initials *WS*. He was impatient. He didn't like Ward being in the house and wanted to get on with it. The woman ignored her husband and told the detective it was nice to meet him. She walked off down the hall and up the stairs.

'Let's step into my office,' Spender said. It was a command rather than an invitation. Spender signalled the door he had come out of. They walked through into a vast room, centred round an 8-foot mahogany desk.

Ward looked round the room. Spender's office was bigger than the press room at Musgrave Street. The back wall was lined with a large bookcase containing rows of leather volumes. Ward didn't think Spender had read any of them. Behind the desk was a high-backed executive chair. The developer took up his position and motioned to a seat in front.

'So, Detective. Where are you with the investigation?'

Ward paused, wondering who Spender thought he was. He ignored the question and got out his notepad, slowly and deliberately. When he'd opened it at a clean page he looked up.

'So. What do you know about the body on your site, Mr Spender?'

'Only what I have seen on the news,' Spender replied.

'And where were you, the night of the murder?'

'I was here with my wife.'

'What were you doing?'

'Probably working.'

'Probably ...?'

'Listen, Detective—'

'And what about Monday morning?'

'I was here.'

'So how did you find out about it?'

'Someone called me.'

'Who called you?'

'The foreman.'

'The *foreman* called *you*?'

'No. He called the office and they put him through. Listen, Detective, I don't know why you're—' Spender was getting increasingly annoyed.

'What time was the call?'

'In the morning.'

'You don't know what time?' Ward asked, a deliberate note of disbelief in his voice.

'Before nine,' Spender snapped back.

'And what did you do?'

'What do you mean what did I do?'

'A dead body turns up on one of your sites. You don't go down there? You don't contact the police?'

'You'd already been contacted. Then you arrived and pulled my whole workforce off the site.'

Ward could see this had got to Spender. The fact that someone was interfering with his empire. He decided to prod.

'Must have cost you a bit, that. Us shutting you down.'

Spender didn't reply.

'Do you know of anyone who might want to disrupt Laganview?'

'No.'

'Locals? Contractors? Disgruntled employees? Anyone with a grudge against you or the company?'

'No. Detective, we're providing jobs down there. Building some of the best property ever seen in Northern Ireland. These apartments—'

'Save it for your investors, Mr Spender.' Ward decided to change tack. 'How long has Tony Burke worked for you?'

'Six, seven years.'

'What do you know about him?'

'I know he is a good foreman. Listen, Detective—'

'Do you know about his past?'

'No. But what has that—'

'You were in the *Belfast Telegraph,* Mr Spender. Corruption and fraud.'

'Once the *Telegraph* checked its facts, it soon let the story drop.'

Ward stayed silent, staring at Spender incredulously. The developer went on the offensive.

'I hardly see the relevance between that and some wee hood turning up dead on my building site. I'm not even sure why you are down here. Wouldn't your time be better spent in the Short Strand? The Markets? Instead of out here, casting aspersions about things you know nothing about.'

'You stick to the property game, Mr Spender. Leave the policework to the rest of us.'

Ward stood up and walked slowly to the wall of Spender's office. There were two framed photographs, showing Spender holding some award, flanked by well-fed businessmen in black tie.

'Who's this?' He pointed at one of the men.

Spender gave a name.

'And this?'

Another name.

Ward went through each person, jotting down names. He took his time, letting Spender see he could make things awkward for him. No smoke without fire. Another showed Spender in a dinner jacket alongside three other men at a charity auction. Ward imagined tables of drunk businessmen playing How Big is Your Wallet? They would try to outbid each other for signed rugby jerseys, tickets to Paris, a spa day for the wife.

'Well, Mr Spender. Let me leave my card.' Ward put his card down on the corner of the oak desk. 'If anything pops up, you'll be sure to give me a call.'

Ward turned slowly. 'And don't worry. I can show myself out.'

Moving into the hall, he heard the sound of footsteps coming down the stairs. He paused at the family photograph and looked at the children. Karen Spender walked behind him.

'Great-looking kids,' Ward offered. 'Still at home?'

'No. Across the water. London and Manchester.' The woman looked briefly at the picture, before continuing down the hall and into the kitchen.

Ward got in the Mondeo and lit a cigarette, breaking the force rule about smoking in pool cars. At the bottom of Spender's drive he sat for ten seconds as the black gates slowly opened and released him into the grey morning.

FIFTEEN

Sean Molloy was raging.

'Fucking wee prick-tease. A pair of bitches. Letting us look after them all night and then sliding off in a taxi.'

Saturday night had run into Sunday morning. The club had closed and he was walking home with Tierney. Until an hour ago this had looked like the least likely outcome of the night.

Molloy had been playing the big man, throwing his money round. They'd been sitting for three hours in Mint with two girls, Tara and Sharon. They must have only been eighteen but, as Molloy told Tierney, a hole was a hole. The two girls fancied themselves and for good reason. They both looked like they'd been poured into their dresses. Molloy had done a line before they arrived so was already buzzing. He ordered a bottle of champagne, even though he would have preferred a pint of Harp. The two girls loved it, sitting there like it was Christmas, hanging on his every word, especially after he gave them a wrap to take into the toilet with them. When they were away he turned to Tierney.

'Fucking gagging for it.'

'Aye.'

'They're all the same, these wee sluts. All want a good seeing-to.'

The girls came back and sidled in beside the men. Molloy put his arm around Sharon. He looked old enough to be her father. The perfume, the feel of her pressing against him and the coke all started working their magic. He told her he was in business. Self-employed. An entrepreneur. She nodded, pretending that she cared. The only thing she knew was that the champagne was free and didn't look like drying up any time soon. An hour later Tierney went to recharge his batteries. Molloy went with him, following his mate to the gents. As they walked back from the toilet Molloy put his arm on Tierney's shoulder.

'She's full of shit this one, but I tell you what, I'm going to buck the fucking hole off her.'

Both men laughed aggressively. When they got to the table, the girls were gone. All four glasses were empty.

'Fucking wee hoors,' Molloy said. He was fuming. He wanted to kill someone and started looking round the room for them.

'I'll wring her fucking neck, next time I see her.'

Tierney led him to the bar where they pushed to the front and ordered two bottles of Budweiser. By the time they finished, the chilled beer had started to cool Molloy's temper.

'Come on,' he said as the bouncer did the rounds, getting folk to drink up. 'I'm calling Alice. Party up at her place.'

Molloy was married but Alice was his thing on the side. She had been for almost three years. There was Louise as well, but she had been doing his head in lately. Alice was twenty-eight now but when she was eighteen she had been one of the most stunning girls in the whole of Belfast. Since being with Molloy she had had two abortions. She was a devil for the coke and Molloy knew he was guaranteed some action, no matter what time of the night it was, provided he didn't arrive empty-handed.

Outside, both men were hammered. There were no taxis but it was only a twenty-minute walk. Halfway along Victoria Street Molloy announced that he needed a slash and turned down an alley. Tierney waited at the mouth of the entry.

'Stop looking at my knob, ya fruit!' Molloy shouted over his shoulder.

Tierney flipped his mate the finger and walked on. He knew they'd get to Alice's and Molloy would disappear with her into the bedroom. Besides, he had some dope back at the house which would help bring him down after the last few hours.

In the alley Molloy put his head back and sighed as the stream of hot piss flowed out of him. He thought about what he was going to do ...

He braced himself as something moved out the corner of his eye.

A 6-inch rat scuttled down the drainpipe next to his head. Molloy breathed a sigh of relief as the rat burrowed into a pile of black bags.

'Aye. You better run, you wee fucker.'

He zipped up his fly and made his way out of the entry, looking for Tierney, who was nowhere to be seen.

'Aye. You run and all, you fucking bastard,' he slurred to himself.

Molloy started walking, thinking about Alice. The road was deserted, except for the odd car with a TAXI sign lit across the roof.

Molloy walked up Cromac Street. Four street-lights in a row had been smashed, creating a darkened stretch of pavement. Broken glass lay across the ground and Molloy swerved at the last minute to avoid walking into a bin. At the side of the footpath, shop doorways formed a series of black alcoves. He was still thinking about Alice. He'd get her high. Then he'd get her to put something on. Her wee black number. Then ...

Darkness.

Something had smashed into Molloy's face. He stumbled and went down, the back of his head cracking off the pavement, knocking him out. A brick had come out of nowhere, out of the empty space of a shop doorway. It struck him square in the face, breaking his nose and sending him to the ground. Six foot four, sixteen stone, lay motionless on the pavement.

A taxi drove by but didn't stop. The driver saw a man fall and assumed it was another steamer, with one too many in him. The car paused at the lights at the bottom of the road. The lights changed to green and the taxi turned the corner into May Street.

Quietly, Joe Lynch stepped out of the doorway.

He was still holding the brick. A small beanie covered his head. He pulled the collar up on his black jacket. He was calm and stood quietly looking down at the prone figure of Molloy.

For three days he had watched and waited. By now he knew Molloy better than he knew himself. It was like the old days. That sense of familiarity, like putting on a pair of jeans you'd already worn. He'd watched and he'd waited. Over three days Lynch had memorized Molloy's life. Every detail.

Where he went, and who he saw. Where he slept, where he drank, where he ate. The wife, the girlfriend, the bit on the side.

Lynch looked at the large frame, lying comatose on the pavement. He kneeled down, crouching next to the body. Molloy was breathing, but he wasn't moving.

Lynch looked at the brick in his hand, then at the body. Blood ran out of Molloy's nose which was now lying sidewards across his face.

'Not so handsome now. Eh, big lad?' he whispered.

Lynch exhaled before he stood up. His eyes swept the street. It was all clear. He walked off, making his way along Cromac Street, staying in the shadows. He was calm, collected, in control. He hadn't felt this steady in months. Since he'd come out of prison, in fact. Around the corner he cut through a side alley into the Markets. He walked past the Lagan, silently flowing by, and threw the brick into the middle of the river.

When he got home, Lynch lit a cigarette and sat in the living room with the lights off. His eyes slowly adjusted and after a few minutes he could see in the dark. He was able to make out the outline of his hand. He held it up in front of his face. It was still. Perfectly still. There wasn't the slightest tremor. He went upstairs and lay on the bed, fully clothed. Lynch closed his eyes and fell into a deep, satisfying sleep.

SIXTEEN

Catherine lay in bed, trying to read. Her mother had given her the book. An Irish family saga. The story of three sisters growing up in fifties Dublin. Sexual repression, domineering parents, sibling rivalry. She wished life was that simple.

She set the paperback down on the empty space in the bed next to her. Catherine was still sleeping on the left-hand side and wondered if there would come a time when she would move to the middle of the bed. She knew it would finally be admitting that the current arrangement was permanent.

She looked at the ceiling, thinking about John. He was on nightshift. She imagined him at Musgrave Street, staring at the computer, his brow furrowed. Catherine had a copy of O'Neill's shift pattern sellotaped to the back of a kitchen cupboard. It helped with arrangements for Sarah. He had been in her head constantly since Jack Ward's visit last week. Sarah seemed to be asking about her daddy more than usual, too. Catherine wondered if it was like buying a car. Suddenly you started to see the same model everywhere. Sarah had also asked about Rex, Ward's dog. Catherine agreed to arrange for her dad to take her the following weekend.

She picked up the book again, trying to concentrate on the words, to put a stop to the memories of John. Ward had sown a seed inside her. If John was anything to go by and if she knew CID, it was exactly what he'd intended to do. Policemen spent their lives performing, one minute feigning ignorance, the next acting as if they were omnipotent. She thought about Ward's hesitancy, his awkwardness. He'd been able to read her as well. Knew she needed to vent, to let go, to let it all out. It was the last thing she would have thought of doing, speaking to another cop. Ironically, Ward was one of the few people she could talk to. It had been like a release valve. Afterwards Catherine hadn't felt nearly as weighed down. She'd let go of some of the frustration. For the first time in months she was able to look past the petty annoyances, the minor disappointments. She caught herself wondering if there might not be hope.

Lying in bed, Catherine began to think about why she married O'Neill in the first place. She thought about the two of them when they first got together. John started in uniform not long after. He would come home from a nightshift at 8 a.m., still buzzing. He'd roll into bed beside her and spend half an hour telling her stories about what the night had been like. He sanitized them, of course, holding back anything that might worry her. On weekends she would have a lie-in, spending the first two hours of the day reading, listening to him snore quietly beside her.

Catherine thought about their second date and the fight she had told Ward about. He had smiled at the story, like he couldn't imagine John doing anything else. She thought about Sarah and how there might be a time when she would be in trouble, when neither of them would be there and she'd need someone to stick up for her. Someone who wouldn't just walk past like everyone else.

The day after Ward's visit Catherine had taken the brown envelope with their divorce papers out of her handbag. She had been carrying it round with her for almost a week. Her solicitor had been right. The best thing to do was just post it. Once it was done it was done. The horse would have bolted and things would take on a life of their own. So why hadn't she? After O'Neill disappeared from the café she had addressed the envelope with the details of the flat in Stranmillis.

Now she had put it into one of the kitchen drawers. If moving into the middle of the bed meant acceptance, then perhaps this was a stay of execution. She thought about John. Her John. Perhaps Ward was right. Maybe he did need her help, after all.

At 3 a.m. O'Neill sat in Musgrave Street, hunched over the case-file for Laganview.

The nightshift had its advantages. Wilson wasn't in the station and he didn't have to worry about any unexpected visits. 'How are things going? What about this? What about that?' They were loaded questions. The only right answer was that he was getting closer. O'Neill told it to Wilson but he also told it to himself. He had to. He was fighting Murphy's Law. The one that says it's the drunk driver who always walks away from a car crash. That says it may be the tenth time he beat her, but she'll still take him back. That says a good peeler will always get fucked on a case no one gives a shit about.

O'Neill had the Laganview file memorized. They had no ID on the victim, no suspects and no forensics. He knew there must be something he wasn't seeing, a detail, something he'd overlooked, an angle that hadn't been considered.

Both the physical evidence and the pathology report had told him nothing he didn't know the morning they found the body. Puslawski had checked out. The foreman, Tony Burke, was dodgy but it didn't make him a murderer. O'Neill knew that people lied to the police for all kinds of reasons. Ward had told him he would look into the Spender angle. 'It's a while since I've had a jaunt down to Cultra.' Meanwhile, O'Neill had compiled a list of the great and the good of the Belfast drug scene. He was looking for mid-level guys, the boys who ran things. They'd be involved, but high enough up not to directly handle any product. The list stretched to 146 names. And that was only the people the police knew about. Any one of them could have done the boy at Laganview.

Uniform had come up with nothing either. They'd spent two days questioning every tracksuited teenager in East Belfast. The kids laughed at them, knowing the police had nothing. They started owning up, like it was some kind of game.

'I done him.'

'No, I did.'

'No, it was me.'

O'Neill thought back to his uniform days in North Belfast. The New Lodge. The Oldpark. The Ballysillan. You'd climb out of the wagon to a row of 'fuck you' stares from fourteen year olds. The rest of his patrol hated them – 'fucking wee hoods', 'a bunch of ball bags'. O'Neill didn't mind. After a year he got to know the faces and some of the names. He would give them a slagging-off – 'Hey McCrory, you still not got laid yet?' He'd pick the smallest in the group – 'Big lad, you know fags stunt your growth.' Or ask them all – 'Where's the birds tonight then? Is this a social club for fruits? Or are yous an out-of-work boyband?' They would laugh and call him a wanker as soon as he was out of earshot.

Life was a game to them. It had to be. The only commandment that mattered was *Thou shalt not get caught.* And it wasn't just the peelers you had to worry about. In fact, the police were the least of your worries. Everywhere on walls you saw the letters UTH – Up the Hoods. FTIRA – Fuck the IRA. There was not one of them didn't know someone who had been done by the Provies, given a hiding, been told to leave the country, or worse. O'Neill thought about Janty Morgan. He must have arrested him half a dozen times. He thought about Morgan's backchat, as if he hadn't a care in the world. It was as if he knew this was it. This was as good as it got. You took the money and ran, and you kept running, until eventually, some day, a hand would reach out and grab you and that would be it. Game over.

Earlier that evening O'Neill had called at the Royal Victoria Hospital to talk to the surgeon who headed up the Orthopaedic Unit. Mr Winters was in his early fifties and for the past ten years had been running the reconstructive team. He was a minor celebrity in the world of knee surgery. Practice makes perfect, O'Neill supposed. They had coffee in the empty canteen of the hospital, a couple of ghosts, existing at odd hours, in spaces vacated by normal, everyday life. They swapped stories, talking about their experience of Belfast's hoods. Winters was quiet, reflective.

'They're pretty subdued by the time they get to me. They will have been medicated in the ambulance and stabilized on the ward. Then they're prepped for surgery. It's sunk in by then. After the shock. Being shot seems to be better than taking a beating. For them, I mean. Not me. A bullet-hole might not look like much ...' Winters paused, remembering who he was talking to. 'I imagine being shot's quicker, maybe less personal. After a beating, when you talk to them before surgery they're always quiet. They've seen enough to know what their life'll be like when they come out. The crutches, the walking sticks. The pins and plates. The pieces of metal. Then there's the aching joints. Not to mention arthritis by the time you're thirty.'

Winters took a drink of his coffee and rubbed his chin.

'I don't think it's the physical injury though. That's not the real damage.'

'What do you mean?' O'Neill asked.

'Well, it's as if there's a change in them. They become sullen. Silent. Resigned. You see it in the follow-up appointments. It's as if they give up. As if the beating is like some final, irrevocable proof. The world, telling them that they really *are* just a piece of shit, that they're completely worthless, that their life means nothing. People can come along, beat you half to death, and no one says anything about it. When they wake up from the surgery you can see it in their eyes – that expression – no matter how well things go in the operation. It's there six weeks later, and at the six-month visit. It's as if, deep down, they always suspected that they were nothing. And now, there's no denying it. They have the proof.'

Back at Musgrave Street O'Neill closed the file and reopened it at page one. He remembered Ward's words when he first joined CID.

'Sisyphus, son ...'

O'Neill thought about all the drug players they'd pulled in over Laganview. He thought about the hoods that uniform had stopped. Records the length of your arm, every last one of them. He wondered what the police's job was in this whole game. They did nothing more than guard the great revolving door – nick them, question them, charge them. Six months later, you were picking up the same people, off the same streets, for the same shit.

O'Neill stretched upwards before hunching back over the Laganview file. He'd have time to go through it once more, before eight o'clock, when he'd head back to the empty flat in Stranmillis.

SEVENTEEN

It was Tuesday night and Marty and Petesy were in the Holy Lands doing their paper round.

Petesy had been walking about with a face on him all night. The plan had been to go round to Micky's after and smoke a few joints. They were going to bring the gear. Micky's mum was due back from Benidorm tomorrow so it wasn't a big one, just a few of the lads. Micky'd nicked a copy of the new *Grand Theft Auto* from the Virgin in town. A night of carjacking, shooting cops and picking up prostitutes. All from the comfort of your own home.

Marty had been bored so he called round earlier in the day but Micky wouldn't let him in. The ski-masks had scared the shit out of him and he still had bruised ribs from where he'd been hit at the door.

'Tonight's off,' Micky told him.

'What are you talking about? Because of Friday?'

Marty and Petesy had sat round the back of the petrol station for two hours before going home. They only heard about the visitors the next day.

'They held a fucking knife to Locksy,' Micky said. 'I can't be having it. My ma will do her nut. She'll turf me out. You can't come round. It's too much.'

Marty couldn't believe what he was hearing. He remembered the cheering when he'd arrived at the party on Friday night. Micky had practically thrown his arms round him and now he didn't want to see him.

'Aye, Micky? Yous are all happy enough to score some gear. Happy to have us take the risks. Get fucked on the pills that we bring. What? And now you don't want to know? It's all different, is that it? Well, away and fuck youself.' A bit of spit flew out of Marty's mouth as he gave off.

'Wise up, Marty. It's not like that. This is only for a wee while. When things—'

Marty turned and walked away.

He walked to the edge of the estate and sat near the bank of the Lagan, looking over at the train-tracks on the far side. The Dublin train went along that route, every couple of hours. Marty wondered what things were like down South. He lit a Regal and began tossing stones into the river. He was on his second cigarette when Locksy came up behind him and sat down. He had a plaster down his right cheek from where the knife had opened him.

'All right, mate?' Locksy said. 'Give us a toke.'

Marty passed the cigarette. Locksy sucked on the butt, took it out of his mouth and had another quick toke before handing it back. The two boys sat for a while, neither speaking. Eventually Marty broke the silence.

'Sorry about Friday night.'

'Aghh. Don't worry about it. They're fucking cunts.'

'Yeah.' Marty took a draw on the cigarette. 'Micky reckoned it was me and Petesy's fault.'

'I wouldn't sweat it. Round here, sooner or later everybody gets a turn. It could have been worse, he could've really started drawing on me with that fucking knife.'

Locksy's face was smooth. He wasn't properly shaving yet. His eyes looked towards the horizon and the Castlereagh Hills in the distance.

'Micky's a bit freaked out,' Marty said.

'Micky's always freaked out. The guy's a fruit. I wouldn't worry. Best you can hope for is what happened the other night. When they come for you, if you're lucky, you're not there. Micky thinks Friday was a nightmare. He's wrong. It was a fucking result. That's what it was.'

Marty pulled out the packet of Regal and offered one to Locksy. They sat by the edge of the river, smoking together. Further along the bank they could hear the rumble of diggers flattening the old Belfast gasworks. The site was being levelled and workmen were erecting blue fence panels to seal it off. The place had lain derelict for years but they were building a hotel and some offices once the weather got better in spring. Marty spat on the ground in front of him. When he had finished his fag he stood up, telling Locksy he'd see him later, he had to collect some more gear for that night.

Later, walking round the Holy Lands, Marty could tell Friday had spooked Petesy. He came out of their first call, a gram of coke on Damascus Street, and found him pacing the pavement. Marty looked at him. Petesy might as well have had a sign on him saying *dodgy* in foot-high letters.

'There's a fucking parked car over there,' Petesy said, his voice shaking. 'The black one. Guy's been sitting for ten minutes.'

'All right. Calm down.'

Marty was casual. He looked up the street, taking in the car without making it obvious. A man was trying not to look out at them, talking into his mobile phone. He was in his late twenties and had a shaved head and a gold earring. Marty could make out a tattoo on his neck which crawled up and out of his collar.

'OK, Petesy. Walk slowly – and be ready to bolt.'

They started down Damascus Street. Suddenly a door burst open in front of them.

A blonde girl came bouncing out, almost running into Petesy. She was wearing thick foundation, four-inch heels and a short black skirt. She bounded over to the car and got in, leaning over to kiss the driver. The car fired to life and peeled off down the street, its bass blaring.

Marty breathed a sigh of relief. Petesy was all over the place. He wasn't thinking and he was getting inside Marty's head now and all.

Normally Petesy was totally cool. He could disappear at the drop of a hat. Even in broad daylight, he'd slide into a doorway, duck behind a hedge or just sit on a wall. He'd look bored, blend in, cloak himself in casual indifference. People walked past him like he wasn't even there. Tonight though, he wasn't at the races. Pacing up and down. Jesus Christ, Marty thought, it was only a matter of time before he came out of a house to see the peelers with Petesy up against a wagon. He was so wired he'd probably get Marty lifted and all. He decided to bring him with him. They'd go in together and at least then he could keep an eye on him.

After three calls Petesy started to relax. He liked going inside, liked looking at the posters on people's walls. He reckoned every second place had the mad one of Jack Nicholson from *The Shining*, his crazy face sticking through the door. Petesy liked the books piled up on people's desks. *Wherever Green is Worn. People's History of America. Utopia.* He wondered what they were all about. He thought about sitting in someone's flat, reading one, maybe having a spliff while he was at it. He wanted to know what was so fascinating that people would sit for hours, just reading. He imagined being a student, going to Queen's. All the birds. It would be just like school, except without the boring stuff. He'd heard that if you didn't like the teacher, you could just get up and walk out. He'd learn about other countries. About America. He had a cousin in New York who had been there on 9/11 when the planes hit them buildings. Now *that* was a terrorist attack. None of this blowing up a bookies or shooting a peeler rubbish.

In a flat on Cairo Street two guys were buying some blow. In one of the armchairs a girl was lounging, reading a magazine. She wore ripped jeans and had long brown hair. Petesy thought she looked like that bird from *Lord of the Rings*. She had a small nose and skinny features, offset by a pair of dark brown eyes. He couldn't stop looking at her, as if something was forcing him. Sure, he knew girls that were wee rides, ones you'd want to have a go at, but this one ... she was really beautiful.

Petesy caught himself staring and looked away. After a few seconds he glanced back and saw her looking at him. He gave a faint smile and she smiled back. Petesy felt like he'd been lifted off the carpet. He wanted to talk to her, to tell her things, to tell her—

'Hey.' Marty was half way out the door. 'Time to go.'

Petesy followed him out of the flat. He wasn't brave enough to turn round but he thought he could feel the girl's eyes on him as he walked out the door.

That was the last call of the night. Marty was happy. He was trying not to think about Sean Molloy or Johnny Tierney, focusing on the fact it was Tuesday and he already had two hundred quid in his pocket. Their fifty-fifty split would mean a hundred each. Petesy barely spoke as they walked out of the Holy Lands and down the Ormeau Road.

'Two hundred tonight.'

'Right,' Petesy said quietly.

'Not bad for a few hours' work.'

'Aye.'

'Reckon we'll double up by the end of the week.'

'Aye.'

'I think I'm a fruit.'

'Aye.'

Marty stopped walking.

'OK. Enough. Will you frigging wise up? This is like working with a zombie. If you don't want to come out, just say so. There are plenty of other guys who'd like to make a bit of money.'

'They don't all have cousins in the Ardoyne though, do they?'

The two of them walked on in silence. Marty stopped at the Shell garage and bought a can of Coke. He handed Petesy a Mars bar he'd nicked while the manager wasn't looking. He smiled at Petesy.

'Don't say I never give you anything.'

Petesy didn't laugh. He carried the Mars bar in his hand, not eating it. Finally he spoke.

'How hard do you think it would be to go to Queen's?'

Marty spat out a mouthful of Coke. He wiped his chin, laughing.

'What the fuck would they want with you?'

'What's wrong with me?'

Petesy was sullen. Marty tried to backtrack.

'It's not that. I mean, what the fuck would you want with them? Have you seen the state of these students? Sitting around all day. All their fucking books. Homework and everything. Didn't you get enough of that shite at St Matthew's?'

'*This* is fucking boring. The same every day. Sitting round. Nicking stuff. The PlayStation. Going round the Holy Lands. Getting wasted. I don't want to spend all day just waiting until Johnny Tierney gets his hands on us. Besides ...'

'What the fuck's wrong with it?' Marty snapped back.

Petesy paused. 'I don't know. I mean, it's just ...'

'What else do you think there is, Petesy?'

Marty was hurt. It wasn't Petesy slagging off what they did, it was the idea of him not wanting to hang about any more. Petesy was his mate. His best mate. Micky could go fuck himself. So could the rest of them. He'd always have Petesy though. Least that's what he'd thought. Butch and fucking Sundance.

'Fine,' Marty said. 'Fuck off then. See if I fucking care.'

'Don't worry. You'll still be able to get the gear off my cousin.'

'Do you think I give a fuck about that?' Marty stormed off, throwing his can of Coke on to the main road. A car blared its horn. Marty gave it the finger and walked on.

Petesy stood by the road, holding the Mars bar by his side as his friend strode off on his own.

EIGHTEEN

Tuesday night dissolved into Wednesday morning. O'Neill lay in bed staring at the ceiling. He'd been watching the clock since twelve. It was almost three. The smell of Chinese food wafted in from the empty cartons in the living room. O'Neill had sat for an hour, rereading the forensics. Taking police paperwork home was a serious offence but what the hell, the ship was sinking anyway. Since the break with Catherine it had given him something to do. Stopped him thinking too much.

The one-bedroom flat was identical to when O'Neill had first moved in. There were no pictures and no plants. A pile of dishes rose out of the sink. Beside the bed sat an unframed photograph, curling at the edges. It was Sarah on the beach at Portstewart. She wore a woollen hat with her hair falling halfway across her face. He had another one of the three of them, but he had put it away in a drawer. He had told himself to wise up, to stop kidding himself. He knew 'a break' meant Catherine didn't have the guts six months ago to tell him it was over. Divorced at thirty-four, O'Neill thought. Well done, son. All he needed was a drink problem and a dodgy past and they'd make him a character in some crime novel.

To stop the self-analysis, O'Neill thought about the case. CCTV from the area round Laganview had given them nothing. There was no murder weapon. No witnesses. And still no ID. The autopsy had found wooden splinters in the head wound. It was pine. Heat-treated. Containing traces of methane bromide. Baseball bats and hurling sticks were made of ash which was strong and flexible. Pickaxe handles were hard wood, something like hickory. Pine was soft, cheap. It tended to be used in furniture or packing material. Forensics had taken samples of all the wood near the body – fence-posts, internal beams, cable drums. The splinters matched some nearby pallets. The heat-treatment and methane bromide confirmed it. They were to prevent Asian longhorn beetles coming in through packing crates from China. Apparently they were munching their way across the forests of Europe.

'Bloody foreigners,' O'Neill had said sarcastically.

The question was, how did it all relate? What did it say about the murder? Whoever did it didn't bring the weapon with them. They grabbed the nearest thing at hand. It took away a degree of premeditation. Perhaps they hadn't intended to kill the kid. Just having some fun and things got out of hand. Maybe they found out something from him and that tipped them over the edge. Something he said which meant he had to go. It was all theory, all conjecture. O'Neill needed more than that.

He thought they must have chased him into Laganview. He imagined the kid running and figuring he could get away through the building site. Scrambling over the fence. Being followed, caught and then given a hiding. Ending up dead. Maybe there was never a decision to kill him, just to give him a good beating. He must have tried to bolt and wound up taking one to the head. Game over. Lights out. Thanks for coming.

The chase didn't chime with a punishment beating though. It was unplanned, impromptu. Punishment beatings were controlled, ordered, disciplined.

By three in the morning O'Neill decided enough was enough and rolled out of bed. He needed to see Laganview the way the victim saw it, the way the killer saw it. Deserted. In the middle of the night. He got dressed and lifted his car keys.

Belfast looked like a ghost town as he drove towards the city centre. He passed a couple of taxis hoovering up the night's stragglers. A white armoured Land Rover was parked up outside Queen's University. O'Neill wondered if Sam Jennings was in the back. He pictured her, hat down, her eyes staring through the blacked-out glass. He caught himself on.

'Calm yourself, son. What are you? Sixteen years old?'

He went back to the case. He needed to see the scene again, to be there alone, away from the distortions of daylight and the whole circus of a crime scene. He parked on Bridge Street across from Central train station and jumped the wall, heading across a patch of wasteground towards Laganview.

The building site was surrounded by 8-foot blue fence panels. Graffiti decorated the side – *UTH* and *FTIRA*. O'Neill walked slowly along the perimeter, scanning the panels as he went. After 20 yards he noticed a muddy smear, 4 feet from the ground. He moved along to the next panel, which was unmarked. O'Neill stepped back and took a run at it, making to shimmy up and over the fence. He stopped halfway and stood back. His foot had hit the wall at almost the exact same height as the other smear.

'Edmund Locard. How did I ever doubt you?'

O'Neill took out a packet of B&H and lit one. He emptied the box and put the loose cigarettes in his pocket before tossing it over the fence and into the site.

Some 500 yards away the security guard slept in his hut, oblivious to the figure examining the fence. O'Neill saw an old oil drum 30 yards from the footprint. Rolling it against the fence, he climbed up and dropped down on the other side. He used his torch to find the cigarette packet, the gold box winking at him in the dark. He stood back and swept the beam of light over the area. The packet of B&H glimmered in the darkness and 3 feet from the box he could make out a pair of prints. The feet were parallel, close together, quite deep. It was a landing. O'Neill looked round him. He was at the opposite end of the site to where the body was discovered. It was no wonder Forensics hadn't seen these. From where he was standing, O'Neill could make out the Nike swoosh in the footprints. It was the same brand of trainers the victim had been wearing. If someone followed the kid over, there would be other prints. He'd get the SOCOs out first thing. Get them to take anything within a 15-foot radius. He left the small gold packet of B&H as a marker, taking another loose cigarette from his pocket and lighting it.

O'Neill walked down through the site to where they had found the body the week before. It was quieter than he remembered it. At the bottom of the bank the black waters of the Lagan flowed by. On the far side the Hilton, the Waterfront Hall and the Court House seemed to look off in the opposite direction. Tourism. Showbiz. Justice. Three silent witnesses, turning their backs as if they didn't want to know.

O'Neill looked at the view. The Black Mountain stood silhouetted in the distance. The white limestone of the Court House was lit up against the dark night sky. It was quiet, peaceful. Could have made a good postcard.

To his right stood four pallets, stacked with breeze blocks, covering the area where the body had lain.

'Business as usual,' O'Neill said.

He imagined the makeshift pine bat and the sound of bones breaking. He tried to hear the cries of pain, the apologies, the pleading. There was no romance here. No poetry. Nothing to write home about.

O'Neill drove back along deserted roads. Red lights stopped him, forcing him to wait and stare across empty junctions. They turned to green and he pulled away slowly. He was tired, but he thought about the prints and felt a little lighter than he had at any time in the last seven days.

NINETEEN

Catherine couldn't remember the last time she had seen Sarah so well-behaved. The five year old sat on the sofa with her coat on and her bag by her side. Every time she heard a car outside she jumped up and ran to the window.

It was Wednesday morning and the schools were on half-term. O'Neill was picking her up at nine o'clock as Catherine had to go to work. They were going to the cinema together to see the new Wallace and Gromit and then out somewhere for lunch. Catherine wondered at the fairness of it all. Why did *he* get to be the best friend and she always had to be the parent? He didn't have to deal with the tantrums, the vegetables, the not wanting to go to bed. It was all pictures and popcorn with Dad. Like being on holiday. Catherine thought if she had to hear the words 'my daddy' once more she'd explode.

She tried to remind herself that it was a good thing Sarah loved spending time with him. A good thing that she got so excited about seeing him. A good thing ... Catherine looked at the clock. Five to nine. John had come off doing a series of nights. She wasn't sure if he had been working last night. If so, he would go home for a shower and swing by and get her. Catherine had seen it before. Not sleeping, working a nightshift, seeing Sarah and then back into work for eight.

No wonder he looked like death warmed up. She imagined him sleeping in the cinema, surrounded by noisy children and the disapproving looks of parents. She had an urge to stand over him, to stare down the other parents, to defend him. She would tell them what he spent his days doing. When someone was prowling round the school gates, who did you think went out there after them?

Sarah's voice called from the living room. 'Mummy? What time is it *now*?'

'It's almost nine, sweetheart.'

She had been asking every five minutes for the last half-hour. In the kitchen Catherine cleared up the remains of breakfast. She moved fast, scraping bowls and rinsing glasses, as if her energy could somehow make John appear. She muttered under her breath.

'You better not let that wee girl down. So help me.'

The hands of the kitchen clock ticked past nine. There was still no sign. Catherine lifted the phone and dialled O'Neill's mobile. It went straight through to answerphone. She sighed and slammed the receiver down, harder than she meant to.

Sarah's head popped round the door.

'Was that him?'

'No, love.' Catherine forced a smile. 'He'll be on his way.'

Sarah went back into the living room and resumed her post as sentry on lookout.

Catherine went upstairs and started stripping the beds. It was a deliberate tactic to avoid having to be in the same room as her daughter. She caught herself looking out the window at the street below. Three doors down, the Brogans were getting into the car. Kevin and Sue must have taken the day off and it looked as if they were taking the boys swimming. Catherine heard the car doors slam shut and the engine start up. She heard Sarah's voice calling up the stairs, 'Mum, what time is it now?' She pretended she didn't hear her.

At twenty past nine Catherine picked up the phone and tried O'Neill again. Straight to answerphone.

She cursed him. It was vintage John. Always the same. First there was the disappointment, then the excuses and then the promises to make it up next time. It wouldn't be him that would have to spend the rest of the day with Sarah, dealing with the tears, trying to make up excuses. Catherine had heard them enough times before. Back when they were directed at her. How could you tell a child though? *Daddy had to work. He's out there chasing a bad man.* There were only so many times ...

At ten o'clock Catherine knelt down in front of her daughter. Sarah fought back the tears. She had seen enough to know that her daddy didn't always come when he said he was going to.

'It's not fair,' Catherine said, as much to herself as to her daughter. She was only a child. She was only five, she didn't know how to guard against the disappointments, to shield herself the way her mother had learned to do over the years. Catherine knew now she'd have to call in sick to work.

'Something must have happened, my love – something really important at work. Would you like me to take you to the pictures instead?'

The girl's mouth turned downwards and she shook her head. Catherine wished she would cry because at least then she could give her a hug. Her eyes were almost unbearable to look at.

'It's OK, Mummy. We'll go next time.'

The girl slowly took her coat off and hung it back on her hook, the one John had put at a special height when they had first moved into the house. She then went upstairs, into her bedroom, and quietly closed the door.

Catherine marched into the kitchen, cursing under her breath. She opened the drawer beside the cooker, rummaging through the old shopping lists and spare batteries until she found what she was looking for. The brown A4 envelope. She grabbed her handbag from the counter and searched for the stamps she knew were in her purse. She put a whole book of first class on the envelope. There was no way it wasn't going to get there.

She called Sarah down from her bedroom and told her: 'Put your coat on, sweetheart. We have to go out to do a message.'

In the flat on the Stranmillis Road O'Neill snored heavily. He hadn't slept much the day before and had ended up down Laganview at four in the morning. He'd planned to have a shower before going to pick up Sarah. He was looking forward to seeing her and taking her to the pictures. They were going to Johnny Long's for fish and chips afterwards. It was Sarah's favourite. On the bed his suit lay crumpled. The phone in the pocket was dead, the battery completely out of charge.

The hot shower had been like a knock-out blow and O'Neill had almost fallen as he stepped out of the bath. He lay down for a few minutes on the bed. The clock said 8.15 so he could have twenty minutes' kip and then head over to get Sarah.

The tiredness dragged him down instantly.

He dreamed he was running through a labyrinth. It was the dead of the night and freezing cold. When he stopped he could see his breath, bellowing in front of him. He didn't know where he was – somewhere among rows of terrace houses. Long redbrick walls were interspersed with wooden doors into back yards. He was chasing someone. A figure in black. But he was always too slow. Every time he turned a corner he'd see a shadow disappearing round the next one. No matter how fast he ran, how much his lungs burned, it was no use. He stopped at a junction, his hands on his knees, sucking in air. He stood up and felt a cold metal barrel held to the back of his head. The last thing he heard was the loud click of a gun being cocked.

O'Neill snapped awake. It was twelve thirty.

He cursed, jumping out of bed and grabbing his suit for his mobile. He saw the blank screen and tossed it aside. Then he remembered he had no landline and fumbled round for the charger. He scrolled through, looking for Catherine's number. The phone at the other end rang five times before going through to answerphone. He heard the recording of his wife's voice and tried to think of what to say. He tried the house phone but there was no answer either.

He threw his mobile across the room. It hit the wall and exploded, falling to the floor in several pieces.

O'Neill looked at the clock. He wasn't due in Musgrave Street until six that night. He thought about the dream, the sound of the gun being cocked next to his head. He picked up his car keys, knowing he couldn't stay in the flat another minute.

On the way into work O'Neill stopped at a mobile phone shop on Botanic Avenue.

'I dropped this,' he said, handing a young guy his handset in four pieces.

The shop assistant looked back incredulously. The phone was broken. Completely broken. O'Neill told him to replace it. The assistant launched into his sales patter about the latest Nokia. He was cocky and presumptuous. It had a camera, a digital screen, extra memory, high speed ...

O'Neill's eyes bored into him. The assistant worried for his personal safety and quickly realized this wasn't going to be an upgrade.

'Same again?' he asked meekly.

O'Neill nodded.

He produced a box from under the counter and rang through the transaction. O'Neill didn't say anything but paid and took the phone.

TWENTY

William Spender closed the heavy oak door of his office. The house was quiet and Karen had gone out. She would be at the hairdresser's, the gym or out to lunch. Whatever it was she filled her days with.

Eight miles away at Laganview, Tony Burke was sitting in the site hut when his mobile rang in his pocket. It came up *Number Withheld*.

'Hello?'

'It's me,' Spender said.

'We need to talk. I think the police—'

'Not over the phone.'

The statement sounded like a threat. Burke was immediately worried and stayed silent, waiting for the other man to speak. He hadn't been in contact with Spender since they took him into Musgrave Street. They'd both agreed it was best to lie low.

Since walking out of the station that Monday, Burke had felt like he was constantly under surveillance. Every time he turned a corner he seemed to come upon a parked-up police wagon. In the town on Saturday two cops had come sprinting towards him. Burke had thought it was all over, and braced himself, but they blew past, chasing some hood in a tracksuit who had come running out of a shop.

On the other end of the phone Spender issued an order.

'Eight o'clock tonight. Usual spot.'

The line went dead before Burke could say anything.

It was the middle of the week and the Ormeau Road was quiet. Burke had walked from his house just off the Ravenhill Road, taking a deliberately circuitous route. Since Spender's call he'd felt even more sure there was someone on his tail. The walk normally took ten minutes but it was nearer twenty by the time he'd doubled back on himself. Burke knew he couldn't afford any risks and had looked round a couple of times, pretending to tie his shoe or light a cigarette. Since the phone call he'd spent the whole afternoon wondering what Spender wanted. Whatever it was, he didn't sound pleased.

Work on the site had picked up again. They had brought in ten more men since losing the previous Monday to the cops. Burke did the usual, gathering the foreign workers at the end of the day and telling them he needed ten more the next morning. That Thursday he'd arrived at seven to find twenty-five guys lined up. Poles, Lithuanians, a few Czechoslovakians, or whatever it was they called the place nowadays. It was that easy. He would keep them on until he didn't need them and just get rid of them. They were always on time, worked themselves to the bone and never complained. It was capitalism as it was meant to be.

At five to eight Burke took up his spot in the empty doorway, across the road from the Errigle Inn. He looked up and down the street, waiting for the black Mercedes to pull up to the kerb. It had started to rain on his way over and the tarmac road shone a sleek black. Across the street a solitary figure stood outside the Errigle smoking a cigarette. A taxi pulled up outside the bar, and the driver glanced over at Burke. The passenger window came down and the smoker approached the car, leaning in the window to say something to the driver.

Burke started to panic. Had Spender turned on him? Was it a set-up?

He looked up and down the road, trying to figure the best way out. Down Sunnyside Street? No. Better the main road. More obstacles. More people. Ormeau Police Station was 300 yards away, squatting by the roadside like an iron fortress. Burke thought about walking up the street, trying to get closer to its protective shadow. Spender would wonder what he was up to though and he might think Burke had said more to the peelers than he was letting on.

The foreman glanced across the street. The back door of the taxi closed and he saw a swish of long blonde hair in the back. The car pulled out into the night traffic and Burke let out a sigh, whispering: 'I'm getting too old for this shit.'

He reached into his back pocket and pulled out a packet of Lambert & Butler. He lit one just as a sleek black Mercedes slowed at the kerb. Burke looked at the fag. It was always the same. He suddenly wondered if this might be his last smoke and took two quick draws before tossing it away. He pushed the thought to the back of his head, telling himself it was all right, everything was dead on. As he rounded the car he checked that the passenger seat was empty and Spender was alone. A somewhat relieved Burke turned his collar up, glanced down the street, and lowered himself into the car.

'Mr Spender, I—'

'Shut up.' Spender was tense and knew he wouldn't have to repeat himself.

As the car eased out into the night traffic Burke was struck by how quiet the engine was. He was about to mention it, but thought better. Spender drove up the Ormeau Road, past the new shopping complex at Forestside. He took his time, keeping to the 30 m.p.h. speed limit. Spender liked being in control and enjoyed Burke's discomfort beside him. The foreman's mind raced. Was he driving with deliberate care? Not wanting to attract attention? No. It was OK. There was nothing to worry about.

The houses started to thin as the car made its way up the Saintfield Road and out of Belfast. They passed Purdysburn, the city's mental asylum. Burke wanted to ask where they were going but stopped himself. You can't be nervous, he told himself. A nervous man's hiding something. He thought about his brother Michael and wished he was there. Michael had been involved and had seen things. Burke didn't know how many operations he'd been on, but a situation like this wouldn't have worried him in the slightest. Why hadn't he brought Michael along?

In the past Spender would park up round the corner from the bar, in a side-street, somewhere off the main road. They were now well out of Belfast.

Just before the Carryduff roundabout the Mercedes slowed and turned off the main road, winding its way down a narrow country lane. In two minutes they were in the middle of nowhere. It was dark, and high hedges crowded in on the car. Burke had no idea where they were. Spender steered the

Mercedes through a gap in the hedge and they emerged into a clearing in front of a 40-foot corrugated iron building. It was disused but looked as if it had been some sort of hay barn.

Burke peered at the gloomy surroundings, half-expecting another vehicle, a van perhaps, with a couple of men at the back doors. There was no one else, a fact that didn't reassure him as much as it should have.

Spender stopped the car and turned off the engine. The car lights went out and the yard was plunged into darkness.

Burke glanced at the door handle.

'Now,' Spender said, turning to his passenger. 'Tell me, have I got a tout working for me?'

TWENTY-ONE

O'Neill arrived at Musgrave Street to find a message from Mike Hessian.

Hessian was part of Civilian Support and was known as Big Brother round Musgrave Street because he worked CCTV and video surveillance. Eight hours a day he sat locked in a cupboard with nothing but a bank of six screens for company. The Health and Safety men would have had a field day.

Hessian was in his fifties and wore a cardigan and a pair of glasses, perched on the end of his nose. He looked like a librarian more than a peeler. Everyone round Musgrave Street knew though: you could cheat on your wife and *she* might never find out, but Mike Hessian would know.

He might not have been a proper peeler but Hessian had locked up more guys than anyone in the nick. He gave you what every crime needed: a witness. And Hessian's witnesses always took the stand. They didn't get cold feet. They couldn't be intimidated. In Musgrave Street you learned pretty quickly: when Bap stabbed Mackers, when Gerry did Jackie, when Micky ran over Carsey, and the whole world happened to look the other way, you went to see Mike Hessian.

Last week O'Neill had spent a day in the cupboard, poring over the CCTV from the street around Laganview. They had this, plus footage from the Court House, the Hilton Hotel and the Waterfront Hall. Everything in the vicinity. He'd come up with nothing. Hessian joked that whatever had gone on at Laganview happened in the only blind spot in the whole of the city. O'Neill had rolled his eyes, knowing he was a fool to have expected anything else.

When he got the message from Hessian he headed straight for the cupboard.

'Mike. How are you doing? Watching *EastEnders* again, I see.'

Hessian laughed. 'Detective Sergeant O'Neill. The very man.'

O'Neill took a seat. The room smelled of black coffee and Old Spice aftershave.

'So what have you got? Please tell me it's someone running from Laganview holding a baseball bat.'

'Afraid not. But you did say if there was anything interesting in the Markets, to let you know.'

Hessian pressed some buttons on the control panel in front of him.

'The Markets is a black spot. Always has been. Cameras don't last more than a couple of days in there. But take a look at this. It was sent over by Central. It's the early hours of Sunday morning.'

The read-out in the corner of the screen showed 03:36. O'Neill recognized Cromac Street, the main road that ran along the edge of the Markets. It was less than five minutes from where the body was discovered at Laganview. The picture was grainy but you could make out four traffic lanes and both footpaths. The road was quiet, except for the occasional taxi.

'Cromac Street,' O'Neill said.

'They don't give you guys those badges for nothing then.'

Little happened on the screen. A traffic-light changed in the black-and-white picture.

'Very good, Mike. *Belfast By Night*. You should enter this in the Turner Prize next year.'

'Hold your horses, Detective. I've got a few friends I'd like you to meet ... Here we go.'

A figure ambled into shot. He had his back to the camera so you couldn't make out his face. He was swaying and had definitely had a few. He continued walking up the road until he was almost out of the picture.

'OK, Hessian. I get it. *Drunk Man Walking*. I wouldn't be practising your Oscar speech just yet.'

'The younger generation – no patience. Just watch the screen, will you?'

Suddenly, the man on the screen went down as if he'd been shot. He lay motionless on the pavement for several seconds. A taxi drove along the road, slowing slightly, before continuing to the lights and then turning into May Street. Ten seconds later, a figure stepped out of the shadows. He stood over the man and looked down on him, holding something in his hand. The figure crouched over the body, as if he was thinking about something. Then he stood up and walked off purposefully. He crossed the street and disappeared out of shot, down a side-street into the Markets.

'Have I got your attention yet?' Hessian jibed.

'Sure. A little bit of Belfast nightlife. But as you know, drunken vendettas aren't exactly my thing at the moment.'

Hessian shook his head. 'Wait until you see.'

He fast-forwarded the tape, stopping it a few minutes later. The man on the ground started to move. His hand went up to his face, touching his nose, inspecting the blood on his fingertips. He stood up, steadying himself against the wall before staggering off in a similar direction to his assailant.

At no time during the whole episode could anyone's face be made out.

'We can't follow them into the Markets,' O'Neill said.

'No.'

'OK. So why am I so interested in all this?'

'Take a look. You think I've shown you the good stuff. That's just the trailer.'

Hessian rewound the tape as the images started to scroll backwards. A series of cars reversed down the road. He typed on the keyboard in front of him, pulling up a video of Victoria Street.

'This is a couple of minutes before he went down.'

O'Neill could make out the same tall figure, swaying drunkenly towards the camera. He got closer and you could almost make him out. The man lifted his hand, rubbing his face, obscuring the camera's view.

'Come on. Stop teasing, you bastard.'

After a second the man on the screen dropped his hand. Hessian hit pause and zoomed in on the face. After a second the pixels adjusted and the blurred outline crystallized into a face.

'Sean Molloy,' O'Neill announced.

'Bingo.'

Molloy was held in freeze-frame, looking sidewards, his expression part-snarl, part-grimace. O'Neill watched intently. Who had the balls to take out Sean Molloy? Moreover, why would you let him live? Molloy wasn't the kind of guy you wanted getting up and coming after you. It was a one-time deal. You had to put him in the ground, first time of asking.

'OK. You can start practising the Oscar speech now,' O'Neill said. 'So what about our friend? Who's the shadow with a death wish?'

'Shadow is the right word. Wait until you see this.'

Hessian pulled the tapes of Cromac Street, Victoria Street and High Street and put them up on separate screens. He slowly wound the footage back, retracing Molloy's progress. Sporadically, in the corner of each shot, a diminutive figure could be made out stealing along, just out of shot. He'd come into view for a split second, before ducking down an entry or sliding into a doorway. He would wait, out of view, and then make another move. When he did step out, he stayed tight to buildings. He had on a black beanie and his collar was pulled up high. When he passed directly beneath the camera on Victoria Street he put his hand up to hide his face.

'You're kidding me. It's like this the whole way down the street?'

'Four city-centre streets. A dozen cameras. There is not a single clear shot on any of them.'

Hessian pulled up a blurred profile. 'It's the best I've got.'

With the black hat and the collar of his coat up high he could have been anyone.

'He knows exactly what he's doing. He doesn't want Molloy to see him but he also doesn't want us to see him. Where did Molloy come out of?'

'A nightclub called Mint. It's on the edge of the Cathedral Quarter.'

Hessian produced up a piece of footage from outside the club. It showed two stocky doormen with shaved heads checking IDs. The clock in the corner of the screen read 11:28.

'This is three hours earlier. Can you see him?' Hessian asked.

'No.'

'Doorway across the street. Forty yards along.'

O'Neill looked. He couldn't see anything. Hessian rewound the tape to 11:24 and the slight figure walked backwards out of the doorway. Again, he was at the wrong angle for the CCTV. The hat was pulled tight and you couldn't make out his face.

Hessian spoke. 'Four hours. Never moves. He just stands there, watching, waiting.'

It was after nine and O'Neill decided to put a call into the Cathedral Quarter, to pay a visit to Mint. He couldn't remember the last time he had been in a nightclub. Since joining the PSNI he had stopped drinking in the city centre. You couldn't go anywhere without clocking a couple of guys you'd arrested. The problem was they normally clocked you as well. They'd be looking over, talking to their mates and you wouldn't know what might be waiting for you outside.

From the cobbled street he heard the dull thud of dance music coming through the thick walls. The club was part of the Belfast regeneration. An area of old warehouses between the docks and St Anne's Cathedral had been restyled with bars, restaurants and designer shops. A large neon sign flashed *MINT* in 4-foot yellow letters, a dollar sign forming the dot over the 'i'. On the door, two bouncers stood guard. They had shaved heads and no necks and would have passed for a couple of rugby props. The doormen were smartly dressed in black suits and long overcoats.

Inside, the bar was a plush mix of dark wood and leather furniture. Chandeliers hung from the ceiling and O'Neill felt as if he'd walked into an MTV video. Men in Armani suits sat on sculpted chairs, while women with fake tans sipped cocktails on bar stools. House music piped into the bar from the club upstairs, making folk shout into one another's ears.

'Whatever happened to a quiet pint?' O'Neill muttered to himself.

He lifted the menu from the bar. Champagne by the bottle. *Moët* – £76. *Veuve Clicquot* – £92. An attractive brunette set a napkin on the bar in front of him.

'Beer?' he asked.

She turned to reveal a fridge full of imported beers. O'Neill didn't recognize any of them.

'One of those will do,' he said dismissively.

The girl opened the bottle and set it down, announcing, 'Four-seventy,' without batting an eyelid. O'Neill laughed, glad that he wasn't buying a round. His change came back on a round silver disk and was left sitting.

Along the bar a couple of men in their fifties filled champagne glasses for two giggling blondes in short, sparkly dresses. The men looked twice their age. One of them was boasting about taking a Maserati for a test drive. The blondes listened intently, eyes wide, pretending to be impressed.

170

O'Neill doubted they'd know a Maserati if it ran over them in the street. Still, the guys were full of shit and so were the birds. They were welcome to each other.

O'Neill left his beer and went to the gents'. The room was like something from a luxury hotel: floor-to-ceiling mirrors, sculpted glass sinks, automated taps. He stepped up to the polished chrome urinal. As he finished he heard a long drawn-out snort from a closed cubicle behind him.

A few seconds later, a man in a Hugo Boss suit opened the door and stepped out. O'Neill looked at him over his shoulder. Hugo Boss stared back as if he owned the place. He took a step forward, pulling himself up to his full height.

'Got a problem, mate?'

O'Neill turned round and pulled out his warrant card.

'CID, dickhead. But by the sounds of things, I'd say you are the one with the problem.'

Hugo Boss swallowed hard, immediately backing down.

'Sorry. I didn't mean ...'

O'Neill didn't have the energy to bust him. He'd be booking him in for hours and it would take him away from Laganview. He fed Hugo Boss his lines.

'You've got a cold. That's what you're telling me?'

'Er ... yeah. That's it. Haven't been well.'

'An early night then, probably the best thing for you, don't you reckon?'

The man nodded.

'So when I come out of here, I don't want to see you ...'

Hugo Boss nodded vigorously. O'Neill turned his back and began rinsing his hands at one of the sinks. The suit backed his way towards the door and out.

O'Neill went back to the bar. His bottle of beer was sitting where he had left it but he ignored it and headed back to Musgrave Street.

O'Neill had spent most of the night buried in Laganview. At 4 a.m. he had gone back to the cupboard and looked over the tapes of Sean Molloy getting done on Cromac Street. Who would want to send Molloy a message? And why do him there? Why not somewhere quiet, more out of the way? And why wouldn't you just kill him?

At 7 a.m. he stood in the car park smoking. A Land Rover pulled into one of the parking bays and three uniforms jumped down. The passenger door opened and Sam Jennings lowered herself to the ground. She saw O'Neill and hung back as the group walked across the car park. She let the door to the station close before she spoke.

'You coming off a nightshift, Sarge?'

'Yeah.'

'Same here.' Jennings paused and glanced over her shoulder. 'Fancy buying a girl breakfast?'

O'Neill paused, momentarily taken aback. 'Sure. Wellington Park Hotel. They do a mean fry. Or muesli, if that's what floats your boat. About half an hour?'

'Sounds good.' Jennings smiled, walking into the station to catch up with her shift.

Forty minutes later, O'Neill sat in the restaurant of the Wellington Park Hotel. He'd been at school with the manager who recognized him as soon as he walked in.

'No problem. Sit where you like. I'll send one of the girls over.'

O'Neill sat at the back so he could look out over the room. Walking through, he had automatically scanned the faces at each table. It was mostly tourists and businessmen. As he waited he tried to remember when all the habits had started. Catherine used to get annoyed.

'I don't want to hide in the back, John, every time we go out for dinner.'

It was a weekday and the place was only half-full. Folk were getting stuck into bowls of cornflakes and cooked breakfasts. O'Neill always liked coming off a nightshift and watching people start their days. That feeling of tiredness. It was a reminder that he moved through a different world from those around him. His eyes were heavy and he knew Sam would be feeling something similar.

He watched her arrive. She wore a pair of jeans and tight red top. Sam looked different out of uniform, less attractive maybe. O'Neill had always thought women's fashion was a waste of time. A uniform, any uniform, did it for him. He saw Sam do a quick sweep of the room as she weaved her way through the tables. They ordered coffee. He caught himself checking her left hand as she picked up the menu. There was no ring.

O'Neill had chosen seats out of earshot of the rest of the room. They made small talk. Police College. Dungannon. Belfast. She laughed about her fractured cheekbone.

'I might have stamped on his balls a few times afterwards. He was pretty high-pitched by the time we interviewed him, I'll tell you that for nothing.'

Sam asked about CID, the move out of uniform, Laganview. O'Neill felt at ease talking to her. He didn't need to pretend, to lie, to put on some kind of performance.

She asked about Catherine. He told her the truth.

'It was the shifts that did it. Or maybe it was always going to happen. Maybe we were too young. Maybe Sarah came along too soon. Fuck, I don't know. I didn't fit in at the dinner parties with the rest of the husbands. I mean, have you ever spoken to a banker for two hours? Fuck me, it's hard going.'

Sam laughed.

'What about James? The fella you had back at Police College.'

Sam was surprised. O'Neill had remembered the name from all those years ago.

'Hightailed it. Said he'd had enough war stories. Said I was married to the job. I mean, it's all right for a man to have a career, to love what he does. But a woman? We're supposed to be secretaries. Make you your dinner, type your frigging letters ...'

O'Neill felt Sam starting to get her back up.

'All right. Easy there, sister. And what about after him?'

'Don't start me on the others.'

O'Neill had forgotten how natural Sam's smile was. The way her eyes flashed to life when she was telling a story. She asked him where he was living and he explained about the flat in Stranmillis.

'God, you're one sad case. Sitting up there, living off Chinese takeaways. Does the man in the shop know you by name? I'll bet he does.'

'Don't be slagging off Mr Wong. He's been a tower of strength through all this.'

They both laughed. O'Neill asked about Sam's shift. He was curious and, given how Laganview was going, a little nostalgic for his own days in uniform. He wanted to hear stories, jokes from back in the wagon, the kind of stuff no one ever believed, unless they'd actually been there.

Sam hesitated. 'It's fine.'

'Who's your Sergeant?'

'Donnelly.'

'What do you make of him?'

'There are worse ones out there.' Sam sighed, looking out the window into the car park. 'The shift's all right.'

'That is not the most ringing endorsement I've ever heard.'

'Ach, I'm tired. I've only been with them a few weeks. They're pretty tight, been together a good few years. I'm the new face. We're all sussing each other out. It'll take a while.'

O'Neill looked across the table, raising his eyebrows. He didn't buy it. Sam had great instincts, always had. He'd seen it in Police College. She glanced sidewards, wondering whether to tell him.

'Who have you got? Peters, Morrow, Savage, McAllister ...'

'Thompson and Cleary. Between us, they're a bit of a law unto themselves. They go drinking together most weekends. Men's men, you know. Think they know everything. Not afraid to put the boot into someone. Tossing them over in the back of the wagon.'

'You sure you're not just annoyed because you're not in the gang yet?'

'Screw the gang, John. I don't give a shit about the gang. But you know when you just have a feeling? Like something's not all it's cracked up to be?'

'Yeah. I know what you mean.'

O'Neill didn't push it. He made a mental note to go back there next time he saw Sam. He could tell she didn't want to go any further, not now anyway, and probably felt like she'd overstepped the mark. It was a secret though. And she'd wanted to tell him, to bring him closer, to show she trusted him.

'How long is it since we came out of Police College, John?'

'Six years, four months, nine days.'

Sam smiled. She had forgotten that things stuck with O'Neill.

'Is it everything you thought it would be? The job, I mean.'

O'Neill's eyes narrowed. 'What are you talking about?'

'I don't know. Maybe it's just me. Maybe it's the new station. Or the shift. I mean, don't you ever wish you had a normal job, like everyone else? Clock in, clock out. Go home. Get on with the rest of your life. Sometimes I look at people coming out of offices at five o'clock and I wonder ...'

'You wonder what?'

'I don't know. I wonder about the job.'

'Let me tell you. This – this here – this isn't a *normal job*.'

'What do you mean?'

'What we do. I mean, it might look like a normal job. You do a shift, get a wage, collect a pension. But that's where the similarity ends. A normal job is sitting at a desk, typing emails, answering phone calls. Pulling pints, serving lunches, waiting tables. Conference calls, sales visits, team meetings. The peelers?' O'Neill raised his eyebrows. 'What we do?' He slowly shook his head. 'Checking beneath your car in the morning, just in case someone's left a bomb under it. Chasing down some burglar who assaults pensioners, then ties them up and cleans them out. Nicking some husband who beats his wife, watching her drop the charges for the fifth time in a row. Parades. Standing in a riot, having stones thrown at you from both sides. Interviewing a forty-year-old man, asking why he raped a nine year old and posted the footage on the internet. The theft, the fraud, the assault. The abuse, the violence, the hatred. That's what *we* do. We do it. Nobody else. And because we do it, the rest of them out there can sleep in their beds at night. This might be many things, but I can tell you one thing. There's nothing normal about it.'

Sam could see it in O'Neill's eyes. He had had the same look in Police College. His face had weathered, there were a few grey hairs, a few lines round the eyes. But that look was still there. O'Neill paused and took a drink of his coffee.

'Why did you join up, John? Can you remember that far back?'

O'Neill exhaled slowly, his eyes in the distance.

'There was a guy in our year at school. We were eleven, but he must have been held back somewhere along the way, because he was a year older. He was a big lad, from up the Ardoyne. His da was involved and was doing time somewhere. Maghaberry. The Maze. No one really knew.'

'You going to tell me this kid stole people's lunch-money, and no one would do anything about it?'

'No,' O'Neill said, smiling at the schoolyard cliché. 'It wasn't that obvious. It was just when we played football. No one wanted to tackle him. To embarrass him. Run the risk of annoying him. He could do what he wanted.'

'So you joined up ...'

'I don't know. I just knew it wasn't right. There are people out there who do whatever they please, and nobody ever wants to put a tackle into them. It's the same everywhere. It's the same at Catherine's work, at Musgrave Street, the same on the street. People just taking things and nobody dares to say anything.'

O'Neill stopped and laughed quietly to himself. 'That's pretty serious for half eight in the morning.'

Sam didn't flinch. 'So that's why you're a peeler?'

'This is me. This is what I know.'

She held his gaze, and after a few seconds excused herself and went to the toilet. O'Neill left money for the bill. Afterwards they stood in the car park, hesitant, not wanting to go their separate ways.

'That was good,' O'Neill said.

'Yeah. I had a really good time.'

They paused, neither sure what to do. Shaking hands seemed naff.

'We should do it again,' Sam said.

'Yeah. I'd like that.'

Before O'Neill could move she stepped in and kissed him on the cheek. He had sat over breakfast, watching Sam eat, wondering what it would be like to put his mouth on hers. He tried not to show his disappointment at the kiss on the cheek. It was something, after all. Sam turned and walked towards her car. She didn't look over her shoulder, but got in quickly and drove away.

O'Neill smiled to himself as he walked out of the hotel car park. He wasn't thinking about anything: not Laganview, not the boy, not the dead ends he'd spent most of last week chasing. His phone rang in his pocket. It was Musgrave Street so he answered.

'DS O'Neill. It's Chief Inspector Wilson.' The voice was angry. The Chief Inspector had taken to calling every morning and every evening, piling on the pressure, giving O'Neill daily reminders that the case was going nowhere.

'Can you tell me why—'

O'Neill spoke into the phone. 'Hello? Hello? Can you hear me? *Hello!*'

He switched the phone off, staring at the handset. There was a bin next to his car. He thought about it, but decided not to and got into the car, tossing the phone on the passenger seat.

'Fucking twenty-first century.'

TWENTY-TWO

Friday morning at Musgrave Street and Doris was on the front desk. She'd spoken to Ward as he made his way through reception.

'I think your boy is getting pretty close to the edge.'

Doris had been around long enough to see cases ruin detectives. It was the pressure, the obsession. Young guys trying to prove themselves but not realizing they were playing with a dud hand. The only thing to do was to fold and wait for better cards. An hour earlier O'Neill had walked past, looking as if he hadn't slept for a fortnight.

Upstairs, half-drunk cups of coffee lay dotted round CID, a present from the nightshift. O'Neill sat between two stacks of folders, not looking up when Ward entered.

'Still not handed in your homework, Detective?'

'The dog ate it.'

Ward knew from Doris that O'Neill had been in well before his shift started. He'd probably spent half the night looking through files he'd sneaked home, thinking no one knew.

'Grab your coat, son.'

'How come?'

'Because I'm the Inspector and you're the Sergeant. That's how come.'

Ward grinned as O'Neill threw down his pen and stood up.

'You know, someone once told me something,' Ward began.

'Yes, Obi-Wan Kenobi?' O'Neill replied.

'If you're in the shit, best thing to do is start throwing some. When everyone else is covered in it, you won't feel so bad.'

'So where are we off to then?'

'We're gonna throw a little shit.'

'Sounds good to me.'

It was just after 11 a.m. when Lynch approached The George. His doorbell had rung at 9.30 that morning. It was one of the local kids who couldn't have been more than ten years old.

'Mr McCann wants to see you. Told me to give you this.' The kid passed Lynch a bullet, a 9mm copper round. 'Said it was time to bite the bullet.'

Lynch looked at the kid who smiled back, pleased at remembering his lines.

'He made me learn it, so he did.'

Lynch imagined McCann making the kid repeat it back to him. Gerry McCann, the great educator.

McCann used The George as an impromptu office. Lynch had been summoned and told to be there at eleven. Before leaving the house, he took the Browning from the shoe-box under the bed and was about to tuck it into his trousers. He knew they'd pat him down though and a pistol wasn't the kind of opening gambit you wanted with McCann. He knew he didn't have much choice and put the gun back under his bed.

As Lynch approached the bar he saw Sean Molloy and one of his boys standing outside smoking. McCann was definitely inside. Molloy had two black eyes and a bandage across his nose. Lynch kept his head down and walked through the double doors into the bar.

Molloy had taken almost all Lynch's attention as he walked up to the George. Not so much though that he didn't notice the two peelers, parked at the end of the street in an unmarked Mondeo. He wondered if McCann's boys had sussed they were there. From the two outside smoking, it didn't look like it.

In the Mondeo, Ward was mid-sentence. 'When we get in there, just follow—'

He stopped as he saw Joe Lynch approach the doors to the bar. O'Neill was reaching for the handle when Ward put an arm across him.

'Hold on a minute. That was Joe Lynch just walked in there.'

'Who's Joe Lynch?'

'Before your time. He did ten years in the Maze. They put four bodies on him but the word was there were a hell of a lot more. Let's hang back a minute. The question is, what's Joe Lynch doing with Gerry McCann?'

The George didn't officially open until midday. McCann sat at the back, near the emergency exit. Lynch crossed the threshold and saw a few figures, dotted around, waiting. No one was drinking. A man stepped forward and put a hand to Lynch's chest, looking him up and down before frisking him. To Lynch's left sat two men in black leather jackets. One of them looked at him with a blank, pitiless stare. Pat down over, the man nodded and pointed at a seat.

Molloy walked into the pub and took up a stool near the door. He made eye-contact with the men in leather jackets.

Lynch wondered if he had been set up but he put on an air of indifference, pretending to be oblivious as he planned an exit strategy. There were two doors. A lot of bodies at the front, so it would have to be the back. There'd be someone in the entry as well, although he wouldn't be ready. Lynch would be on him before he knew what was what. Then he'd be away.

McCann sat at a table at the back of the bar, talking to Johnny Tierney. He handed over a white container the size of a car battery.

'Three parts of this, to one part of the good stuff.'

Tierney smiled. 'What's it this time?'

'Don't you worry what it is,' McCann laughed, shaking his head. 'These fuckers round here will snort anything.'

Tierney joined in the laughter and handed the cutting agent to two young fellas in tracksuits. The three of them walked from the back of the bar, stopping to speak to Molloy before leaving.

The man who had frisked Lynch signalled that it was his turn. Three stone overweight, McCann sat before a large Ulster fry – eggs, sausage, bacon, fried soda, fried potato bread.

'Joe Lynch. I was beginning to think that you didn't like me.'

McCann pointed his knife at the plate. 'Best fry in the whole of Belfast. Or so they tell me. Wife says these things'll kill you. But sure if the Brits never managed it, what chance have a few rashers got, eh?'

McCann laughed at his own joke. The *bonhomie* was all part of the show, acting like he didn't have a care in the world. The Master of the Universe, all under control. Lynch kept his guard up. With McCann you were only one wrong word away from getting your throat slit. Back when he was nineteen, McCann tea-bagged a guy, putting eight holes in him with a flick-knife, in the toilets of Durys in Blackstaff Square. The guy had offered to buy McCann's bird a drink. He didn't know who she was, let alone that she was with McCann. The club was full but not a single person came forward to the police. It was how things were.

'So how are you enjoying being back, then?'

'Fine.'

'Having a bit of trouble sleeping, I hear.'

McCann raised an eyebrow. Lynch wondered who he had been talking to. Dr MacSorley? Marie-Therese? No. His house was being watched.

'Bit sad, don't you think, lying awake all hours. Is it nightmares? Have you tried sleeping with the light on?' McCann laughed sarcastically. 'Are you lying there thinking about your wee cell back at the Maze? Wishing you'd never got out? Liked doing your time for the Cause? Our Joe, the big martyr. Do you want your war back – is that what it is?'

Lynch didn't answer. McCann hadn't done a day inside so what the fuck did he know.

'Do you want to know why it is that you can't sleep?'

Lynch remained silent.

'It's because you're not doing anything. And I'm not talking about walking round, going to the shops, getting on like an auld housewife. You need to get busy, get yourself involved, get the blood pumping, the juices flowing. Men like you, Joe, men like me – we can't just sit around.'

McCann put a piece of sausage in his mouth and chewed it slowly, thinking.

'Let me tell you a story. When I was a wee lad my da took me up to Bellevue Zoo. We were going to see the lions, the tigers, everything. I was so excited, I wouldn't shut up in the bus the whole way up the Antrim Road. I'd seen them on TV, chasing zebras, hunting antelopes, attacking buffaloes. When we got there though, it was shite. There was this big lion, sitting there in his cage, just staring out. He no more looked like he could kill you than our neighbour's cat. All day long he just sat there. Rocking back and forth, like some mental patient in Purdysburn.'

McCann pierced a bit of soda bread with his fork and pointed it at Lynch.

'I don't know the kind of shit you've heard. Peace Process. New Northern Ireland. The Assembly.' He paused. 'It's a load of balls. Meanwhile you're pacing back and forth, staring out of the bars of a cage you don't even know you're in. Is this what you did ten years for? A shitty wee house and a portable TV – is that what it was all for? All the time, all the jobs, all the sacrifice?'

Lynch remained expressionless. Inside he was on fire. Partly it was sitting there and being lectured on sacrifice by someone like McCann. The other part was hearing McCann voice some of his own thoughts since he'd returned to Belfast. Maybe the man was right. Who was he kidding, walking round, trying to pretend he was normal? How many normal people had the thoughts he had? Still, he wasn't a criminal. He knew that. Thatcher had tried to tell them they were criminals. Ten men had died on hunger strike proving her wrong. No food for forty days. Death by starvation. They had shown her what real willpower was. *That* was discipline.

Lynch slid his chair back and made to stand up.

'Where the fuck do you think you're going?' McCann raised his voice. Along the bar one of his men got up from his stool.

'Sit the fuck down. I haven't finished with you.'

Lynch looked down the bar. The man who had frisked him stood where he was. He sat down as McCann loaded his fork and shovelled it into his mouth. He chewed slowly, showing Lynch he was in no rush. He could keep him there as long as he wanted.

'You owe me,' McCann said.

'How do you figure?'

'The fucking punchbag sitting at the end of the bar – Molloy. He hasn't worked for a week. The peelers have been on him like flies round shite. That's bad for business. Costs me money.'

'I don't know what you're talking about.'

'Aye, dead on,' McCann said sarcastically. 'You're going to do a bit of work for me. Pick up a package and deliver it. There's five hundred quid in it for you. Take the money, treat that wee tart you have your eye on, take her out to dinner or something. She'll be sucking your dick by the end of the week.'

Lynch stared at McCann.

'Aaagh, stop being so fucking sensitive, will you? We're all men here. She's a good-looking bit, or at least that's what the boys tell me. A bit young for you, mind, but sure, who the fuck am I to say?'

'I'm not interested.'

'I don't give a shit if you're interested or not. Molloy's not the sharpest tool in the shed, but he's a mean fucker once he gets an idea in his head.'

'Come again?'

'Don't play the innocent with me. It didn't work when the RUC grabbed you ten years ago and it's not going to work now. Molloy's young. He hasn't been round the block as many times as me and you. He doesn't know it takes a special kind of person to do what someone did to him. A person with patience. A person who can follow a target for days, weeks even. A person who can bide his time, wait until things are just right. Who can do a job and then vanish. Who doesn't need to sit in a bar all day, boasting about what he's done.'

Lynch sat in silence. McCann looked into his eyes. He had only been half-sure before, but meeting Lynch again, face to face, erased any doubts.

'And sure, Joe,' McCann lowered his voice, 'if none of this interests you I can always send the boys round to that wee slut of yours.'

'I don't even know her. She's nothing to do with anything.'

McCann shrugged his shoulders. 'That's not my problem.'

He ate another piece of sausage, chewing slowly before pointing at his mouth.

'Cookstown sausages. Really good. You should try some.'

The two men sat in silence.

'Who knows, Joe, you might even like it. Get the taste back. If you do, there is always work. Anyway, you'll be picked up outside here at two on Thursday morning. Now fuck off till I finish my breakfast.'

187

Ward and O'Neill watched Lynch walk out of The George. He put his hands in his pockets, turning in the opposite direction from the Mondeo.

'Forget McCann,' said Ward. 'He'll be an easy find when we need him. Let's have a word with Joe Lynch. Find out what he's doing so far from home.'

At the end of the street Lynch looked left into the oncoming traffic. He crossed the road and headed down May Street, towards the city centre. Ward started the car and O'Neill jumped out on foot. May Street was busy with cars. O'Neill took out his mobile phone, dialled Ward and held it to his ear. He looked like any other office worker, nipping out to grab a sandwich. Lynch looked over his shoulder at the traffic, then crossed to the other side of the road before turning down Joy Street.

Ward ditched the car and joined O'Neill on foot. They were 100 yards back and broke into a jog as Lynch crossed the road at the end of Joy Street.

They arrived to see him disappear into SS Moore, a sports shop on Chichester Street. Moore's was a local business, one of the few shops that hadn't been taken over by the big chains. O'Neill and Ward picked their way between the traffic and entered the shop. At the counter a woman was buying a hockey stick for her teenage daughter. The girl looked mortified at having to be in the town with her mother. Near the back of the shop, a middle-aged woman inspected a rack of swimsuits. O'Neill did a three-sixty.

Lynch was gone.

A small alarm sounded behind the counter. The shop assistant sighed and spoke to the mother.

'That alarm will be the death of me. I swear it has a mind of its own ...'

O'Neill looked at Ward. 'Fire exit.'

The younger detective sprinted out the front of the shop, wheeling round towards the side of the building. Ward knocked over a clothes-rail in his hurry to get to the changing rooms where a green sign pointed to the emergency exit.

He got there to see a set of double doors swinging open on their hinges. Ward burst out into the entry as O'Neill rounded the corner. At the far end Joe Lynch stopped running. He paused at the corner and looked back. His eyes met O'Neill's. The peelers had seen him, but he had seen them too. After a second he turned and took off, vanishing into a crowd of Belfast shoppers.

TWENTY-THREE

It was three days since Petesy had seen Marty. Three days since he had told him he'd had enough, that he wanted out, that he wanted to do something else.

Petesy sat with Micky in his bedroom playing *Grand Theft Auto* until two o'clock in the morning. He'd told Micky he was done with dealing. On the game they had just jacked a new car and were busy driving round, looking for the cops to get a chase.

Micky kept telling Petesy what to do. Go here. Do this. Do that. Petesy missed one of the turnings and Micky laughed, calling him a dozy bastard. Petesy didn't care. It was only a game. He thought about his mate. Marty never told him what to do. Never slagged him off, even when he made a balls-up of something.

Petesy left the house just before three. He had texted Marty, who was sitting smoking round the back of the Maxol garage. He said he'd come over and meet him.

It was awkward when Petesy arrived. Marty was still pissed off at him. His white Kappa top had a stain on the sleeve.

'What have you been up to?' Petesy asked.

'Riding that Cara one. Dirty wee hoor. Can't get enough of it.'

'You're full of shit.'

'I'm telling you, she loves it. Tits?' Marty exhaled between puckered lips, shaking his head. 'I could sit there all day, just feeling them.'

They laughed together. Marty tossed Petesy the box of cigarettes. He took one, lighting it from the smouldering end of his friend's fag.

'Micky's a dick by the way,' Petesy said.

'What? Your new best mate?'

'Grand Theft Arsehole.'

Marty smiled at his friend's joke. He finished his cigarette and lit another one straight away.

'Listen, Petesy. If you want to go to the Tech, go back to school and all that, it's fine with me. You're going to need money for pens and books and everything though.'

'Aye.'

'Well, your granny can hardly afford it. So what about if I sponsor you? Keep you sweet? You better become a lawyer or something though, because the chances are I'm going to need one sooner or later.'

Petesy smiled. 'Sounds good.'

'There's one catch,' Marty said.

'Oh aye?'

'You have to bring me to any parties you get invited to. Introduce me to the birds in your class. The snatch down the Tech is supposed to be phenomenal. There's loads of it. I'll stick a few books under my arm, nick a pair of glasses from somewhere. They'll never know.'

Petesy laughed. Marty would never change. They started to walk home. As they turned off the main road Petesy caught Marty grinning to himself.

'What the fuck are you smiling about?'

'Nothing.'

'Fuck away off and tell me.'

'A gentleman never talks.'

'Is it Cara again?'

'She's a wee ...'

They stopped in their tracks. Two figures were coming towards them. They were 100 yards away, but as soon as the men saw Marty and Petesy they started running. Instinctively the boys bolted, sprinting back in the direction they'd come from. By the end of the road Marty was ten yards in front of Petesy.

Another man came round the corner, wearing a dark green combat jacket. He tried to cut them off. Marty was quick, swerving between two parked cars.

'Come here, you wee cunt.'

A hand lunged out and tried to grab his tracksuit top. Marty could feel him right behind him. He kept his head down, kept going, expecting to go down at any moment.

Marty cut down an entry between two rows of houses and burst out of the Markets. On the main road he swung right and sprinted up the Albert Bridge. He didn't let up until he'd gone 500 yards. His lungs were burning. He slowed and looked back over his shoulder. The man had stopped where the entry hit the main road. Even from that distance Marty could make out the figure in the semi-darkness. It was Tierney. He scanned the street behind him, looking towards Oxford Street. There was no one to be seen. Where the fuck was Petesy?

Tierney walked forward under a lamppost. He wanted Marty to see him, to see who he was. After thirty seconds he turned and went back into the Markets. Marty waited a few minutes before crossing the road and starting back. There was no traffic, not even a taxi. He felt alone, incredibly alone. Where was Petesy? Everybody else could go fuck themselves. His ma. Micky. Janty. Even Cara. Petesy was the only one that mattered.

He took the long back way into the Markets, lowering himself over a wall and picking his way along the bank of the river. There was a patch of wasteground that separated the edge of the estate from the water. It was the same place as he'd had a fag with Locksy a couple of days ago. Marty could make out some muffled voices at the far end, hidden by the new fence around the disused gasworks.

Marty crept closer, bracing himself to bolt at any moment. He peered round the corner. There were three figures standing. Tierney, Molloy and another. Petesy lay on the ground at their feet. He wasn't moving. Tierney kneeled down, grabbing a handful of hair and lifting his head off the ground. He let go and Petesy's skull bounced off the concrete. Tierney stood up and goaded him.

'Where's your big talk now, you fucking wee hood? Do yous think this is a free market or something? That you can just do whatever you want? You and your fucking mate. Where's your mate now, eh? Fucked off on you, has he?'

Molloy laid a boot into Petesy, who groaned and curled into a ball.

Marty looked round for something. A bottle. A stick. There was nothing.

Fuck it.

He put his head down and sprinted, making for Tierney. He was at full pace when he came out of the dark. He hit

Tierney in the face, knocking him off his feet. Marty stood over Petesy to protect him.

Tierney picked himself up. 'You fucking wee cunt.'

Marty hadn't thought this far ahead. What did he do now?

'There must be a special offer on or something,' Molloy said from the side. 'A two-for-one on hoods.'

The three men barred any escape route. Molloy walked casually to the wall and lifted a hurling stick that was lying on the ground. The end of the stick had a series of nails protruding out of it. He gave a few practice swings as he walked back to the group. Warming up.

'So what the fuck are you going to do now?' Molloy asked.

He took a swing and Marty jumped back wards. The two others rushed him, knocking him to the ground. They were all over him. Punching him in the head. Then they stood up and started laying boots into him. Marty felt the wind go out of him and blackness start to close in.

The two men stood up. Molloy held the hurling stick at his side.

'You know something? It's your lucky day. We're only going to do one of you. The other one of yous is going to come and work for me. We'll put those entrepreneurial skills to some use.'

Marty heard the words, vaguely somewhere in the distance.

Molloy started pointing back and forth between the two boys on the ground.

'Eeny – meeny – miny – mo – catch – a nigger – by the – toe. If he – screams – let him – go. Eeny – meeny – miny – mo.'

His finger stopped on Petesy.

The two men dragged Marty away from his friend. One knelt on his back, pressing Marty's face into the gravel. They would make him watch.

Molloy methodically straightened out Petesy's legs. He stood back and took off his coat before stepping up and cocking the hurling stick over his shoulder. Then he swung it down, smashing the stick into Petesy's legs.

Petesy screamed. It was a raw, animal sound. He screamed with each blow. Molloy hit him five or six times on each leg. Afterwards Petesy lay there gradually quietening to a series of moaning whimpers.

'Not such a hard lad now, you wee cunt.' Molloy laughed. 'Don't take it personally, mind you. It's only business.'

The three men walked away, leaving the two boys on the wasteground. They joked among themselves, making imitation screams, revelling in the pain they'd inflicted.

TWENTY-FOUR

O'Neill was going to church.

It was the first time in twenty years. He hadn't seen the light. Laganview was nothing but darkness. It was almost two weeks and the body still didn't have a name.

St Mark's was tucked away in the city centre of Belfast, dropped among office blocks and apartments. It sat two streets back from the green copper dome of the City Hall. The building dated from the 1840s, when Dunvilles had the whiskey distillery next door. The distillery was long gone. O'Neill wondered how long before churches went the same way. Congregations were shrinking. He had heard of places across the water being turned into restaurants and nightclubs. Northern Ireland wouldn't be far behind.

O'Neill was not desperate. He'd been desperate a week ago. Desperate was a distant memory. Everyone else was off the case. He was alone. Just him, the body and a total lack of suspects.

St Mark's parish included the Markets and the lower Ormeau Road. The peelers had been stonewalled by everyone on the street. Even their regular informants knew nothing. O'Neill needed something, even if it was just a whisper – a rumour. *Anything*. Some kind of lead, something he could work from. He was still waiting on Forensics coming back with the footprints and wasn't hopeful.

Outside St Mark's a glass case contained notices of Mass times. There was a Polish Mass at 10 a.m. every Sunday. Above the sign was a question: *Looking for answers?* O'Neill ignored it and walked into the church.

The door thudded shut behind him, sealing O'Neill in the quiet of the building. He had stopped going to church when he was sixteen. He hated being told what to do. All that stand up, sit down. People droning their prayers like cattle.

Father Donal Mullan had been at St Mark's for ten years. He had hoped to be retired in some country parish by now. Visits to the elderly. Cups of tea. 'A wee bun there, Father?' Instead, the Bishop had given him St Mark's. Recruitment was at an all-time low. 'All hands to the pump, Donal.'

Fr Mullan felt as if he'd done his fair share of pumping. He'd been in Belfast schools for over thirty years. O'Neill had been one of his pupils at St Malachy's College. Mullan regarded the Catholic boys of Belfast as his own particular penance. He taught History and Religion, but his true love was Gaelic football.

'Dribbling is for babies,' he used to say. 'Soccer? An English game. Grown men falling over themselves like a bunch of women.'

Inside the church, forty pews stretched out in front of O'Neill. The altar was a large stone table. Confession boxes were built into the wall along the side of the church. Above the three doors, small lights showed they were all engaged. The priest sat in the middle. A sinner on either side.

Two pensioners sat nearby waiting. O'Neill took a seat near the back. He looked at the pensioners, wondering what they could possibly be there for. He thought about the files they had on people at Musgrave Street. The assault, the robbery, the rape. He wondered did that stuff get an airing in the darkness and quiet of the confessional.

One of the doors opened and an old man walked out, head bowed, face penitent. O'Neill thought about what must have been said in those boxes over the last forty years. The bombings. The shootings. What did you get for killing a man? For following him home. Putting three bullets in him in front of his wife and two children. A few Hail Marys? A whole rosary? He suddenly had a deep loathing for the Catholic Church. Did they forgive these fuckers? Were slates wiped clean? Any SOCO would tell you, you can never entirely get rid of a bloodstain.

The last pensioner came out of the confessional. O'Neill waited. It was getting late. There'd be no one else coming. He got out of his seat and pulled the handle of the heavy door. It took him a few seconds to adjust to the dim lighting inside. In the box there was a kneeler and a chair. O'Neill sat.

He heard the priest in the adjacent box clearing his throat. The divider slid back and a gravelly Tyrone voice came through the wire mesh.

'In the name of the Father, the Son and of the Holy Spirit. The Lord God is a just God and forgives the sins of the world. How long is it since your last confession?'

'That's a good question, Father.'

'O'Neill.'

Mullan's tone changed, reverting to the streetwise school teacher.

'Now there's a voice I haven't heard for a few years. Someone told me you'd joined the mighty Police Service of

Northern Ireland. Is there something on your mind, O'Neill? You haven't been beating up the suspects, have you?'

'Just a visit. Thought I'd see how you're doing. Catch up on old times.'

'Oh aye. I've heard that one before.'

'How's the God business these days, Donal? Plenty of bums on seats? A lot of sinners, a lot of sins.'

'Don't mock, son. It doesn't suit you.'

O'Neill could smell the waft of tobacco coming through the grille.

'Still at the Dunhills, I see. You know those things'll kill you.'

'Well, I've got to do something to get out of here. Forty years in Belfast – a life sentence by any man's reckoning.'

'You've not seen the news then? The Promised Land. The new Northern Ireland.'

'I'll believe it when I see it.'

There was a pause in their conversation.

'I need your help, Donal.'

'You need my help? Or the PSNI needs my help? Because you see it's interesting. The PSNI spend their days harassing my congregation and then they come round here asking for help?'

O'Neill had almost forgotten Mullan's style. He was like a bantamweight boxer. A conversation was a sparring match. He had taught the same way. St Malachy's had had 700 teenage boys and they all had an answer for you. There wasn't much choice.

'You know about Laganview, Donal?'

'Saw it on the news.'

'I'm in the dark. Completely in the dark.'

'We're all in the dark, son. That's how the world works.'

O'Neill knew Mullan was a strong Republican. According to him, Irish history taught its own lessons. It was a list of wrongs, a litany of sins against Irish Catholics, first by the British, and then by the Protestants in the North. Mullan used to tell them: 'A creed. A man's got to have a creed.' O'Neill could feel the door closing on him and the priest retreating into his shell.

'Do you remember Raymond Burns, Father?'

'I remember you all, O'Neill. Every last one of you.' Mullan sighed. 'Burns was from the Ardoyne. A cheekier wee bastard you wouldn't want to meet.'

'Let me tell you about Raymond Burns. He has a wee brother, Jackie Burns, ten years younger. Wee Jackie is sixteen. Thinks he's a big lad. Decided to have a go at nicking cars. He got away with it, or at least he did for a couple of months. One day he's walking to the shops when a couple of men grab him off the street. Broad daylight. They know what he's been doing and he needs to be taught a lesson. They put him down a manhole. And put the lid back on. Wee Jackie's screaming. Begging. He's claustrophobic, you see. But fuck it, down he goes. These wee bastards, you see, they never listen. Now those manhole covers are pretty thick. Six inches of heavy iron. It fairly muffles the screams.'

O'Neill felt the priest listening on the other side of the mesh.

'They left him there for three hours,' he said. 'Three fucking hours. By the time they let him out he'd lost his voice. He'd shredded his vocal cords screaming so much. He'd pissed himself and shit himself. Sixteen years old, Donal. Not shaving yet. They're laughing as they lift him out. "Dirty wee bastard. Look at the state of you." And they leave him there. Just lying by the side of the road.'

O'Neill cleared his throat.

'You probably saw the rest of it on the news. The anti-depressants. Wouldn't leave the house. In the end he hanged himself. His mother found him in the entry round the back of the estate.'

O'Neill stopped talking. He could hear the priest breathing on the far side of the grille.

'But you've probably seen this all before, Donal. The seventies. Wee girls kissing soldiers. Hoors, the lot of them. Chain them up. Shave their heads. Get the tar. Teach them some lessons, eh, Donal? Pearse, Connolly, Collins – I forget which one spoke about torturing kids. A man's got to have a creed. That's right, isn't it?'

O'Neill stopped. He had gone too far. The frustration of the past two weeks had boiled over. It was all mixed up inside him. The images of Laganview, the kid's legs, his blood, his face. The story filled the confessional, making the space seem smaller, as if the air had been breathed too much.

'Laganview, Donal. Somebody out there knows something.'

O'Neill slid one of his PSNI cards under the mesh. He then got up and left the confessional, walking through the empty church, out of the heavy wooden doors. The sky had greyed over while he had been inside. As he got into the car, specks began to appear on the windscreen. The rain was starting up again.

Back in Musgrave Street, Ward was thinking about Spender.

201

He'd gone fishing after his visit to Cultra. The projects Spender had been involved in: the houses on the High Town Road, the investments in the Cathedral Quarter, Laganview, and the next one, the Ormeau Gasworks. Apart from the retracted complaint, twenty years back, the man looked clean. He might be rich, and he might be an arsehole, but so far, none of that was illegal, Ward told himself.

On his way into work Ward had stopped at a ESSO garage to get petrol. He watched two teenagers getting out of car. The girl had long blonde hair, just like …

That was it. Spender's kids.

When he got to Musgrave Street he ran both kids through the Police National Computer. The daughter, Zara, was clean. The son, Phillip, was a different story.

A string of minor offences went back to 1999 when he was seventeen. Shoplifting, theft, possession. It had drugs written all over it. In 2001 it had stopped for six months, then a couple more, this time in Manchester. Ward remembered Mrs Spender saying the kids were across the water. He must have gone away to university, cleaned up for a while, or at least had a student loan to cover his habit. When that ran out he would have needed to get busy again.

Ward imagined how it would have gone. The parents cutting off the money. He started stealing. It escalated from there. He sighed, knowing he could pull out a thousand files with exactly the same story.

Ward looked in his notebook, picked up the phone and dialled a number. A secretary answered.

'William Spender, please.'

'Can I ask who's calling?'

'DI Ward, Musgrave Street.'

'One moment, please.'

He didn't think Spender would talk to him, but the call would get the girls in the typing pool going if nothing else. Ten seconds later the secretary was back.

'I'm sorry, Detective, Mr Spender is busy. Can I take a message?'

'Just tell him I called.'

Ward had found out what he needed to know. He grabbed the car keys for the Mondeo and left the office.

Twenty minutes later in Cultra, a black iron gate slowly opened, admitting the navy Mondeo. At the front door Ward was greeted by Spender's wife. He knew he would be.

'My husband's not at home, Detective.'

'If it's OK, I'd like to ask *you* a few questions, Mrs Spender.'

Ward was unassuming. Kind yet assertive. Not giving her anywhere to go. He knew if you started easy you could always press harder.

In the kitchen Mrs Spender sat at the table. The room was expensively furnished. Polished granite counters. Large chrome cooker. Sliding glass doors. Outside, a wide patio with steps to the lawn, swept down to the waters of Belfast Lough.

Mrs Spender was nervous and kept glancing towards the door. Ward did nothing to put her at her ease. He took his time, allowing the simple fact that he was there to discomfort the woman. Mrs Spender lifted a cup of coffee. Ward figured it was to give her hands something to do. She didn't offer him one.

'You know what this is about, Mrs Spender?'

'No, I'm not sure I do.'

'Did your husband say why I came to see him last week?'

'He didn't.'

'So you've absolutely no idea?'

'I watch the news, Detective. The body on the building site. Makes sense you want to speak to people – my husband included.'

'Did he tell you any more than that?'

'My husband's a busy man.'

Ward paused as the woman took a sip of coffee. She was gathering confidence, attempting to hide behind a wall of ignorance.

'Why did you lie to me, Mrs Spender?'

'I beg your pardon?'

Ward repeated the accusation.

'I didn't lie.'

'You didn't tell me about the drugs.'

'What drugs?' The woman went on the defensive. 'My son isn't involved in drugs.'

Ward stopped and looked at Mrs Spender. The words hung in the air, revealing that she had overstepped the mark, said more than she meant to.

'Who said anything about your son?'

Mrs Spender realized she'd been caught by Ward's bluff. The detective started pressing home his advantage.

'Lying to the police is a serious offence, Mrs Spender. You can go to jail.'

The woman was unnerved. Ward could see the tears, hidden just below the surface. As quickly as he saw them rise, she forced them back down. Ward imagined she'd had plenty of practice keeping them at bay. All the dinner parties. The questions. *How are the kids? How is Zara? And what about Phillip? You'll have to bring them round.*

Ward wondered what it must be like to love someone and then be worried, embarrassed and ashamed, all at the same time. He walked to the counter and lifted down a framed photograph of the two Spender children. He held it in his hands before setting it down on the kitchen table.

'How old is Phillip in this?'

'Seven.'

'Amazing. I'll bet you can remember it like it was yesterday.'

Ward watched the woman's eyes look up and to the right as she remembered. She was thinking about Phillip as a boy. Seven years old. Still a kid. Ward kept working.

'Seven, eh? What was he into? Action Men? Star Wars? Those Ninja Turtle things?'

'Star Wars. He had every one of those bloody figures. I used to end up standing on them and having to buy him new ones.'

Ward laughed gently. 'How old is he now?'

'Twenty-two.'

'Where is he?'

'Manchester. Or so we think.' There was a sadness in the woman's voice. As if she was talking about someone who had recently passed away.

'When was the last time you heard from him?'

Mrs Spender's nose started to run. She sniffed, having to hold back the tears again. Ward handed her a tissue.

'Sixteen months ago.'

It was as if a release valve had been turned in her.

'How long has he been a drug addict?'

'It started when he was seventeen – so we think, anyway. He was doing his A-levels. Didn't like school so decided to do them at the Tech in Belfast. He must have fallen in with the wrong crowd. Started going into the town at weekends, Friday night right through. He would come home Sunday morning with bags under his eyes. As if he hadn't slept for days. We tried everything. Stopped his money. He wasn't allowed out. He climbed out his bedroom window and went anyway.'

Mrs Spender looked past Ward, into the middle distance.

'He went to Manchester for university. Things seemed to settle down. The first Christmas he came home he looked OK. By the summer he'd lost half a stone. His skin was a yellowy grey colour. He would disappear for weeks at a time. Then he'd turn up out of the blue. He started stealing from us – from his own family. It was my fault. I raised him, William was always busy. The next Christmas, he never came home. We got a letter saying he'd been thrown out of the university at the end of his first year. We haven't heard from him since then. Sixteen months.'

Ward had a sudden sinking feeling. Could the body at Laganview be Phillip Spender? The police hadn't released a photograph, only a description and an appeal for information. What if he had come back? What if he'd owed some people money? Someone could have tried to get to Spender through his son.

Ward sighed. There was nothing else for it. He produced a photograph of the victim from his jacket pocket.

'Mrs Spender, do you recognize this boy?'

The woman suddenly realized what Ward was trying to ascertain. The colour drained from her face. She looked at the photograph with an expression of horror, then shook her head. It wasn't Phillip.

'Mrs Spender, that feeling you've got – the one for Phillip – the hurt you feel for him. Because you're his mother. Because you carried him round inside you for nine months. Because you gave birth to him, because you fed him, because you were everything to him. There is another mother out there, feeling exactly the same thing – except her son is lying on a slab in the Belfast morgue. She doesn't even know he's there. He's alone. Completely alone. She needs to know what happened to him. She needs to come and get him.'

Ward stopped talking, setting the photograph on the table, beside the framed picture of the two Spender children.

'You can help this woman. You can help her by helping us.'

Karen Spender looked round the room, searching for something to hold on to. Her mind was racing. Was it William's fault Phillip had turned out the way he had? The arrogance. The greed. Never having time for him. Or was it her? Had she been too soft on him? Just letting him do what he wanted? And would someone out there speak up if something like this happened to her Phillip? If he was lying somewhere with the same lifeless expression?

The emotions whirled through her. She felt sick. Ward was offering her a way out.

'There was a book,' she said thickly.

'A book?'

'A small black book. William found it in Phillip's room a couple of weeks ago. It had phone numbers in it – Belfast numbers. There were initials beside them. We figured it was the people he was getting his drugs from.'

'Where is it now?'

'I don't know. William took it.'

'And where was William on Sunday evening, a fortnight ago?'

She hesitated for a second. Then: 'He was here.'

Ward noticed the pause. She was lying outright or else trying to cover something up. Mrs Spender looked at the detective. A veil fell from her eyes as if she had suddenly awoken. She remembered where she was and who she was talking to. The kitchen, with all its familiarity, seemed to rally round, to prop her up.

'Detective, my husband is a respectable businessman. If you have any questions about his affairs, I suggest you take them up with him.'

She stood up.

'If you'll excuse me, I have quite a lot of things to get on with.'

'One last thing, Mrs Spender.'

He produced a photograph of Tony Burke, one they'd lifted from the video recording of his interview. He also had one of Michael Burke, a copy of his arrest mug shot from an old RUC file.

'Do you recognize these men?'

'No.'

'Are you sure?'

'Yes.'

Ward held the woman's gaze for several seconds before picking the photographs from the table.

As he walked down the hall he caught sight of the family portrait hanging on the wall. The kids were twelve or thirteen. Everyone was smiling. William Spender included.

TWENTY-FIVE

William Spender admired himself in the full-length mirror. There was something about black tie he'd always liked – the polished shoes, the white shirt, the tight collar. It was like a dress uniform for the successful. He tilted his head back, straightening his bow tie. Not bad, for the son of a builder, he thought. Black tie had become almost a monthly fixture on Spender's calendar. It seemed businessmen across Northern Ireland couldn't wait to get together and congratulate themselves on how well they were doing. The trousers had been a bit of a squeeze and Spender wondered if he needed to finally go up a size. He patted his gut softly, thinking about his favourite restaurants – Deane's, Cayenne, The Merchant. Venison steak, pan-fried scallops, Dundrum mussels.

'How could a man not get fat?' he said out loud.

Tonight was the Chamber of Commerce awards dinner. It was an annual event. A five-course meal at the City Hall and anyone who was anyone would be there. His friends from Planning, as well as a few folk from the City Council. It would be a good chance for him to see them, make sure they were all on side for the upcoming Gasworks project. The favours for Laganview had all been paid up.

The Chamber of Commerce had some doll from UTV presenting the awards. Spender Properties were receiving one for their work in the Cathedral Quarter. Spender laughed at the idea – as if you needed to be rewarded for making money! It was money that mattered. Money spoke louder than any bit of Waterford crystal ever could. At night, when he couldn't sleep he'd drive round Belfast in the Mercedes, doing a loop of the various developments he'd built. It was a counting exercise and not a little bit of self-congratulation. There were the houses up the Hightown Road, the Cathedral Quarter, Laganview, and now the Gasworks project. Spender would sit in the warmth of the car, listening to the hum of the engine, whispering to himself: 'She's mine. So's she. So's she.'

He knew the Chamber of Commerce do would be good publicity and would undoubtedly bring more investors on board. From the plans alone they'd sold half the apartments at Laganview. In Northern Ireland people couldn't get enough. It was as if they'd been let off the leash after years of straining. Folk walked round show apartments and pulled out their cheque books. The banks were everyone's friend, and were giving out money hand over fist. With Laganview they'd be able to raise the price by a hundred grand per apartment when they released the second phase. The important thing was that work was back on track. It was easy. A few more Poles swinging pickaxes and the thing was on schedule again. The police were a joke. Strutting around like they owned the place. They didn't, Spender reminded himself. *I do*.

Karen walked into the bedroom from her en suite. Something was up with her: she'd had a face on her since Spender walked in the door an hour ago. He didn't know what she had to be unhappy about – she'd just put on the black

211

silk dress, the Yves Saint Laurent number that cost the guts of two grand. She sat at her dressing-table, putting the finishing touches to her make up. Karen had been stunning when they had first met. She was still attractive and had kept her figure well. Spender glanced at her in the mirror. He liked walking into a crowded room with her on his arm. Heads turned. The men looked at her leeringly and women as if they wanted to slit her throat. After their entrance though, he could never wait to get rid of her. He'd park her with the rest of the wives. Let them talk about whatever it was that they talked about. He could go off with the men. Talk business. Tell them how well Spender Properties were doing.

He finally got the bow tie fixed and stood back from the mirror. From the dressing-table behind him, Karen's voice piped up.

'That policeman was back again today.'

She tried to feign indifference, as if she was asking about the weather or what he fancied for dinner. Spender turned and looked at his wife.

'What did you say?'

'I said the policeman called again. He was looking for you.'

'What did you tell him?'

'He was asking about the body. I told him I didn't know anything.'

'You don't know anything.'

'That's what I said.'

Spender walked to within striking distance and stood over his wife. He pointed a finger in her face.

'What did I tell you about talking to people about my business?'

Karen tried not to look at her husband. It only made him angrier. She'd learned that a few years after they were married when the kids were still wee. She knew she needed to hang in there for them. Spender hadn't raised his hand to her in years. But that person was still there, still inside him, she could see it now, just below the surface. She used to wonder if he had changed or whether she got better at reading the signs and staying out of trouble. Her husband's eyes bored into her now and she sensed a storm brewing.

'What else did you say?'

'He knew about Phillip.'

Spender flew into a rage. 'Did you invite the guy in?'

'He just wanted to talk. Ask a few questions. What was I supposed to do?'

'What did he want to talk to *you* about?'

'I don't know. The body. Phillip. Drugs.'

'What did I tell you about running your mouth off? When it's something you know nothing about ...'

Spender remembered the Cavehill Road development ten years earlier. He had been about to finalise contract negotiations for a block of shops with eight apartments. Karen had been talking to someone at the gym or the hairdresser's, the wife of Paul Bartholomew, a property solicitor in Belfast. Next thing, Mrs Bartholomew goes home and tells her husband, who tells one of his clients – and bingo! The deal gets stolen, right from under Spender's nose. The development was due to net him over half a million.

Spender took a deep breath and tried to rein in his temper. He needed to know everything that had been said. What the detective wanted to know and, more importantly, what she'd told him. Karen didn't know anything, but you couldn't be too careful. He knew he wasn't going to get anything out of her if it turned into a slanging match.

He went downstairs and poured himself a large Bushmills. He made up a gin and tonic for his wife and set it on the kitchen table. They could be late for dinner. This was more important. After five minutes he heard Karen's heels click along the hall.

'Have a seat before we go out,' Spender said calmly. 'I'm not cross with you. It's those frigging cops. They cost me thousands ... cost *us* thousands, shutting down the site for most of last week. If they have their way they'll do it again. All over some wee hood that no one gives a damn about.'

He got Karen to talk him through the conversation with Ward. She told him about Phillip, about the drugs, the stealing, the fact he'd been gone for over a year. She told him about the black book, the one with the numbers. The one he had taken off her when she showed it to him.

'Is that everything?' Spender asked. Her eyes shifted.

'He wanted to know where you were the Sunday night the boy was killed.'

'I was here. You know that.'

'That's what I told him.'

Spender sensed there was more.

'You were up late though.'

'I'm up late most nights.'

'Well, I was in bed. Asleep. But I thought I heard the car leave.'

'No, you didn't. I was working downstairs until three in the morning, getting figures ready for the accountant. Busting my balls, Karen, so you can go to dinner parties in frigging Yves Saint Laurent dresses.'

Spender felt the heat rising in him again. How could she be so stupid? The word 'divorce' popped into his head, as it did most weeks. He dismissed it. His solicitor had run out the numbers, twice now, on how much it would cost. It was cheaper to keep her around, keep her in haircuts and designer dresses. He could always get his kicks elsewhere.

'How do you think all this gets paid for, Karen? The house, the new kitchen – that wee coupé you're driving out there? I work for it. Me. *I* make it happen. Do you want it all to suddenly vanish? Are you that frigging stupid?'

Spender's wife slowly shook her head. Her husband drained his glass.

'They're just trying to stir things up. They come out here, see we're doing all right for ourselves and they want to have a go at us, try to take it all away.'

Karen looked at her husband. He smiled, wanting to let her know it was OK. She might have messed up but he forgave her. At the same time his head was racing, wondering what the cops were doing, what they would make of what his wife had told them.

'Let's get in the car and go. And if the cops call again, then you don't answer the door. All right?'

Karen nodded her head and the two of them stood up from the table.

TWENTY-SIX

1.57 a.m. The road outside The George was deserted. From the mouth of the alley, Lynch could see the full length of the street. He'd been there since eleven. He looked at his watch. McCann's boys wouldn't be late.

He reached down to his ankle, running his hand over the duct tape that held the Browning in place. It was secure, still hidden. He knew it would be. He also knew there was a good chance he'd have to use it. They might be trying to get him back in the game but it could also be a set-up. McCann had a tendency to see things in black and white. It was an easy logic. People picked a side. You're with us or you're against us.

McCann had guessed that Lynch was behind Molloy's accident, and Molloy was one of his boys, so anything that happened to him might as well have been directed at McCann. As far as he would be concerned, Lynch was a liability. People like him didn't just settle down, get a nine to five, pint down the local, football on weekends. And if he could do that to Molloy, he couldn't just be ignored. Lynch wondered if the operation was meant to test the waters, McCann giving him a chance. If he wasn't interested, would there be instructions to get rid of him when the job was done? A working interview? Either way, Lynch knew there was no more stalling. He was backed into a corner and it was time to choose.

A grey Honda approached The George and parked up, turning off its headlights, but keeping the engine running. One man sat behind the wheel. Even from 40 yards, Lynch could make out Molloy's profile. He jogged over, going behind the car to check the footwell of the back seat. It was an old trick, to hide someone in there. The target got in and before he knew it he had a gun at the side of his head. It didn't leave much room for negotiation.

Molloy had lost the white bandage from his nose. The swelling in his eyes had gone down, and the purple bruising was a mild discolouration, a brown and yellow stain. Lynch got into the car. Pretending he hadn't shut his door properly, he reopened it. It might have been tampered with, have the child lock flicked on. At least now he knew he could get out, make a run for it if he needed to. Molloy didn't look at him and drove off without speaking.

The two men sat in silence as the car made its way up the Newtownards Road. They passed Stormont, its white imperial face lit up against the black night sky. Lynch looked at the building, the home of the Northern Ireland Assembly. For decades it had been a symbol of everything that was wrong with the North. From there, successive Unionist governments had put the boot into Catholics. Now everyone was round the table, the Chuckle Brothers, playing Happy Families. It was easy to be happy when you were taking home thousands every year for sitting round talking all day.

The roads were quiet, except for a few solitary cars, weaving their way through the dark.

'We're playing taxi tonight. Making a pick-up,' Molloy said. 'Taking it to a drop off. Easy money.'

Lynch imagined Robert De Niro in *Taxi Driver*. Was it Travis Bickle, he was called? He remembered the bulging eyes, the psychotic voice. '*Are you looking at me?*' He wondered who fitted the part better, him or Molloy. Molloy liked to think he was dangerous, that he lived on the edge. Lynch smiled quietly to himself, remembering there was only one of them that had been to see a shrink in the last few weeks.

The car turned off the main road into a large council estate. Rows of pebble-dashed houses, once white but now a dull grey, were lit up by orange sodium street-lamps. On every corner the kerbstones were painted red, white and blue. Molloy pulled up beneath a 30-foot Loyalist mural. A masked gunman loomed over the car, clutching an AK-47. *Prepared for Peace. Ready for War.*

Lynch didn't like it. Peace Process or no Peace Process. A couple of Catholics, parked in Ballybeen at two in the morning?

'Don't panic there, Lynch,' Molloy said. 'This isn't a trip down Memory Lane. It's the new Northern Ireland. You've got to remember we're all in this together.'

Lynch felt his senses sharpen. They had been slowly tightening all day and were now razor-sharp. He felt as though he was aware of everything. The estate outside – he'd immediately scoped the four places someone might come from. He had an escape route for each scenario. He could sense Molloy's hands and knew where the other man's eyes were looking. He heard the other man's breathing, sensed its rhythm. He was looking for a sign. Anything. A split-second head-start. Half a chance. It might be all he got.

'So what's the story?' Lynch asked.

'You don't need to know that,' Molloy answered. After a few seconds he continued: 'It's purely business these days.'

'I see.'

'You don't need to see, Lynch,' Molloy told him. 'That's not your job. You just need to *do*.'

Lynch rolled his eyes. Molloy had memorized every bad gangster film he'd ever seen. The more Lynch looked at the estate, the painted kerbstones, the mural, the more he wondered if *he* wasn't in fact the package. Might McCann be delivering him up to somebody?

Molloy reached into the back seat and pulled out an Adidas bag. He took out a handgun, tucking it into his trouser belt before tossing one to Lynch. It was heavy steel, black, almost new. Glock 19. Standard issue PSNI. Molloy saw Lynch's surprise at the make of weapon.

'We've got friends all over the place these days.'

Lynch slid the magazine out of the handle, checked the ammo and hit it home with the heel of his hand. He slid back the chamber, the mechanism snapping back on its spring. He was ready to go.

'Bag's got the money in it. Anything seems wrong, we keep hold of the cash and get out,' Molloy said.

'You don't know these guys?'

'Know them? Yes. Trust them?' Molloy raised his eyebrows and exhaled. 'That's a different question.'

Molloy now was markedly different from the man Lynch had followed along Victoria Street. He might be full of shit, but he was in control. The adrenaline was pumping through Lynch's body. He'd been there enough times to know that, even if his heart was pounding, his hands would remain still, his voice steady. Lynch didn't know why. He couldn't explain it. It had always been that way.

Molloy looked at his watch. He left the headlights off and pulled the car round the corner, parking in front of a pebble-dashed house.

'Right. Let's go.'

Driving back down the Newtownards Road, the relief in the car was palpable. Everything in the house was as it should have been. The door had opened and they went in without exchanging words. There were two men. A blue sports bag sat on the coffee-table. Four kilos of white powder, wrapped in clear plastic and duct tape. One of the men spoke.

'Do you want to check it?'

'Don't need to,' Molloy answered. 'I know where you live.'

The three men laughed at the old Northern Irish threat. Lynch didn't imagine it was the first time any of them had said it.

When they were out of Ballybeen, Molloy had taken the Glock back off him.

In the city the car headed along Ann Street, turning in behind the huge stone edifice of the Belfast cathedral. For a second, an 80-foot Celtic cross towered over the vehicle. Behind the cathedral, the narrow cobblestone lanes glistened from the rain. Molloy navigated his way through several tight turns before pulling up at an unmarked door. It looked like an emergency exit.

'What's this place?' Lynch asked.

'Enough of the questions. Christ, it's like being out with Anne Robinson.'

The two men got out of the car, Molloy carrying the blue sports bag. He kicked the steel door. After thirty seconds it opened and a squat figure with a shaved head stared out at them. Lynch recognized him. It was one of the bouncers from Mint.

'Right, Ivan?' Molloy said.

The man stood aside, giving Molloy space to enter. Through the door Lynch could see a commercial kitchen. Stainless-steel counters and white tiles were illuminated by powerful lights. He went to follow but the bouncer put a large hand in his chest.

'Who this?' he asked in a thick Eastern-European accent.

'He's with me.'

The man looked at Lynch as if he was a piece of shit someone had walked across his new carpet.

'No.'

The heavy steel door closed in Lynch's face.

He stood in the alley, wondering if Molloy would reappear. He didn't and after a couple of seconds Lynch walked off in the direction of the docks. He rounded the corner and saw the unlit sign for the nightclub overhead. He walked past the doorway where he had waited for four hours the week before.

He had done the job. His debt was paid. McCann couldn't complain.

TWENTY-SEVEN

It was two in the afternoon. Musgrave Street smelled like cold coffee, stale sandwiches and packets of crisps.

O'Neill was looking through the material Ward had put together on Spender. He'd brought him up to speed on his visits to Cultra. O'Neill had done some more digging but Spender came up clean. The best O'Neill could do was the complaint from twenty years back and a couple of parking tickets. The son's record was interesting. It had the classic drug pattern – high on desperation, low on execution. Junkies didn't make for the most subtle or patient of thieves.

How did this relate to Laganview though? And what about the notebook? Would Spender go so far as to have someone killed? Was it revenge on whoever got his son into drugs? Did someone go after his son? Was someone sending a message to Spender himself?

The other DCs on the shift, Kearney and Larkin, were both at their desks typing up. Kearney finished and clicked 'save' in theatrical triumph.

'Have some of that, you little bastard.'

O'Neill's eyes drilled into the back of his head. Everything felt like an accusation, as if the world was rubbing his face in Laganview. For two weeks the walls of Musgrave Street had been closing in on him. It seemed as if he couldn't walk down the corridor without bumping into Wilson. The Review Boards were coming up in ten days. O'Neill knew that the Chief Inspector was going to make a move to get him out of CID, and this would be where he'd do it. It would be a committee job. On the surface it would read like standard protocol. But Wilson would have the deck stacked long before the meeting. It would be all polite smiles. They would simply be asking questions. Trying to ascertain O'Neill's competency in his current role. O'Neill knew Laganview would be the final nail in the coffin. Proof that he wasn't right for CID. It would be in everyone's best interest. A fresh start for him. A new challenge. All that bullshit.

O'Neill looked around CID, wondering if someone had put two more desks in when he wasn't looking. It felt that way.

Kearney and Larkin were leaning back on their chairs.

'Did I tell you about going to the ice hockey last weekend?' Kearney asked.

'No. I never had you down for all that carry-on.'

The Belfast Giants were the latest must-have ticket. They had started up the year before in the Odyssey Arena. It was a new sport, free from the religious baggage of football and charging enough money to make sure the riff-raff stayed out. The Giants were made up of Canadians and Americans and played against teams from such exotic locations as Nottingham, Hull and Dundee. They won their first season and journalists had fallen over themselves, writing that it showed what Northern Ireland could do, now that the dark days of the past were behind them.

'The kids had been on at me to take them for weeks,' Kearney said. 'Guess how much it cost?'

'Don't know.'

'Fifty quid.'

Larkin raised his eyebrows.

'Yeah – fifty quid. To watch a bunch of Americans beating the crap out of each other. I mean,' Kearney continued, 'for fifty quid you'd want to beat the crap out of your own American.'

Both men laughed. O'Neill rolled his eyes. It was as well they had something to laugh about.

Kearney and Larkin chatted on, talking about the jobs they were on. They schemed and plotted, figuring out ways to catch folk out. O'Neill couldn't stop himself from listening in. He was jealous. Jealous of the variety, the different bits of work, the pace of things. Right now, anything looked better than Laganview. One body, no name, no suspects.

The phone rang on O'Neill's desk.

'DS O'Neill? John McBurnie down at Forensics. I ran through those additional footprints you had us cast at Laganview last week.'

'Yes?'

'Well, you were right. The Nike prints coming over the fence were the victim's. Looks like that is where your boy came in.'

'Anything else?'

'Location? Parallel pair of prints, 2.8 metres out from the fence. Suggests he was in a bit of a hurry. If he's sneaking over you'd imagine he lowers himself down. The prints would also be facing backwards, towards the fence. They'd be closer too.'

'Agreed.'

'He's not hanging about. He climbs, jumps down and is off again. Someone's chasing him.'

'Yeah. There were other prints in that area as well.'

'That's right. There is one set which have a similar pattern. Quite deep and facing outwards. Someone following him over the fence, most likely. They have the kind of sole you see on an Army boot. I can't trace the make from the prints though – they aren't good enough. I am getting someone to drop the pictures over to you in the next hour or so.'

The prints confirmed what O'Neill had guessed. The chase and the jumping of the fence. The military boot though – where did that leave him? Maybe there was an army connection. Maybe it was nothing. You could buy Army gear in a load of shops in Belfast. He grabbed a set of car keys.

'Oh, O'Neill,' Kearney said. 'Forgot to tell you. Some girl called in for you. No name, foreign accent. Said she saw the boy from the river in a nightclub. Some place called Mint. Sounds like a hoax though. That place is pretty ritzy. I'm sure they're not letting wee hoods in these days.'

'Yeah. Thanks.'

O'Neill thought about the call as he drove into town. Kearney was right. He doubted Mint were letting wee hoods in. Sean Molloy drank there though. Maybe that was the connection. O'Neill had also seen someone hovering in the toilets, so there was the possible drug angle. The phone call: it might have been a vendetta. It might have been some wee girl. She gets knocked back by the bouncers and decides to stir things up, create a bit of trouble for the place.

O'Neill parked the car on a double yellow line. Police privilege. He thought more about the call. Most people used the *Crimestoppers* number. It rang through to a call centre, so you were guaranteed anonymity. This one had come through to CID's direct line. She'd asked for him by name and all. How did she get the number? And how did she know it was him she needed to speak to?

O'Neill thought about all the people he'd left his card with since the investigation started. He couldn't remember any young girls, and none with foreign accents. He could almost hear the culchie accent of Fr Mullan, somewhere in the background. 'Forty years in Belfast. A life sentence by any man's reckoning.'

O'Neill left the car illegally parked and took the photographs of the boot-print to Alcatraz in Corn Market. The place sold ex-Army gear, along with an array of compasses, camping kit and knives. O'Neill looked at the 12-inch bowie knife in the window, wondering what kind of a Boy Scout needed one of those.

Inside, the shop had the stale fug of second-hand clothes. It mostly sold to students and grunge kids. It was old German stock, and small flags – black, red and gold – adorned the shoulders of green shirts. Along the wall hung pairs of combat trousers with large leg pockets. At the back of the shop they kept the boots. O'Neill pulled one down, feeling how heavy it was. He recalled his own Magnums from his days in uniform, remembering the confidence he felt putting them on and lacing them up. The leather on the Army boot was worn but still in good condition. He thought about the places that it might have marched: Bosnia, Belgrade, Baghdad. He went through each boot on display. None of the soles matched the photograph.

'Can I help you there, mate?' A man in his mid-thirties with a large beard came from behind the counter.

'Trying to match a boot-print.'

The man looked at the photograph.

'It's none of these,' he said, pointing to the wall. 'They're too old. You see how thick the treads are on the boot you're holding? It is standard issue, German Infantry. Leather. Durable. The photograph is probably something lightweight. Goliath. Viper. Magnum. One of those makes. It is the kind of thing you find with Special Forces. You can run all day in them. Run across entire countries if you need to. A lot of police wear them as well.'

O'Neill looked sidewards at the man. He put the leather boot back on the wall.

'What do you want to know for?' the shop assistant asked.

'Just curious,' he said, cutting him off.

O'Neill threaded his way out, through the racks of clothing. Freed from the shop, the air felt fresher and cleaner.

O'Neill didn't want to start thinking about the possibility that the PSNI were involved in this. Still though, it might explain the utter lack of evidence. And Kearney had said it himself, it was one less hood on the streets. He thought back to breakfast with Sam. She hadn't taken to her new posting. Jennings had great instincts about people and she'd deliberately held back, not wanting to tell tales on the rest of her shift. Going back, the police in the North always had a reputation for bending the rules. On a good day a suspect took a beating, on a bad day it was worse. But that was the past. The PSNI were different, they had to be. Whiter than white, that was the promise.

O'Neill imagined himself as the cop who investigated other cops. Nobody came out of that a winner. There was no surer way to career suicide. Fuck it though. If there were dirty cops in Musgrave Street, if they were involved in Laganview, they had to go down.

He tried to consider the other angle. Special Forces. It was equally unappetising. Everyone knew the SAS ran covert operations in Northern Ireland during the Troubles. But that was years ago. Why would they be here now? Why would they be chasing kids into building sites? Leaving them for dead?

O'Neill didn't want to go back to the station. The thought of his desk, the file, and now a set of boot-prints that could put the PSNI or the British Army in the frame. He imagined the headlines: *PSNI Death Squad*; *British Special Forces Still in Northern Ireland*. If that wouldn't bring the Assembly down, he didn't know what would.

O'Neill got in his car and headed out to the Ravenhill Road. He turned into a side-street and parked the car; 150 yards away sat 56 Ravensdene Park. It was Tony Burke's house. O'Neill wanted to do a door knock. See what he could stir up. He wondered how much of it was not wanting to think about the other two possibilities.

In the car he hesitated. It was the size of Burke's house. When he'd given his address, O'Neill had imagined one of the small terrace houses at the lower end of the Ravenhill Road. This was leafy suburbia though. Detached and semi-detached villas. It was all bay windows, driveways and gardens. Burke might be a foreman but he'd said he was a labourer before that. So how did a labourer end up in a place like this?

It was after five. Burke would be home from work soon. O'Neill waited, watching. Radio Ulster hummed at a low volume in the car. Gerry Anderson was reminiscing about showbands and dance halls, a Belfast O'Neill never knew, but had heard about from his mother. It sounded cosy. But then, nostalgia always did. The radio announced that rush-hour traffic was building on all the usual routes.

O'Neill's mobile rang. It was Ward.

'How you doing, Sergeant?'

'Still alive. Or just about, anyway. I'm outside Burke's. Going to make a house call.'

'Sounds good. A bit of community relations work.'

O'Neill thought about telling him about the boot-prints, about the potential link back to the police or Special Forces. He wondered what Ward would say. The RUC had bent the rules to the point where some people asked themselves if there *were* any rules. The ends justified the means. But what about now?

Just then a white Transit van pulled up outside number 56, and a man got out. Same height, same build as Burke, but it wasn't him. The man put a key in the door and entered the house. It looked natural, as if he'd done it a million times before. O'Neill still had Ward on the phone.

'Sir, can you run a registration for me?'

'Go ahead.'

O'Neill gave Ward the licence-plate.

'Nissan Almera. Red. Registered to a Martin Cushnan, 28 Ladas Drive, Newry,' Ward read out.

'What would you say if I told you your red Nissan was a white Transit van?'

'I'd say false plates.'

'I'd say you're right, sir. And it's parked outside Burke's. The driver just went in. Looked like he'd lived there all his life.'

'Newry licence ... Do you want to take a bet on the brother, Michael?'

'DI Ward,' O'Neill said, feigning surprise. 'The same brother Burke told us he hadn't seen in six months? You're not suggesting someone *lied* to the PSNI, are you?'

Ward laughed. O'Neill looked at his watch and yawned.

'How do you want to play it?' Ward asked.

'I'm going to hang back. See if Tony comes home. Can you put in the request for Burke's phone record? He's just lost his innocent bystander status.'

'Anything else, Sergeant? A nice cup of tea? A wee portion of fish and chips, perhaps?'

'Sounds good. And plenty of salt and vine—'

Ward hung up on him mid-sentence.

He sat back in his chair in Musgrave Street. Ward knew the Review Boards were less than two weeks away. He also knew you couldn't force a case. It was like trying to grab the soap in the bath, his old Sergeant had once said. The tighter you squeeze, the more it slips out of your grasp. Still, none of that was going to help O'Neill.

Ward realized the younger man was being hung out on something the rest of the world had forgotten about a long time ago. Last week Laganview had made its procession back through the newspaper. It went from Tuesday's front page, to page four on Wednesday. By Thursday there was a single paragraph on page eight. It sat beside a story on the latest

Northern Irish contestant in *Big Brother*. Stuart Colman's words echoed in Ward's head: *footballers and soap stars, who's shagging who*.

O'Neill sat and waited. The radio show ticked over. Five o'clock came and went. Then six. Then seven. The traffic eased as folk arrived home. O'Neill was hungry. Across the North, people were tucking into their tea. He tried not to think about it. Egg and chips, bowls of stew, plates of lasagne. He lit another B&H and wound down the window. He looked into the packet. There were only three left.

O'Neill glanced at the clock. He had been supposed to come off-duty an hour ago.

At around eight, a Ford Mondeo pulled in behind him. A figure got out of the driver's side and O'Neill's passenger door opened. Ward slipped into the seat beside him. He tossed a fresh packet of cigarettes on to the dashboard, handing O'Neill a cup of coffee and a stale bun.

'You been baking again, Inspector?'

'Canteen leftovers. You don't want to see what you might have won.'

O'Neill took a bite and a drink of coffee. He immediately felt his spirits lift.

'Did your date cancel on you again?' he asked.

'Listen, Billy No Mates. You're not exactly in a position to talk.'

O'Neill agonized over telling Ward about the boot. He felt sure the Inspector would tell him to follow the investigation, wherever it took him. But where *would* it take him? Getting the shoe-size of every uniform in Musgrave Street? Cross-checking it with who was working Sunday night and who was off? O'Neill's stomach turned over at the thought. He imagined the comments from other cops.

'That's him there.'

'Bangs up his mates.'

'Whose side does he think he's on?'

By ten o'clock the Burke house was in darkness. No one had left. The brother's van was still outside.

'Not seen him for six months? My arse,' O'Neill said.

'Looks like that's him for the night,' Ward pronounced.

'Think so.'

'Let's get to our own beds then.'

Ward got out of the car and into his own. He drove off, turning right down the Ravenhill Road.

O'Neill was about to turn on the ignition but stopped. He sat on for another twenty minutes. Finally, he cursed Burke, him and his fucking brother, and turned the key. The engine caught first time and he drove across town to the empty flat in Stranmillis.

The next morning, O'Neill got a call from Rob Leonard at the pathology lab.

'I've been working some more on Laganview, looking at your body.'

Still it was O'Neill's body.

'I've got something you're going to want to come and see. Can you make it up to the Royal Victoria Hospital this morning?'

'I'll be there in twenty minutes.'

O'Neill was relieved. Anything to get out of the station, away from the paperwork, which only reminded him of the dead weight of Laganview round his neck. He was a day closer to the Review Boards and still nothing. He'd seen Burke's brother last night and was going to pay him a visit later that day. It might be something. Then again it might not.

The State Pathologist's Department was a thirteen-man operation, located in a nondescript building within the RVH. Every year, thousands of hospital visitors parked in its shadow without any idea what they were next to. At the entrance to the hospital, people clutched flowers and bottles of Lucozade, gazing up in bewilderment at signposts for various wards. Old men in dressing-gowns stood on the steps smoking, their oxygen canisters wheeled out, standing beside them. They held their cigarettes between two fingers, a defiant gesture to the Grim Reaper or whatever the end might look like.

O'Neill remembered Leonard from the autopsy two weeks before. For sixteen years he had headed up the SPD at the Royal. Two decades' worth of death. Every body since 1989 had passed under Leonard's nose. He had signed off them all. If you were looking for a ferryman to the next life, Leonard was your man. He had seen all the ways people end up making the journey.

O'Neill arrived as the pathologist hunched over some papers on his desk. He was a short man, five-eight, with thinning grey hair. A pair of half-moon spectacles sat on the end of his nose, and he looked at the detective over the top of them. Leonard was everything you wanted in a pathologist: steady hand, cast-iron stomach and a sense of curiosity.

'O'Neill. Good to see you. Looks like Laganview's added a few years to you since we last met.'

'Thanks.'

'I wouldn't worry. How do you think Jack Ward ended up looking like he does?'

O'Neill laughed.

'How is he, by the way?'

'The Inspector's the Inspector. What can I say?'

'I miss him, you know,' Leonard joked. 'He never phones. He never writes.'

Ward and Leonard had history. When the pathologist heard he'd been made DI, he sent a jar with a cancerous lung down to Musgrave Street. It was part-joke, part-jibe, a dig at Ward's lifelong sponsorship of Benson & Hedges.

'Is he still on the fags?'

'Off them six months.'

'You're a shit liar,' Leonard said, smiling. He turned to three brown envelopes sitting on his desk.

'OK. Let's have ourselves a mini-pathology lesson. See if you're as clever as Jack Ward thinks you are.'

Leonard opened the first envelope and poured out its contents: three photographs of male legs, each one skinny, bruised and badly contorted.

'What do you see, O'Neill?'

'Three sets of legs. All male. All pretty skinny. Not a lot of meat on them bones. Is this a bit of compare and contrast, this morning?'

'Spot on. Look here. This one's a jumper, eighteen years old. Similar age and build to your boy at Laganview. Leaped from a warehouse. Fell forty feet. Shattered both knees.'

There were large areas of discolouration, purple and pink bruising, covering more than half of the limbs. The surrounding area had started to turn as well. Shades of brown, green and yellow.

'You've seen the site at Laganview, Rob. My guy's not a jumper.'

'I know. It's the bruises we're interested in. Now take a look at this.'

Leonard swept the photos aside and brought forward the second envelope.

'I got these from one of the orthopaedic surgeons upstairs. Again, similar age and build. This is a straight-up knee-capping. They took a bat to him. Shattered both knee-caps and both ankle-joints. He lived, but will probably be on sticks the rest of his life. And you don't want to know about the early-onset arthritis.'

O'Neill studied the bruising on the second set of photographs. They were similar to the first. Large patches of discolouration. Purple and pink, spreading out from the knee area, covering over three-quarters of the surface area of skin.

Leonard then produced the photographs from Laganview.

'OK. Now this is your boy.'

O'Neill looked at the limbs stretched down the steel plate of the autopsy table. There was less than a quarter of bruising on him than on the other two. A couple of small purple patches, but nothing like the others. He saw it immediately.

'Post-mortem bruising.'

'That's right.'

The body at Laganview was already dead. The heart had stopped beating so the haemorrhaging as a result of the blows with the bat was much smaller.

'Judging by the amount of bone breakage, he took just as much punishment as contestant number two.'

'So who knee-caps a dead body?' O'Neill asked.

'You're the detective, O'Neill. I am merely the State Pathologist for Northern Ireland.' Leonard shrugged. He could sense O'Neill's frustration at this latest turn. He knew the police still hadn't arrested anyone, let alone brought charges.

'I'll tell you one thing though – Jack Ward's no mug. And if he put you up front on this thing, it means you've got what it takes.'

'So *why* does someone do that – knee-cap a corpse?'

'You were closer with your first question. It's not about "why". It's about "who".'

'You're right.'

'For what it's worth, I'd say you've got a straight-up murder. Someone wants you to think it's a punishment beating, but it is murder, pure and simple.'

As he walked back to the car, O'Neill's mobile rang in his pocket.

'You still up at the RVH?' Ward asked.

'Yeah. Why?'

'The surgeon from Orthopaedics called. You told him to get in touch if they had any more punishment beatings from Belfast. He just operated on someone last night. I ran the name. Peter Kennedy. Sixteen years old. He's from the Markets.'

This might be the breakthrough he'd been after. O'Neill felt optimistic for a second, before he remembered the fact that they were no longer after a punishment beating. Laganview was something else. Still, it couldn't hurt to talk to the kid.

TWENTY-EIGHT

Petesy was asleep when Marty arrived. He swaggered along the corridor in tracksuit and trainers, trying to follow the signs. A nurse in her forties glared at Marty as he passed her station. There had been an increase in people stealing from the hospital. It was sometimes patients, but mostly visitors. They took computer equipment and drug supplies off the ward. Staff had been told to be extra-vigilant, and the nurse left Marty in absolutely no doubt that she was watching him.

In Ward 16 Petesy lay still, dozing in and out of sleep. Both of his legs were in plaster and hung in front of him, elevated by a system of pulleys. The tibia and femur, left and right, were both broken. The right knee was shattered and had had to be replaced by a metal insert. The ligaments in both knees were torn and were repaired with cartilage taken from the patient's hip. Marty looked at his mate, remembering the crunching sound of the bat and Petesy's screaming.

Ward 16 had ten other beds in it. Old men mostly, in for hip replacements. Marty felt their eyes on him as he sat beside his friend. He knew what they were thinking.

'Joy-riding scum.'

'Wee cunt, got what he deserved.'

'There's another one.'

It was pure hatred. Marty wanted to flick the brake on the bed and wheel his mate out of there. He didn't need to lie there and have these auld bastards staring at him, their yellow faces, their teeth in jars beside the beds.

The room was warm and smelled like old people, mixed with disinfectant, bedclothes and piss. Petesy was asleep. Marty picked up the copy of *FourFourTwo* from the bedside cabinet. He flicked through, looking at pictures of footballers. He wondered what his friend must have thought, seeing the magazine. Petesy was a shite footballer. That wasn't the point though.

A quiet, croaky voice came from the top of the bed.

'Does this look like a library?'

Marty looked up and smiled. 'If it is, it's a shite one. It's only got one frigging magazine.'

Petesy gave a faint smile, before wincing and inhaling through clenched teeth. The medication was starting to wear off and had wakened him from his sleep. He reached down to his side, lifted a small white remote, and clicked it twice. It was connected to an anaesthetic drip. In thirty seconds the jagged edge started to ease off.

'Is that morphine?' Marty asked.

Petesy nodded.

'You lucky fucker.'

'Aye?' Petesy looked down at his legs. 'Do you think so?'

Marty didn't know what to say. He glanced round the ward, anything to avoid Petesy's eyes. He reached into the bag at his feet.

'I've brought you some presents. Thought they might cheer you up.' He pulled three books out of the bag and showed them to Petesy. 'Three history ones. No pictures. Especially for smart cunts, these ones. Eh? Mr Queen's fucking University.'

Petesy smiled as Marty set the books on the bedside cabinet.

'Where did you get them?'

'Waterstones in the town. I tell you what, nicking stuff there's a total piece of piss. No one on the door. Just some old boy in a grey cardigan behind the till. Almost made me want to take up reading.'

'What are they about?'

'Ah, I don't know. Revolutions or something. I figured I'd go for big ones. Size matters, you know. Least that's what the birds keep telling me.'

Petesy smiled again. Marty tried to ignore the two large casts that floated in front of his face.

'So what about the nurses then? That one at the desk's a bit of a boot. Are there any fit ones? Have you had a bed bath yet? I heard they sometimes can give you a wee ...'

Marty whistled in and out. Petesy laughed.

'What do you think *you* are doing here, Martin Toner?'

Petesy's granny stood at the end of the bed, her mouth pursed, her face scowling. She had been looking for a row for days now. Marty somehow got the feeling he was her big chance.

'I hope you're happy with yourself. This is all your fault. It should be you lying there, you frigging waster. Hung up like some bit of dirty washing.'

Marty didn't know what to say. There was nothing he could say. She was only saying what he had been thinking, ever since Petesy got done.

239

'Our Peter would never have gotten into any of this if it wasn't for you. Go on, take yourself off. If I ever see you anywhere near our Peter again ...'

Marty was going to tell the old woman to go fuck herself. What the fuck did she know about anything? He caught his tongue though. Petesy loved his granny and he could see how upset she was. She needed someone to blame. But deep down he knew she was right. Petesy *would* never have had the balls if it hadn't been for him. Yeah. It should have been him. He was the one that deserved it, not Petesy.

Marty looked at his mate, lying in the white hospital bed. He stood up and walked past the old woman. It *was* his fault. The whole thing. He turned and marched out of the ward. Round the corner he sniffed and rubbed his sleeve under his nose, fighting back the tears.

In the corridor Marty pushed between two men in suits. He didn't look up, focusing all his energy on not crying. The nurse glared at him again as he passed her station.

'Fuck you,' Marty mumbled, walking on, not looking up.

The nurse felt smug, glad that she had been right about him. Marty took the stairs down to the main doors and walked out of the hospital. He headed down the Grosvenor Road, walking under the stern gaze of a wrought-iron statue of Queen Victoria. The plump woman stared pitilessly out over his head, her eyes fixed on the horizon in the small corner of her once-mighty empire.

O'Neill and Ward approached Peter Kennedy's bed. They looked down at the two legs, covered in white plaster. The kid had had the shit beaten out of him. There was no other

240

way to describe it. O'Neill knew they were wee bastards, a bunch of hoods. He didn't think they deserved this though. You wouldn't do it to an animal.

An old woman had settled herself near the head of the bed. She looked up at the two men, clocking them instantly for who and what they were.

'What do yous want?' she demanded.

O'Neill introduced himself and Ward. Petesy's granny remained stone-faced, barely masking her contempt.

'We need to talk to Peter,' he told her.

'*You* need? Where were you three nights ago, when *he* needed you?'

O'Neill had to change tack, bypass the old woman, talk to the boy. The kid was on morphine and would be pretty high. He could distract him, make him forget they were peelers, if only for a minute or two.

He caught sight of *FourFourTwo*. It had a picture of the Liverpool midfielder Steven Gerrard on the front cover.

'Please don't tell me you are a Liverpool fan.'

The boy looked up. 'Man U, actually.'

'Even worse. Beckham, Giggs, that crowd? Posers, the lot of them. Spend half their lives combing their hair. And the Nevilles? Don't get me started. Talk about Dumb and Dumber.'

'Aye. So who is your team?' the boy shot back.

'Everton. A real football team. No primadonnas or wannabe fashion models.'

'Everton. Are they First Division? What's the last thing they won?'

'FA Cup, 1995.'

Petesy laughed.

'FA Cup? Try the treble. League title, FA Cup and the Champions League. *That's* a real football team.'

The grandmother was shrewd and saw what was happening, where the cop was trying to lead him.

'I don't care what you know about football,' she snapped at O'Neill. 'He's got nothing to say to you.'

O'Neill turned to the boy. 'Is that right, Peter?'

The boy looked round the room. The two men across the ward were pretending not to be interested. Petesy had felt their stares for two days though. He knew they hated him. If he spoke to the peelers, people would find out. Not only would he be drug-dealing scum, he'd be a tout as well. He saw the expression on his grandmother's face. She was right. Where were the peelers two nights ago? And they wouldn't be there if Molloy and Tierney came for him again. He remembered the pain, lying there waiting for the ambulance, his legs on fire, wishing someone would just cut them off. That was what he needed to remember. The pain, only the pain.

He pinned his gaze to the two white casts, hanging up in front of him.

'I've nothing to say to yous.'

O'Neill stared at the bed. The kid was right. He didn't have anything to say. Even if he knew who did it, which he probably didn't, he couldn't say. There wasn't a single peeler lived in the Markets or any of the areas where these punishment beatings happened. The cops didn't have to leave their house looking over their shoulder, worrying about more of the same. The only thing more dangerous than being a drug dealer was being a tout. O'Neill left his business card on the end of the bed. If Peter changed his mind ...

As they walked down the corridor O'Neill remember the kid in the white Kappa top, the one who'd brushed past him. He stopped at the nurse's station.

'How's the hardest-working nurse in the hospital?'

The nurse frowned at him. She'd heard it all before and was having none of it. O'Neill read the signs and went for the easy route, producing his warrant card. The nurse relaxed a little, feeling the unspoken bond between the two professions. O'Neill asked about the tracksuit, whether he had been visiting the boy who'd had his knees done. The woman glanced from side to side. They weren't allowed to talk about patients. Strict hospital rules. She gave an almost imperceptible nod of agreement before announcing for her colleague four feet away, 'I'm sorry. We're not allowed to discuss anything to do with patients.'

'I understand completely,' O'Neill said politely. 'Thanks.'

The two men turned and headed for the lift. It took them to the ground floor of the RVH and back on to the street again.

TWENTY-NINE

Lynch walked along Cromac Street on his way into town. It was drizzling and he moved quickly along the pavement, his head down and collar up.

He had slept for twelve hours after being out on the job with Molloy, dozing off as he replayed the night in his head. The sounds and smells became a form of mood music: the car, the orange street lamps, the sound of Molloy's breath, the weight of the Glock. As Lynch relived each sensation, his eyes began to grow heavy and sleep came and took him. A pressure valve had been released. He didn't take any tablets. He didn't need to. It was the job that had done it. Lynch knew it. Walking along Cromac Street in the rain, he knew it. Just being there, being involved. It had been enough.

A silver Mercedes slowed and pulled in alongside Lynch. Its tinted rear window slid down and Gerry McCann's voice came out of the back seat.

'Joe. Come on in out of the rain. I need a word with you.'

Lynch looked up and down the street before ducking into the car. The Mercedes pulled out quietly into the morning traffic. The car was stopped at traffic-lights halfway down Victoria Street. The rumble of a building site came through the tinted glass windows. McCann pointed to his left.

'Look at the state of that, would you? Another frigging shopping centre. I swear, these guys are better at flattening this city than we ever were.'

Lynch looked at a pair of steel cranes rising high over the city skyline.

'Molloy told me you were good the other night. Said he reckons you might have what it takes.' McCann laughed at the idea. Molloy, still in his twenties, providing a reference for Joe Lynch. 'These kids, Joe. No sense of history. They think the world didn't exist before they strode on to the scene and took centre stage.'

McCann knew it would work in Molloy's favour, not knowing too much about who he was partnering. He was a good worker, reliable, and remorseless when he needed to be. Sometimes a bit of ignorance could be bliss.

McCann tossed a brown envelope on Lynch's lap. He picked it up, not needing to open it.

'Here. That's five hundred quid. You've earned it. Take that wee girl out for a drink. Get yourself laid. I'm sure it's been a while.'

Lynch held the envelope in his hand, feeling its weight. He didn't want it. He didn't want cars slowing at kerbs beside him. He didn't want heads turning when he walked into a bar. He didn't want people watching their words when they spoke to him. And he didn't want the likes of Molloy thinking they were on the same side. He knew though that giving it back would provoke more hassle than it was worth.

Outside the car, people hurried along Victoria Street under umbrellas, trying not to get wet.

'I have a proposition for you, Joe. Another job. This one's a little more, how would you say, technical. Needs more than a bit of taxi driving. Needs a man with some subtlety, some patience, some experience.'

Lynch stayed silent, trying to plot his way out of the car and whatever it was McCann was thinking up for him.

'Ten grand. That's what it's paying.'

It was a hit. Lynch knew straight away. He waited though, wanting to hear McCann say it. The other man paused, allowing the money to hang in the air for a while, allowing Lynch to imagine what he'd do with it, the doors it would open, the possibilities. After ten seconds McCann spoke.

'Could you kill a peeler?'

McCann asked the question like you might ask for a light. He turned to Lynch, reassured by the lack of reaction that he'd picked the right man. Lynch wasn't Molloy, he wasn't like anyone in the crew. They were all keen, but they were young. They wanted to prove to the world how hard they were, how ruthless. Lynch knew the lie of the land though. He could do something and shut up about it. He didn't need to brag or try and make a name for himself. Discretion. Professionalism. That was it. He was a professional.

'What has he done?' Lynch asked.

'You don't need to worry about that.'

McCann had barely said the words when he realized it wouldn't work with Lynch. He wasn't some twenty-one year old with a high opinion of himself. He couldn't just be given an order and expected to blindly follow it.

'He's one of Jack Ward's. He's messing with my business, lifting people left, right and centre. We've become an itch he can't scratch. Nights off he's camped outside The George. He's sniffing round Mint. Asking people questions – the kind of people that don't want to be asked questions. He's not going to go away on his own. So we're going to help him go away.'

Lynch could tell from McCann's voice that this was a done deal, no longer a question of 'if' but rather 'how'. The peeler was already dead, he just didn't know it. The clock had started.

McCann resumed his sales pitch. 'This is your out, Lynch. One last job. A one-time deal. Twenty grand – think what you could do with that. A man could start over, with that amount of money. Head off to the sun. Maybe even take a girl and her wee one away with him. If he was inclined that way.'

Lynch looked at the rain bouncing off the grey Belfast pavements.

'Picture it. Walking along some Spanish promenade. A wee breeze off the sea, the sunshine. No one knows who you are, no one cares.'

Lynch pictured Marie-Therese in a summer dress and a big straw hat, pushing the buggy in front of her. He imagined them stopping at an ice-cream joint, the kind with wicker chairs out front. A cold beer for him, an ice cream for her. The sun would have just started to dip.

'Who is he?'

'It's a soft target. We have an address and all. He lives alone, in a flat off the Stranmillis Road.'

McCann passed Lynch a photograph. It was one of the peelers who had followed him. The man looked to be in his late thirties. He was walking through Castlecourt shopping centre and the shot had been taken as he turned his head to the right.

'What's the name?' Lynch asked.

'O'Neill.'

'Killing a peeler brings a lot of heat. It's more trouble than it's worth.'

'You let *me* worry about that.'

'What about Stormont? The Peace Process? The Unionists will say this is business as usual, that nothing's changed. They'll want to bring the whole thing down. Get the Brits back on the streets.'

McCann smiled ruefully.

'You've been away too long, Joe. Or maybe you read too many books in prison. United Ireland? Great Britain? It doesn't matter any more. No matter who you vote for, the government still gets in. These days, the only countries that matter are Colombia and Afghanistan. It's about product, not politics. Politics is dead. The only kind of green that people round here care about is in that envelope I just tossed you.'

McCann ordered the driver to stop the car.

'The peeler needs to be done, Joe.'

Lynch remained silent. McCann patted him on the arm, laughing.

'That's what I thought you'd say. It needs to happen this week.'

Lynch got out of the car. In the centre of Belfast the rain had worsened. He walked along Donegall Avenue looking into shop windows advertising the remnants of January sales. He felt the envelope in his pocket and thought about buying something for Marie-Therese, or maybe the wee one.

He hesitated outside a shop, thinking about the money. Was he a criminal now? Is that what had happened? He felt like a tout. Like someone who had turned his back on his friends. Had he sold them out?

Lynch thought about night-time in the Maze, lying in his cell, six by eight foot. He had nothing in there. But it didn't matter. He had a reason. He'd taken a stand. Burton was right. He'd been backed into a corner. You couldn't just sit there and take it. Pretend it was OK, waiting for someone else to come along. It was the only way. Someone had to do the hard yards, get their hands dirty, put themselves on the line.

This was what Lynch had told himself. Night after night, listening to the screws walk up and down the corridors, trailing their sticks along the doors to keep the prisoners awake, fucking with them just for the fun of it. This was what he told himself to placate the ghosts, the faces that visited him as he lay trying to sleep. The off-duty RUC man, the part-time soldier, the fourteen-year-old boy. The last one was an accident. The bomb went off before the coded warning was called in. 'Collateral damage' was what they called it. It was a war. Things happened.

What about now though? The five hundred quid. The twenty grand. What was that money for?

He thought about the hunger strikes. Bobby Sands and nine others. Starving themselves to death. All to tell Maggie Thatcher they weren't criminals. Was she right though? Was this what they were? Was this what they'd become?

A woman pushing a child in a buggy went past Lynch, hurrying into a shop out of the rain. Ten grand. This was his chance. He could leave Northern Ireland for good. Start over.

It had been a mistake coming back. What had he expected to find when he returned from London? The buildings were different, sure, but the place was the same. The same faces, the same bullying, the same bragging. The same men, telling the same stories in the same pubs. Was it McCann? Was it people like him? You couldn't get rid of him. If you did, someone else would step in and fill the void. McCann was right. It wasn't about your country, your comrades, your cause. It was about money, pure and simple. Lynch looked at people rushing into shops, hurrying to buy things, to get the latest gadget, the latest designer jackets. Money didn't have a conscience. It didn't care about flags. It didn't care where it came from.

Lynch's eyes narrowed. He pulled up his collar and turned down Donegal Avenue. He could do one more. One more, then out for good. It was the only way.

Ward was furious.

He had been sitting in his office after a briefing meeting when Wilson had knocked on the door. There had been an unofficial complaint made against O'Neill. Ward's ears had pricked up immediately. An 'unofficial' complaint? You either had a complaint or you didn't. And if you did, then be man enough to at least stand behind it.

O'Neill had been spotted in the middle of the night, climbing over the fence at Laganview. Ward went on the attack.

'He's investigating a murder, sir.'

'I know what he is doing, Inspector.'

'So what's the problem?'

'Climbing back into a crime scene at four o'clock in the morning? It's not exactly how we want people to see the police operating, is it?'

'A murder investigation? I think people want to see the police arresting people and putting them away. I don't think they care how many fences have to be climbed to get it done.'

'You know what I'm talking about, Ward. Anyway, this isn't an argument – I'm telling you. Next time, O'Neill's getting an official warning. Conduct unbecoming.'

Ward knew Wilson would have liked to have gone the whole hog this time. He couldn't though. If the complaint wasn't official there'd be no record and you couldn't go after someone with a piece of hearsay.

How did it end up on Wilson's desk though? These things normally went through official channels which always bypassed local command structures. There was only one person who'd have the balls to call in with something like that, and call it in directly to Wilson – Spender.

Ward grabbed a set of car keys from his desk and stormed out of the office. In the corridor he blew past DC Kearney who was on his way to see him. 'Inspector War—'

Ten minutes later, Ward was outside a glass office block on Linenhall Street. He parked on double yellow lines. Policeman's privilege. Inside, he took the elevator to the twelfth floor where he was greeted by walls of glass. At reception a girl sat beneath the large stylized logo of Spender Property. She looked up.

'Can I help —'

Ward walked past her as if she wasn't even there. He heard her lift the phone behind him. 'Security ...'

A few twists and turns, and Ward found Spender's office. He marched past the PA and opened the heavy wooden door.

'Excuse me! What do you think you are doing?' a shrill voice demanded from behind him.

The office was empty. Ward turned and rounded on the girl at the desk.

'Where is he?'

The girl was in her thirties, immaculately made up. The kind of girl who is attractive and definitely knows it. Ward had seen the type a million times. There wasn't a PA in the world who wasn't on a power trip. They controlled access to the MD and always thought they were the most important person in the whole company.

The girl was affronted that someone could dare to walk into the office and make demands of her like that. She made to dig her heels in. She'd heard Carol on reception call down for Security and they'd be there any minute.

Ward leaned over the desk, six inches from her face, seething.

'Listen to me, love. And listen carefully. If you don't want to be arrested right now for obstructing a police investigation, you'll tell me where he is.'

The girl wobbled under the threat. Ward saw it in her eyes and closed in, speaking quickly.

'I'm going to count to three. One. Two. Thr—'

'Laganview. He's at Laganview. They have a meeting down there with ...'

Ward turned on his heel and was off, halfway down the corridor.

At reception Carol stood next to a security guard, pointing at Ward as he marched towards them. The guard made to come forward. The detective pulled out his warrant card as he walked past.

'Don't even think about it, son.'

Ward slipped between the doors of the lift as they closed behind the security guard.

Ten minutes later, the Mondeo skidded on the makeshift gravel car park at Laganview. There was a lot of expensive tin in the car park – two Jaguars, a Land Rover and a couple of Mercedes.

He looked down into the site and saw a group of men in suits and yellow hard hats. Spender stood in the middle, holding court, pointing out various aspects of the construction to the visitors. On the perimeter another man stood clutching a mobile phone, pointing at it in an attempt to get his boss' attention. Ward knew it would be the office, letting them know he was on his way.

He walked in front of the group, positioning himself in their line of sight. He held up his warrant card and spoke in a loud voice, almost shouting.

'Mr Spender. DI Ward, Musgrave Street CID. I need to ask you a few more questions about the murder on your building site.'

Spender's bonhomie suddenly evaporated. The expressions on the surrounding faces changed from being impressed to prurient interest. Spender turned to the man holding his mobile phone, his face hiding his anger. Ward wondered if the guy would still have his job by the end of the day.

'Paul, can you take our guests round and show them the walkway and the view of the river? I'll join up with you all in a minute.'

The crowd were chaperoned away, leaving Ward and Spender alone. The developer waited until his guests were out of earshot, before hissing, 'What do you think you're playing at, Ward? I'm going to have you for this. This is police harassment.'

'Harassment? Don't start putting ideas in my head. Or maybe you'd just like to put in another private phone call to Wilson. Tell him his boys aren't playing cricket. Is our wee investigation messing with the value of your portfolio? Is that what it is? Is that *all* it is? Because at the moment I'm beginning to wonder.'

Spender looked towards the group of men. Ward continued:

'If you want to make an official complaint, then fire away. Just know that while you're stirring the pot, I'll be busy working my way through every planning application, every tax return, every single piece of paper with your name on. You see, I'm old. No hobbies. I've a lot of free time on my hands. The Hightown Road. The Gasworks project. The Cathedral Quarter. I imagine there'll be a few interesting names in there. A few city councillors, perhaps? I am sure this would be something the *Belfast Telegraph* would be pretty keen to hear about. So by all means, complain away. I'll look forward to it.' Ward walked away, leaving Spender alone.

The developer stood where he was, watching the detective as he left the building site. He looked over at the group of businessmen on the other side of the apartments' steel skeleton. A few of the group were watching the police officer as he picked his way back to the car park.

Spender cleared his throat and straightened his tie. As he returned to the group he thought of the questions they'd now have and how he would set about repairing the damage.

THIRTY

Marty carried Petesy for days. He was carrying him when he phoned his cousin in the Ardoyne. He was carrying him when he went into the Holy Lands for Thursday's paper round. He was carrying him when he saw Cara and her mate, and they pretended not to see him. He was carrying him when Micky's ma answered the door and told him to sling his hook. He was still carrying him at three in the afternoon, walking across the Albert Bridge, when a black Mondeo pulled up alongside him.

The window rolled down and a peeler shouted his name, telling him to get in the car. Any other day, Marty would have bolted. Across the road, between the cars and off. He'd have been away before the peeler could have lifted his radio. Today though, he was tired – tired of the weight, tired of the guilt, tired of carrying his friend. Marty slumped into the passenger seat of the car. After all, it was only the peelers. What was the worst they could do to you?

After the hospital O'Neill had run Peter Kennedy through the Police National Computer. He found a string of minor offences: possession, affray, shoplifting. He looked at each offence, seeing that Kennedy had twice been arrested along with someone else: Martin Toner. He'd pulled Toner's file. The mug shot showed a fifteen year old, staring defiantly at the camera. O'Neill recognized him. It was the same kid he'd passed in the corridor of the Royal Victoria Hospital. Toner's record was longer than Kennedy's. It featured similar offences: theft, assault, possession. They were both registered to the same school. O'Neill phoned the Principal who hadn't seen either of them for over a year. 'Thick as thieves, those two.' His voice didn't suggest he wanted to see either of them any time soon.

Toner was registered at an address near the bottom of the Castlereagh Road. O'Neill ran it through the computer. The occupier was a Siobhan Toner. Thirty-six years old. She also had a record: theft, drunk and disorderly, affray. Two years ago she'd received a suspended sentence on condition of attending an alcohol rehabilitation programme.

O'Neill staked out the address. Just after four he watched Toner come out of the house. The teenager wore a white hooded tracksuit and a baseball cap pulled so low it almost covered his eyes. When he walked, his shoulders rocked slowly from side to side with the classic hood's swagger.

The detective thought about lifting him there and then but held back. He couldn't make his move yet. People would see. If there was any hope of getting something out of the boy, no one must see. The kid would never risk being labelled 'Toner the Tout'. If he did, it wouldn't be long before he was joining his mate in the RVH.

He made his move on the Albert bridge. With Toner in the car O'Neill did a U-turn and headed up the Newtownards Road, out of Belfast.

'Not going to the station?' Marty asked, gazing out the window, his voice distant.

257

'Not today,' O'Neill replied.

'You're not some kind of fruit, are you?'

O'Neill smiled at the backchat.

'You should be so lucky.'

They continued up the Newtownards Road in silence. Rows of terrace houses gave way to larger, suburban homes. At the edge of the city the carriageway skirted past the Loyalist Ballybeen estate. O'Neill saw the boy glance at the red, white and blue kerbstones. They drove past the estate, the carriageway rising as they left Belfast. For a moment the car felt like a plane taking off. O'Neill was about to mention it but stopped, wondering if Toner had ever been on a plane. He doubted it.

'So where the fuck are you taking me then?'

O'Neill didn't answer.

At the top of the hill Marty made out a small town on the other side. A sign read *Welcome to Newtownards. Drive Carefully.* The car slowed at a large roundabout with a shopping centre squatting on the other side. The car park was busy with folk doing laps, searching for a parking space. O'Neill drove in and turned towards the Burger King. He went to the drive-thru and ordered two Whopper meals with Coke.

He took the last exit from the roundabout and began driving along a country road, away from the town. After a few turns the car started to climb a hill. At the top was a gothic tower over 100 feet tall. Scrabo Tower was built by the Victorians and looked like a cross between a chesspiece and something from *Lord of the Rings*. O'Neill pulled into a deserted car park from where it was a few hundred metres up a path to the base of the tower. He opened the car door.

'I'm eating. You can sit here on your tod if you want.'

O'Neill got out of the car and walked up the path. After a few seconds Toner followed, walking up the hill ten yards behind the cop.

At the base of the tower was a flat piece of grass with three benches. Each had a small brass plaque, dedicated to someone. You could see for miles. On one side was an expanse of water, Strangford Lough. Two arms of land reached down either side of the large inlet. On the horizon, a low winter sun was starting to dip below the grey band of cloud. Newtownards stretched out to the left. You couldn't make out Belfast, which was out of sight, hidden behind the Castlereagh hills.

On the nearby golf course, an old boy in an Argyle sweater was teeing off. He made a swipe, topping the ball which scuttled away into some gorse. The man was 200 yards away and out of earshot. It didn't stop Marty though.

'You're shee-ite. And so's your jumper.'

'Sit down,' O'Neill said to him.

He opened up the brown paper bag and handed the teenager a small square box with a burger in it. Marty took it suspiciously.

'What?' O'Neill asked. 'You're going to tell me you're a vegetarian?'

The boy smiled slightly, taking a bite of the burger. He took several chews before speaking with his mouth full.

'You can buy all the burgers you want. I'm not telling you fuck all.'

'Dead on,' said O'Neill. 'It's your call. I mean, it wasn't my best mate that just got seven shades of shite beaten out of him.'

The two sat eating in silence. Marty took the pickle out of his burger and flicked it away.

'Frigging pickles.'

They watched the golfer poke around in the gorse looking for his ball. He scraped it out with a club before standing up to take his shot. This one was much better. The small white dot bobbled down the fairway, coming to rest just beside the green.

'I spoke to Mr Johnson at St Matthew's. He said he hadn't seen you for over a year.'

'School? Don't make me laugh.'

'He remembered you though. Said you were a hell of a footballer. Hat-trick in the Belfast Schools Cup. He said Glentoran had been looking at you. There was even a chance you could have gone across the water.'

Marty smiled. He remembered the hat-trick as if it was yesterday, the boys jumping on him down the back of the bus on their way home.

'I know what you've been up to, you and Petesy. You've been working. Out there grafting.'

Marty sat up straight. He could get done here if he wasn't careful.

'Out on your own. Fuck Molloy and Tierney and those boys, right? Yeah. You've got yourselves some gear and gone it alone.'

O'Neill was fishing, voicing his theory as to why Peter Kennedy might have been done. He seemed to be on the money so far.

'We have almost nothing on you. That's how I know. You and Peter have been at this a while, but you've managed to keep a low profile. Stay under the radar.'

O'Neill paused, taking another bite of his burger. He looked at the open space in front of him. The golfer had arrived at his ball on the green, 500 yards away.

'Bet you he gets it in two,' O'Neill said.

They watched as the small figure knocked his ball on the green. He walked over and tapped the ball towards the hole. It didn't disappear.

'Hey. What do I know about golf?' O'Neill mused. Then: 'Thing is, Marty, you're doing what you've got to do. That's all. The problem's not you. It's not Peter. The problem is the guy in the Hugo Boss suit, standing in the toilet of a nightclub, hoovering a gram up his ... Or the wee student at Queen's, skinning up, dropping a few Es, then back to his lectures on Monday.'

O'Neill paused.

'None of these guys are lying in the RVH like your mate. None of them are getting a baseball bat taken to them. None of them will be on walking sticks the rest of their life. I mean, sure, we could arrest you. Lock you up. But so what, right? Out here, we're the least of your worries.'

O'Neill stopped talking. They sat there in silence, looking at the expanse of land stretching out below them. He was deliberately quiet, trying to get the kid to speak, to say something. After a minute Marty spoke.

'It's fucked up,' he said. O'Neill thought he could feel an opening, but just as quickly, the silent stand-off resumed.

They sat for a few minutes. O'Neill had another go.

'Have you ever thought it's not fair? Like, why does it have to be yous always taking the hiding? Where were you when Peter was getting a beating? Hospital told me it was a bat with

261

some nails through it. They hit him twelve times. Where were you, Marty? I thought you were his best mate? Aren't best mates supposed to stick up for each other?'

O'Neill could sense the teenager tensing up beside him. He kept pressing.

'We spoke to his granny at the hospital. Had she told you to take yourself off? Was that why you stormed out, holding back the tears? Did she blame you, Marty? Petesy didn't seem like the kind of guy to go up against Molloy and Tierney. Was it *your* idea?'

Toner stared out at the horizon. It was cold. He felt as if he was in a different country. The coastline, the water, the green fields stretching off in the distance. Belfast seemed miles away, the streets around the lower Ormeau, almost another world.

Marty was half-listening to O'Neill; the other part of him was back by the side of the river, his face shoved into the gravel as the bat came down on Petesy.

'Do you blame yourself, Marty – is that what it is? Have you been walking round, thinking it should have been you instead of your mate? Do you want some revenge – is that what you're looking for? Because if it is, this is your chance. You're not going to go up against these boys on your own. I'm the only way you can get to them. You need to use me. You need to help me. You need to tell me who it was that did Peter.'

They sat on for ten minutes. O'Neill went back to the well several times, evoking images of Peter Kennedy, the beating, the effects it would have on him. The teenager went back into his shell, shutting himself away from the cop, away from what he was saying. O'Neill eventually gave up and got to his feet.

'Come on. Let's go.'

They drove back into Belfast, the car-heater warming them after the cold outside.

'You're not a tout, Marty. You're sticking up for your mate. Get the fuckers that did it to him. This is the only way. What else are you going to do? I know why you don't want to talk. We don't live where you live. We're not going to be there when someone kicks your door in at three in the morning. Sure. You could call 999. You'd be as well asking for an ambulance though, by the time we got to you. It's fucked up. You're right. The whole thing's fucked up.'

The traffic outside was starting to thicken. From the dual carriageway on the top of the hill the car looked down on Belfast. Church spires were sprinkled across the horizon, jutting up from rows of terrace housing. The two giant yellow cranes of Harland & Wolff straddled the docks.

'Thing is, Marty,' O'Neill continued, 'eventually, someone's got to take a stand. They shouldn't get away with doing that to you. You guys take the risks – and for what? So they can come and beat the shit out of you when they don't like what's going on?'

Marty spoke for the first time since he had shouted at the golfer.

'I'm not telling you who did Petesy. There's only two people that know, me and him. They would know who'd told. And if they couldn't get to me, they'd come back for him. And he's had enough.'

O'Neill thought about it. The kid was right. He couldn't talk. There was no way.

'Fair enough. But you need to give me something. It's the same people, right – the ones who did the kid we found by the Lagan the other week?'

'That one. Yous are still after that?'

'That's right.'

Marty gave a short laugh. 'That one's a mystery.'

'What do you mean?'

'Nobody knows.'

'What do you mean, nobody knows?'

'I mean nobody knows.'

'OK. Forget who did him. Who's the kid?'

'I just told you. Nobody knows.'

The teenager could have been lying but O'Neill didn't think so. He'd thrown the comment away as if it was the least interesting thing he'd ever said.

As they neared the centre of Belfast Toner slumped down in the car seat, pulling his hat low over his face. O'Neill turned off the main road, driving under the bridge that used to lead to Central Station. It was deserted and dark. He slowed the car. The wheels hadn't fully stopped before the door was open and Toner was gone. O'Neill looked in his rearview mirror, trying to pick out a shape in the darkness, but it was too late. The kid had already disappeared.

THIRTY-ONE

Lynch had been shadowing for two days now, watching, waiting. He knew O'Neill inside and out, almost better than he knew himself. As soon as he saw the photograph, Lynch had clocked him for one of the cops who had followed him out of The George. The other one must have been Ward.

O'Neill had been on an early shift, eight to six, though he wasn't leaving Musgrave Street before nine. Lynch saw straight away why McCann wanted him dead. He was a peeler with no life. He worked, he slept. That was it. Not the kind of person you wanted sniffing round, asking questions. Fat and lazy, you could work with. Someone who could turn a blind eye, who could take a hint, who could be told. Lynch could see that wasn't O'Neill.

The last two nights, after a ten-hour shift, he had driven round to May Street and parked up. For four hours he had sat and watched the comings and goings at The George. Lynch wondered how much he knew about McCann's operation. He was there though, so he must know something.

The following morning in Stranmillis, O'Neill left for work just after seven. Thirty minutes later, Lynch dandered round the back, picked the lock and broke into the flat. At the front door lay a pile of unopened mail. On the top lay a brown A4 envelope with an entire book of stamps plastered to its front.

Someone wanted to make sure that arrived, Lynch thought, stepping over the post.

Inside the place looked as if O'Neill had just moved in and was waiting on his stuff arriving. On the mantelpiece an opened electricity bill said he'd been there five months. The kitchen cupboards were bare apart from coffee, baked beans, a packet of digestives. On the counter sat a loaf of bread, a week out of date.

'It's an existence,' Lynch whispered. 'But I wouldn't call it a life.'

O'Neill's flat reminded him of his own place. It was functional, but not much more. On the bedside cabinet he saw a photograph of a woman giving a little girl a piggyback. They were running along a beach under a brooding grey sky with big Atlantic waves crashing in the background. It looked like Portstewart strand or somewhere in Donegal. Long brown hair fell across the woman's face. She was attractive and the photo caught a moment – part-smile, part-laugh. The little girl looked like her mother.

Lynch started putting the pieces together. 'So this is why you don't go home at night,' he whispered to himself.

His mind automatically kicked into gear. He knew if the woman and the girl were in the North, he'd have no problem finding them. McCann would have contacts in the Civil Service. Addresses were easy – Electoral Register, council tax, water rates. In the past they'd recruited sympathizers, people who wouldn't pull the trigger, but who wanted to help, do their bit for the Cause. These days it would be a simple question of money. Everyone had their price. You passed on a brown envelope and a few days later you had an address.

Lynch wondered, was it necessary for the peeler to die? If the mother and daughter were brought into the equation, would O'Neill back down? He'd seen it before. All it took was a public place and a quiet word.

'I want to talk to you about Ashfield Drive.'

He'd done it himself and watched as the implications slowly dawned on people's faces. You didn't need to raise your voice. They knew who you were, what you were capable of, and now you had an address. Sometimes folk didn't believe you, so you gave them more. The sister, the mother and father, the cousin. Skegoneill Road, Eia Street, Henderson Avenue. Eeny, meeny, miny, mo ...

Lynch stood in the bedroom, surprised at how easily the old patterns, the familiar logic of intimidation and threat, re-formed in his head.

Would O'Neill back down? For some reason Lynch didn't think so. Anyway, it didn't matter. He knew McCann would never buy it. He wanted the peeler gone, off the street, eliminated. It wasn't a discussion, it was an order. There was only one way this was going to go down.

That night in the Markets, Lynch crashed on to his bed and fell sound asleep. The job had given him a focus, a purpose. He had been filling his head with the minutiae of O'Neill's routine and it had worked like a drug. When the alarm went off at seven he felt as if he'd slept for a week.

Lynch had decided on the spot. It would be outside the flat in Stranmillis, just as O'Neill arrived back from work. McCann could have someone at The George, watching the Mondeo. They would call when it pulled up and again as it left. Lynch would lie in wait, ambush him as he put the key in the door. It would be late, which meant little chance of witnesses and plenty of time to disappear.

Before leaving the house, Lynch took the shoe-box out from under his bed. He lifted out the tea-towel and unwrapped the Browning. He kneeled on the floor and took the pistol apart and cleaned it. He worked slowly and methodically, wiping and oiling each piece, before reassembling the weapon. This had been a ritual from years ago, before heading out on a job. The last thing you wanted was a gun jamming or a misfire at the critical moment. He knew two trigger men who had been shot themselves because of it.

At 11 p.m. Lynch was in position. There was an empty house on the opposite side of the street, three doors down from O'Neill's flat. A hedge, 6 foot high, hid a small front garden. He hunkered down and waited. O'Neill was outside The George for the third day in a row. He had gotten sloppy, either that or he was desperate. It didn't really matter, it was going to be the end of him. After an hour and a half, Lynch's phone vibrated in his pocket. O'Neill was on his way.

Three miles away, the Mondeo pulled out of May Street and away from the bar. O'Neill was tired and had gotten nowhere in the last three days. Even taking the kid out to Scrabo, choked up as he was, hadn't given him anything.

He drove up the Ormeau Road, away from the city, away from the station, away from The George. He thought about not going home, just driving through the night, getting out of there. It was a romantic idea, like something from the movies. He heard Ward's voice in his head: *'Too much TV.'*

Eventually O'Neill found a parking space and stepped out of the car, glancing up and down the street. It was dead quiet. There was no one around, not even the odd student, heading back from the pub.

O'Neill was lost in his thoughts, trying to imagine life after CID. Would he carry a reputation, forever be one of the ones that didn't make it? As he approached the door he heard a twig snap behind him. He ducked instinctively and turned his head. A figure emerged from behind a hedge across the street.

The guy swayed, almost tripping down the step. He had long hair and ripped jeans and a Dead Kennedys T-shirt. He stopped and fumbled through his pockets, pulling out a cigarette and lighting it. Another drunk student. It was the price you paid for living in South Belfast.

O'Neill turned and climbed the three steps to the door, hesitating before knocking. The door opened six inches and a shaft of light spilled out on to the porch. Sam Jennings looked down at him.

'Evening, Detective,' she said.

O'Neill looked up at Jennings.

'I'll not ask how you got my address then.'

O'Neill wondered for a second why he was there, but who was he kidding? He knew why. He knew it looked sleazy. He'd promised himself he wouldn't just turn up, unannounced with some puppy-dog face. At least you're not drunk, he thought.

Jennings pulled the door back. O'Neill was about to speak, to try and explain himself, to tell her what ...

'I guess you better come in then,' she said.

For three hours Lynch sat on, opposite the flat in Stranmillis. After the first hour he knew O'Neill wasn't coming but he stayed, tucked behind the hedge, turning things over. He thought about O'Neill. Had someone tipped him off? Had McCann tried to set *him* up? Lynch pictured him, sitting in The George. The bar would be empty, having closed two hours ago. McCann would be there though, one way or the other, waiting near the pay-phone. He thought about Marie-Therese, imagining what she'd say if she could see him, hiding behind a hedge, about to do someone for a few grand. Would she care where the money had come from?

Lynch looked at his watch. It was after three. O'Neill wasn't coming. He stood up and checked the street. The coast was clear. He stretched his legs, pulled his hat low and headed home.

At eight the next morning Lynch left the house. A cold mist hung over the Lagan and had spread out into the Markets. He could see his breath in front of him. He walked with his head down and hands deep in pockets.

He glanced at Marie-Therese's house. The light was on in the front room. He thought of calling in and asking her right out about coming away. He could lie. Say he won it. It was a family holiday and would go to waste otherwise. A wee bit of sunshine? Take the chill off your bones? He caught himself smiling, unsure at first, but slowly warming to the idea.

The week before, he had bumped into her in the town and they'd gone to Bewley's for coffee. They got on well and Lynch asked her questions, happy to sit there and listen to someone else's life. Marie-Therese enjoyed the company, enjoyed talking to another adult. Someone who wasn't obsessed with babies. She was a natural storyteller and liked making people laugh. They left, agreeing that it had been fun and that they should do it again.

Lynch looked at the sliver of light, shining through the curtains. He would ask her later. Wait until she was leaving the house and bump into her. Keep it casual.

He turned his eyes down the street and saw the Mondeo parked near the bottom. The registration read *KXI* ... He didn't need the rest. It was O'Neill. They were after him.

The front seat of the car was back a ways, but Lynch could still see the top of a head. Without breaking stride, he took a hard right down a side entry. He paused, out of sight of the car, and listened. The door opened immediately and he heard O'Neill's voice and a faint crackle of static. He had back-up. It would be swinging round behind to cut him off.

Lynch instinctively reached to the small of his back. He was halfway there before his mind caught up. He didn't have the Browning. He looked down the entry, wondering if he could make it home. It was too far.

He stepped back and ran at the entry wall, shimmying up six foot and dropping silently down on the other side. He checked the yard door and saw it was secured with a large deadbolt.

In the yard Lynch stood still, his back pressed against the wall. He could hear a set of footsteps, coming down the entry. O'Neill had stopped running and was walking slowly and cautiously. Lynch could hear him pressing his hand against each yard door as he went.

Lynch heard the door of the next yard swing open, followed by a foot pivoting on wet concrete. O'Neill would

271

be sweeping his gun over the empty space. The sound was followed by a couple more steps. Lynch felt his heart racing in his chest. It was loud and he was sure it could be heard from the other side of the wall. He forced himself to slow his breath. O'Neill was close; the only thing separating them was half a foot of red brick. Lynch stood stock still. He could almost *feel* O'Neill's hand stretching out towards the door. The wood panels moved a millimetre before catching on the deadbolt. The door rattled but held firm.

Lynch listened as O'Neill moved on, exhaling a long, quiet, controlled breath.

He heard the cop work his way down the entry, counting the steps as they grew more faint. Sixty seconds. O'Neill was 100 feet away. If they didn't find him now they'd seal the block and go house-to-house. Lynch knew this was his chance.

He reached up and slid the deadbolt as if it was a detonator pin. He then sprang the door, running towards the near end of the entry. He heard O'Neill turn but didn't look back. Lynch kept his head down and sprinted. A set of car tyres screeched somewhere behind him. He cut off the road and ran down a narrow pedestrian walkway. Lynch burst out of the Markets and on to the main road, two cars skidding to avoid the figure that suddenly appeared in their windscreen. Running full speed, Lynch made it across four lanes of traffic and away.

O'Neill arrived ten seconds later and caught a glimpse of him as he turned down a side-street and made off in the direction of the city centre.

O'Neill put his hands on his knees. His lungs were on fire, burning in his chest. Thirty seconds later, Ward pulled up in a navy Mondeo. O'Neill got in the car, still heaving, trying to get his breath back.

'You see? What did I tell you about jogging?'

Back in Musgrave Street O'Neill stood in the car park and worked his way through three cigarettes, lighting one from the other.

They would lose Lynch after that. He'd go off the radar completely. Mike Hessian in CCTV would watch everyone who came in and out of the Markets. O'Neill would have someone sitting on the house and someone opposite The George in a disused office block. He'd be given two days. After that, the additional manpower would have to be reassigned. Resources were scarce and O'Neill would be on his own again.

The day he and Ward had sat outside The George and then followed Lynch was what had done it. Walking behind him down May Street, O'Neill couldn't help feeling he knew Lynch, that he'd seen him before. A couple of days later it clicked. The attack on Molloy. He'd gone back to the CCTV. There were only three seconds where the attacker was walking in the open. O'Neill had watched it over and over. He had Hessian pull up the afternoon video of May Street from when they had followed him. It was the same walk, the same shoulder roll, the same head down.

They'd pulled Lynch's address from his probation record. Last registered in Brixton, South London. O'Neill checked the records to find out who he had celled next to in the Maze. Jackie Hurson, a lifer from Derry, was on one side. On the other was Peter Hughes. He was from Belfast. The Markets. Bingo.

They'd blown it though. Lynch had vanished. He would have left Belfast straight away and headed across the border. They'd never find him. O'Neill fought hard not to think about the Review Boards the following week. What would happen would happen. If Wilson came for him then fuck it, there wasn't a whole lot he could do about it. Laganview might bury him, but so what – it would have buried anyone. He still had a week though.

O'Neill stubbed out his cigarette and headed back into the station.

THIRTY-TWO

O'Neill came off his shift at eight, thinking about another stint outside The George. The day had dragged after getting so close to Joe Lynch, only to have him slip away. He was hungry and decided to stop off at a place near the City Hall. He knew he'd make a better decision on a full stomach.

The Last Stop café was mostly used by city-bus drivers as Donegall Square was the main terminus. The waitress was in her fifties and looked as if she'd been on her feet all day.

'Yes, love?' she asked, as O'Neill took a seat.

'What's good?'

'Stew.'

'That'll do.'

Tucking into the bowl, O'Neill looked out at Belfast, settling into another gloomy evening. A steady succession of buses pulled up outside, rattling the windows as they accelerated away. A few late-night shoppers stood queuing – two girls clutched shopping bags, a man read the *Irish News* and two old dears nattered away to each other.

O'Neill pierced a piece of potato and lifted it to his mouth. The woman had been right, he thought, the stew's not ... His fork froze in mid-air. The man at the bus stop had folded up his paper and sat looking at him.

It was Joe Lynch.

Their eyes met and held each other's gaze. Lynch had got away twice and yet here he was, presenting himself to O'Neill.

As if he read O'Neill's thoughts, Lynch raised his eyebrows and stood up from the bus stop. He folded the paper, tucked it under his arm and casually walked away, inviting. O'Neill dropped his fork and hurried out of the café.

'Here – you!' the woman shouted from behind the counter, but O'Neill was out the door.

Outside he could make out Lynch, picking his way between the number sixteen and the forty-five. He kept up a steady pace but didn't seem to be in a hurry. At the street, Lynch turned and glanced over his shoulder, checking O'Neill was there. The detective wondered what he was playing at. Maybe he wanted to talk. Maybe it was some kind of set-up. O'Neill glanced behind him and set off after Lynch, dodging between two parked cars, watching him cross the main road and head down Donegall Avenue.

Belfast's main shopping street was crowded with late-night shoppers. O'Neill reached for his mobile and dialled Ward. He cursed when it went straight to answerphone. Lynch turned right towards Corn Market, past British Home Stores and Mothercare. O'Neill studied him carefully. He had looked back a couple of times, checking on the progress of the detective. O'Neill felt safe: the streets were packed and there would be plenty of witnesses. Lynch wouldn't try anything. From what Ward had told him, Lynch was a pro, someone who knew what he was doing. He wouldn't take a chance on something like this.

They walked down High Street, then into North Street and the Cathedral Quarter. The road narrowed into a cobbled entry with the designer shops and restaurants on either side. Lynch slowed as he approached Mint, heading for the door to the bar. He paused at the bottom of the steps and looked over his shoulder, straight at O'Neill; then he turned and acknowledged the 16-stone bouncer who stood watch over the door. The detective waited at the end of the cobblestone street as Lynch disappeared into the bar.

O'Neill dialled Ward again, this time getting through.

'Just hold fire, do you hear? I'll be there in five minutes.'

O'Neill remained in his place at the end of the entry, watching the door. He was back at Mint. All the pieces were there. He had everything he needed, he just had to put them together. A voice in his head was telling him he'd missed Lynch twice. How many times was he going to let him get away? He could see the main door from where he was, but there'd be fire exits. Lynch could slip out. If you lose him a third time, O'Neill thought, you don't deserve to call yourself a peeler. He knew the bar would be crowded and there was the look at the bus stop as well. Lynch had wanted to be followed. He had wanted to bring O'Neill there.

'Fuck it,' he said out loud. 'In for a penny ...'

O'Neill set off down the alley towards the bar. The bouncer stood aside and let him in. If he remembered O'Neill from the previous night, he didn't show it. Inside, Mint was starting to fill up and O'Neill felt reassured by the number of people there. It was an after-work crowd – men in suits, girls in dresses.

O'Neill clocked Lynch, sitting alone in a booth at the back of the bar. Less than ten feet away, the green sign illuminated the emergency exit – an escape route if more police arrived.

There were two bottles of beer sitting in front of him. Lynch flicked his head, acknowledging O'Neill. The detective walked over and sat down, face to face.

'I ordered for you,' Lynch said. 'I hope you don't mind.'

O'Neill didn't recognize the label on the beer. It was some foreign brand, white with red writing – *Tyskie*. Lynch lifted a bottle, tipping it towards the other man, before taking a drink.

'I don't normally drink with murderers,' O'Neill said.

'Don't worry, I don't normally drink with peelers. You should try that though,' he gestured to the bottle. 'Foreign stuff. It's not bad. That's Belfast for you these days. It's all exotic imports. Used to be you'd be lucky to get more than a pint of Harp.'

'Those would be the good old days, I suppose?' O'Neill asked sarcastically.

'That would depend on who you were talking to.'

The two men sat in silence, sizing each other up.

'Ward on his way?' Lynch asked.

O'Neill didn't answer.

'Told you to wait, didn't he? But that's not really your style, is it?'

O'Neill remained silent, staring at Lynch who raised his bottle and took another drink.

'You know, when I was in the Maze, I used to dream about stuff like this. Simple things. Sitting in a bar. A cold beer. It got so that it was the most amazing thing I'd ever tasted. That's what happens, when you're lying there alone, staring at the ceiling, thinking about something for so long.'

Lynch paused.

'It's funny. Things are never the same in real life. It's never like they tell you it's going to be. Not like you imagined it. Never like they promise.'

'Try telling it to the families of the three people you killed.'

Lynch sighed and looked around the room. O'Neill was trying to get under his skin. What he didn't know was that Lynch had seen those three people every single day since he'd been released. He'd be sitting watching TV and suddenly, out of nowhere, they'd be there in his head. Asking him, 'Why me? What did I do? How are you sitting there watching TV?' The questions. Over and over again. Lynch pushed the thought to the back of his mind.

'You know one or two things about disappointment though, don't you, Detective? About life not always turning out like you'd planned.'

O'Neill was growing tired of the philosophy.

'What do you want, Lynch?'

The other man looked him in the eye.

'I want to save your life.' Lynch paused. 'I want to be on the other side, just for a change.'

'Very noble. I'm not sure—'

'Listen. There's a contract out on you. You're a target. Whatever you're doing, it's pissing folk off. You've been sticking your nose where you shouldn't be.'

'Laganview?'

'I wouldn't like to say. But I'll tell you this. You've upset a few people and they don't like it. Word's been sent down. You've got to go.'

'So what are you then, the friendly warning?'

'Not really my style, O'Neill. Ask Ward, he'll tell you. I'm the doer, not the talker. My face is the last thing you see, before the lights go out.'

Lynch's voice was casual, as if he was stating the most ordinary, everyday fact. It was this, more than anything, that convinced O'Neill he was telling the truth.

'Who the fuck are you threatening?'

'I'm not threatening. I'm just telling.'

O'Neill thought about arresting him there and then, charging him with threatening the life of a police officer. It would be his word against Lynch's, however. There were no witnesses, no one to corroborate the story. It wouldn't go anywhere and it wouldn't get him anywhere near Laganview. He thought about why Lynch had brought him to Mint. Why here? He could have walked into the Last Stop and sat down. They could have spoken anywhere. Or could they? From what Ward said, Lynch wasn't the sort of person who issued warnings. O'Neill looked across the table.

'The plan's changed, hasn't it? In your head anyway. I mean, you're sitting here, talking to me. We could have done this anywhere. There's CCTV all over this place. Plenty of witnesses, plenty of folk to see us talking. You'd be the first in the frame if anything happened to me.'

'Very good, Detective.'

'But there's more. It's this place, Mint. You *want* to be seen talking to me – you want certain people to see. Whatever your game is, you're now just as likely to get shot as I am.'

Lynch raised an eyebrow and nodded slowly.

'Perhaps the PSNI aren't as stupid as people say they are,' he noted. 'Hell, if there's hope for you, there's hope for us all.'

'So why? Why the change of heart?'

Lynch gave a small shrug.

'A man's got to have a creed,' O'Neill prompted.

'You're right there. As for why, that's a tough question. Why is a psychologist's question, not a peeler's. Why is not something you need to worry about; you just stick with the who.'

O'Neill had all the pieces. Laganview. The George. McCann. Now this place. They were all connected.

'So how does it all fit?'

'You're the detective, O'Neill. You tell me.' Lynch drained his beer and made to get up and leave. 'I will say one thing though. Sometimes the answer's right there, right in front of your face. In fact, it can be so close, you look right past it.'

Lynch got up. 'Do me a favour and tell Ward I had to rush off.'

O'Neill watched him weave his way through the bar and out the door. What the fuck just happened? He took the untouched bottle in front of him and lifted it to his mouth. A young waitress in a short skirt swooped up to the table. She was beautiful, with long blonde hair and a thick Eastern-European accent.

'Is this finished?' she asked, reaching for Lynch's bottle.

'Yes, it ...'

O'Neill's voice trailed off mid-sentence. He looked at the girl, then at the bottle of beer in his hand.

'Where you from, love?'

'Czech Republic,' the girl answered defensively.

'And what about this?' Lynch held up the bottle of *Tyskie*.

'Is Polish. We have others if you prefer.'

281

O'Neill looked at the bottle. 'No. It's fine.'

The kid at Laganview hadn't shown up anywhere because he didn't have a record. He didn't have a record because he was a foreigner. No one had reported him missing because he wasn't here long enough for anyone to know him. Czech Republic, Poland, Lithuania. O'Neill wondered how often all these young ones phoned home. The boys would be the worst. His folks might not even know he was missing.

And what about the beating? He was murdered, but they had tried to make it look like a punishment beating. O'Neill's eyes searched the room. He caught sight of the doorway and the bouncer, with his shaved head looking out towards the street. He remembered Lynch and his nod of recognition as he'd walked in.

Ward appeared at the table, flustered, breathing hard.

'Thought I told you to wait.'

'Don't worry. I'll talk to you in the car. Let's go.'

On their way out the door, O'Neill pretended to drop his lighter. He bent down to pick it up, glancing at the bouncer's footwear. He was wearing some kind of black Army boot, with thick soles and canvas uppers.

At the end of the alley he stopped under the pretence of lighting a cigarette. He looked back at Mint and observed the bouncer in the doorway, the way he held himself, the way he owned the space around the door. He was ex-Army, O'Neill was almost certain.

When the two detectives turned the corner, Ivan Walczak stepped away from the door. He walked across the alley, away from the other doorman and the people entering the bar. The bouncer flipped open his mobile phone and dialled a number. Someone answered. Walczak looked both ways, up and down the lane, before speaking.

'We've got problem.'

Back at Musgrave Street, O'Neill pulled the CCTV from the Molloy attack. He watched the footage outside Mint as people went in and out of the bar. Molloy was drinking inside and Lynch was hidden in the shadow of a nearby doorway. On the door the two bouncers stood, slowly letting people in and out. The shorter one was there again, along with another taller one.

Every twenty minutes or so the bouncer with the shaved head would disappear from the door, leaving his partner to hold the fort. He'd be gone for a few minutes, somewhere inside the bar. If he was dealing, he'd know the club's CCTV, where the blind spots were. It was the same with every doorman across the city. The rule was, if you were going to give someone a hiding, you made sure you knew where your black spots were.

On three occasions O'Neill watched the bouncer cross the alley for a smoke. From there he could keep an eye on the door and step in if he needed to. O'Neill watched him take a final drag of his cigarette and toss it along the wall.

That was it. That was his evidence. Every contact leaves a trace ... the science didn't lie.

At four in the morning O'Neill drove back down to the Cathedral Quarter. The place was dead and everyone had gone home.

He got out of the car and walked along the alley, hugging the wall. When he was level with the doorway, he bent down. Sure enough, scattered in a 6-foot area were four fresh cigarette ends.

O'Neill snapped his hands into a pair of white rubber gloves and put the cigarette butts into a plastic evidence bag – a little present for Forensics in the morning.

THIRTY-THREE

The main forensics lab was in Jordanstown, five miles along the coast from Belfast. It was a three-storey glass building, surrounded by a 30-foot perimeter fence and with round-the-clock security. At 7 a.m., O'Neill's was the only car in the car park. He'd flashed his warrant card and Security lifted the barrier. The guard said he could wait if he wanted, but no one would be in until at least half eight.

O'Neill sat in the Mondeo, burning one B&H after another. He stared across the grey waters of Belfast Lough. Dotted along the other shore were Bangor, Holywood and Cultra. He wondered if Spender was at his desk, busy carving up the city before most people were out of their beds. On the passenger seat beside him sat a clear plastic bag with four cigarette ends.

Cars started to dribble in after eight. O'Neill was out and at the door before the first arrival, a man in his fifties, had even swiped his card. The detective showed his warrant card.

'O'Neill. Musgrave Street.'

The man's brow furrowed, unimpressed at being stopped before he was even in the door. It was always the same with CID. They thought the whole world revolved around them. And when they were making house calls, you just knew they were after something.

'Do you know what time McBurnie gets in at?' O'Neill asked.

McBurnie was his man. They'd only spoken briefly, over the boot-print, but it would be enough. He was young and wouldn't mind bending the rules, putting a rush on something if O'Neill asked.

'He's not in today. Friday is his day off. Was he expecting you?'

The man spoke like a headmaster, offended at O'Neill's impertinence. It was the old CID arrogance, showing up unannounced, clicking their fingers and expecting the world to jump to attention. There were rules, regulations, procedures. That was how things worked. Not flashing a badge and expecting everyone to fall at your feet. The man walked through the door, leaving O'Neill on the other side holding his clear plastic bag.

O'Neill turned round and looked across the car park, embarrassed at having been denied. He walked back to the car and waited. If the bouncer had done Laganview, there was a tiny window of opportunity. He would have known Lynch and seen him talking to O'Neill the night before. He'd realize something was up. Shit ... there was a good chance he'd taken off already! If he left the country, they'd never get him. O'Neill felt a ball of nausea growing in the pit of his stomach. He imagined himself at his Review Board, facing Wilson and three others across a large desk. He wasn't going to lose Laganview over some senior lab tech, some jobsworth who loved his rules and thought it was his duty to enforce them.

Five minutes later, a Renault Clio pulled into a spot near O'Neill. A woman got out and started walking towards the entrance. She swiped her card and pulled open the door.

'Hold it!' O'Neill called, hurrying from his car. She didn't flinch, clocking O'Neill for CID and knowing if he'd got past security, he checked out.

'Hey, could you help me out? I'm supposed to get this to John McBurnie, but it's his day off so I'm going to leave it for him. He's on the first floor, isn't he?'

'No. Second.'

'I'm always getting lost in this place.'

'Out the lift and go right.'

'Thanks,' O'Neill replied.

In the second-floor lab his 'friend' was putting on a white coat as O'Neill entered.

'How did you get in here?' he demanded.

'Listen. I need to apologize. We got off on the wrong foot,' O'Neill said. 'I know you're coming here with sixty million things waiting to get done, and the last thing you need is some guy from CID grabbing you before you've even got your coat off.'

He held out his hand. 'John O'Neill.'

The lab tech reluctantly shook his hand.

'Robin Bradley,' he grunted. 'You know there are procedures round here, Detective. That is how we work. That's how things get done.'

'I know,' O'Neill agreed. 'And you do an amazing job. I can tell you, from the front line, the number of people we've put away on the back of what you do ... real scum of the earth, doing horrific things. Robbery, assault, rape. They only go down because of you guys. We might grab them, but they'd be right out the door again if it wasn't for you.'

The man reluctantly started to soften. He looked at the clear plastic bag in the detective's hand.

'I always think it's a pity you never get to see what happens out there,' O'Neill continued. 'See the results of everything you do. The faces of the victims, when they know the guy who mugged them, who put them in hospital, who raped them, is going to go down. Or the old-age pensioners, their tears of relief, when the guys who robbed them of all their savings gets five years. It's you guys who do it. It's the labwork that gets the convictions.'

O'Neill was laying it on thick and Bradley rolled his eyes. He knew exactly what the cop was doing, but deep down inside, he liked hearing it and wanted to believe him.

'So what's in the bag then?'

'A murderer.'

'They look like cigarette butts to me,' Bradley answered dryly.

'We're working the boy at Laganview. The sixteen year old. He was beaten to a pulp and left for dead. He's someone's son, but he's still lying at the morgue. Hasn't even been ID'd, let alone claimed. McBurnie got us this far with the boot-print and I think we've got our man. I've got one more ask though – and we need it yesterday, otherwise this guy's going to split. Leave the country. And if he goes, we'll never get him.'

O'Neill held up the plastic bag of cigarette ends.

'I need a DNA match on these – cross-checked against the samples taken from the scene at Laganview.'

Bradley sighed, resigning himself to breaking one of his own golden rules.

'OK. The test takes a couple of hours to run. I can probably have a result for you by lunchtime.'

'A couple of hours? I thought this was the twenty-first century?'

'It's the twenty-first century, not *Star Trek*.'

'Fair point. Listen, thanks for doing this. I appreciate it.'

'I'll get it done and call you as soon as it comes back and I've run the comparison.'

O'Neill spent the rest of the morning walking the corridors at Musgrave Street, punctuated by drinking cups of coffee and smoking in the car park. He had been pacing up and down outside CID when Ward stopped him.

'Are you digging a trench in that lino?'

O'Neill forced a pained smile.

'Go and sit down somewhere. You're making me dizzy.'

He had pulled a name and address for the bouncer from Mint's Inland Revenue returns. Ivan Walczak. He was Polish and had been in Northern Ireland for three years. He lived at 56 Glandore Avenue, a two-bedroom terrace house off the Antrim Road.

At noon O'Neill couldn't wait any longer and called Jordanstown.

'You know, Detective, you've got even less patience than my wife.'

Despite his desperation, O'Neill liked that Bradley was making fun of him. It meant he had another friend in Jordanstown – and you never knew when it could come in handy.

'The results are just back. I'm running the cross-check. Give me ten minutes,' Bradley said. 'And *I'll* phone *you*.'

O'Neill sat at his desk looking at his watch. It had been twelve minutes. He sighed, tapping his hand on the telephone handset.

Thirteen.

Fourteen.

The phone beeped and O'Neill snatched it up before the first ring had time to end.

'O'Neill!'

'Good news, Detective. I've got two exact matches. A cigarette end and one of the samples lifted from the kid's clothing.'

'Thanks,' O'Neill said, banging down the phone. He stood up and marched out of CID, shouting as he passed Ward's door.

'This is us. Let's go.'

THIRTY-FOUR

O'Neill and Ward stood at the back of the armoured Land Rover. They had on bulletproof vests and Ward had had to suck in a breath to get the Velcro round his.

'I'm too frigging old for this.'

O'Neill adjusted his own vest, feeling reassured by the weight of the Kevlar.

They had assembled a couple of streets away to suit up and brief uniform before taking the door. They had three patrols with them, one for the assault team and two for either end of the street.

In the back of the wagon the uniform listened as O'Neill ran through the drill. There was an air of giddiness. O'Neill stamped it out, pointed to each man in turn and demanded to know if he'd taken a door before. They all had. Earlier, O'Neill had caught himself looking at the officers' footwear. All four were wearing black canvas Magnums. He tried not to think about it.

O'Neill took control, telling them that once the place was secure, they'd all need to step out. The plan was to bring in the dogman and go room-to-room. Ward and O'Neill then climbed up into the Land Rover, shouting at the driver to go.

As the white vehicle rumbled along the street, one of the uniforms, Terry Carson, leaned over to the man next to him. He had to shout above the noise of the engine.

'Kicking in doors. Love it, fucking love it!'

The other man nodded, a nervous smile.

On Glandore Avenue two kids on BMXs stopped riding and stood watching in silence. On the opposite side of the street a curtain twitched and a nosy neighbour shouted to her husband, 'Come here and see this!'

The front officer banged on the door, shouting 'Police! Open up!' He stepped aside and immediately the heavy steel battering ram began blasting the door. Normally a door popped on its first or second hit. Walczak's took six. It had been reinforced and triple-bolted. Each blow made a deep, medieval noise.

When it popped, uniform piled into the house, shouting, 'Police!' at the top of their voices. They fanned out into the rooms, three running up the stairs. From the front door O'Neill heard shouts of, 'Clear, clear, clear...' as each room was secured.

He cursed under his breath. No one was home.

After a few minutes uniform slowly backed their way out of the house. Ward had reminded them beforehand that it might be a crime scene, and that the first man to touch something would be on foot patrol for a year.

O'Neill and Ward let the dogman in, trailing a small brown and white spaniel, its tail wagging as if it had never been happier in its life. The dogman pointed at things, opened cupboards and ran his hand under furniture. The spaniel sniffed its way round the house, in seeming ecstasy. Near a chest of drawers the dog suddenly stopped and sat down, looking up at its master. The dogman gave a treat and had a quick rummage through the drawers but couldn't see anything. It might only be a trace on the clothes. He turned to O'Neill, making sure the detective had seen it before he moved on with the dog. The spaniel stopped and sat three more times but each time the dogman couldn't see anything obvious. Once the spaniel was back in the van he came to talk to O'Neill.

'This place is definitely hot. Or at least it was, not too long ago.'

O'Neill thanked him and went inside, starting a room-to-room search. The kitchen cupboards were sparse, containing tins and jars with various foreign labels that he didn't recognize. *Dzem. Makrela. Pinczow.* Walczak lived alone and there was no sign of a woman, something O'Neill confirmed when he went through the clothes upstairs.

In a living-room cupboard Ward found a 12-inch bowie knife and an improvised baton, made from heavy-duty cable, twisted and held by masking tape.

'Nice guy,' O'Neill muttered, holding up the weapons.

The bedrooms didn't contain much and only had the most basic furniture.

'This guy lives like a monk,' he said to Ward on his way out of the bedroom.

The first sweep found nothing and O'Neill had gone back to the four spots where the dog had sat down. He still couldn't see anything. He bagged the clothes from the chest of drawers, some more forensic evidence for his new friend Robin Bradley.

Then O'Neill went back and started over at the front door. He went from room to room again, this time going through the litany of secret spaces, the secluded hiding spots that every criminal thought he was the only person in the world to have thought of. He checked the carpet in the corners, listening for loose floorboards. He pulled back the side of the bath and lifted the cistern. He tore apart the beds and pulled kitchen units away from walls. He sliced open the sofa and felt up the chimney. With each new empty space, O'Neill could feel his chest tightening.

Under the floor in the cupboard, he got his breakthrough. It wasn't drugs, it wasn't a gun. It was better.

O'Neill lifted out a shoe-box and called Ward in from the next room. He placed the box on the bed and slowly took off the lid.

Inside were a couple of photographs. One was a picture of some soldiers in full combat gear, their faces blacked up. They were crawling through a forest and looked to be on some kind of training exercise. In another picture, a group of three men stood side by side. They looked lean and menacing, all with shaved heads and black combat uniform. Again their faces were camouflaged but O'Neill could make out Walczak. On the back of the photograph were the letters *WS RP*, followed by *Wojska Specjalne Rzeczypospolitej Polskiej*.

'What do you want to bet WR SP is Polish Special Forces?' O'Neill asked Ward.

'Looks like it to me.'

The box also contained a plastic bag with at least twenty SIM cards for mobile phones. He'd be switching SIM cards all the time to make it difficult to trace his calls. At the bottom of the box were six passports, all of them Polish. O'Neill flicked through them, expecting a series of false identities for Walczak. They weren't. They belonged to different people.

In each one the face of a young man, no older than sixteen, was framed in a 1-inch passport photo. O'Neill held the fifth passport in his hand, showing it to Ward. It was their victim.

'It's him.'

O'Neill read the name. *Jacob Pilsudski*. He was from somewhere O'Neill had never heard off. Pomorskie. Born 11 December 1989. He was sixteen years old.

'Yeah. That's him all right,' Ward said. He picked up the passports and flicked through them.

'They're all Polish,' O'Neill said. 'They're kids. He has them dealing for him. He takes the passports off them – a bit of extra security. That was why he knee-capped this one after he killed him. He knew we'd end up running round in circles, chasing after anyone with a paramilitary past. Shit, it's not as if there's a lack of suspects for something like that.'

'So what now?' Ward asked.

'Mint. It's our last chance.'

THIRTY-FIVE

O'Neill and Ward swung by Musgrave Street and swapped the black Mondeo for an unmarked white van. It belonged to the Proactive Unit but Ward pulled rank and commandeered it.

At half four they parked up in Waring Street and waited. They had a clear view down Henry Street and into the Cathedral Quarter. Halfway down the cobbles were the doors of Mint. O'Neill knew this was the only thing to do now, wait and hope. They'd closed Walczak's door and left two units hidden at either end of the street in case he came back. There was a good chance a neighbour had seen the action and tipped him off though. If that was the case he'd go underground and try to slip out of the country. The airport, ferry and train stations had all been put on alert and a picture had been circulated. A description had been sent round the entire PSNI with officers instructed to stop and search anyone resembling.

They needed to be lucky. O'Neill thought about everything he'd done over the last month, the hours he'd spent sifting the case-file, sitting outside Burke's, staking out The George, chasing Joe Lynch. And still it came down to luck. He needed a bit of luck to get Walczak. How did that work? How was that fair?

He looked at his watch for the third time in ten minutes.

'Will you stop looking at your frigging watch?' Ward said.

'I seem to spend my life sitting in cars. Waiting.'

'Hey, that's the job. If you haven't figured that out by now, you never will.'

O'Neill shifted in his seat trying to get comfortable. The van smelled of stale crisps and cigarette smoke.

'This thing reeks,' he said.

'So would your car, if you spent twelve hours a night sitting in it.'

O'Neill watched pedestrians walk down Waring Street. At the bottom of the road a couple of men stood smoking outside the Northern Whig. The bar had opened a few years ago in the former newspaper offices.

'So tell me, Detective,' Ward asked. 'How do a bunch of Polish kids end up dealing on the streets of Belfast?'

'Same way Belfast kids do. It's about money. All they're doing is working. Trying to get by. Doing what it takes.'

'And what about our friend Walczak?'

'He's involved with somebody. A middle man. There is no way the local boys would have allowed him to set up shop on his own. He controls the door to one of the biggest clubs in town though. The customers come to see you. A guy that's on coke will drink all night. He'll never get pissed, never pass out. If the place is making a killing over the bar, everybody's happy. It's one big party and everyone's winning.'

'So what about Joe Lynch and Gerry McCann?'

'Good question. I don't know.'

'And Burke? Spender?'

'They're dirty. Up to something. How it all fits is another question.'

The clock on the car ticked forward. O'Neill reckoned the doormen came on at seven and as it got closer he could feel his legs starting to itch. Ward was gazing out the window, trying to figure out who would be at O'Neill's Review Boards ...

O'Neill tapped on his arm. He looked up and saw Walczak illuminated in the doorway of the club. He was with the same man as the previous night. Both wore dark suits and long black coats. Business as usual.

'Is this that karma stuff you were on about?' Ward asked, arching an eyebrow.

The two detectives got out of the car and started walking down the cobbled street. Neither man looked at the door, trying to pretend they were a couple of guys, out for a pint and a spot of food.

Walczak glanced down the road, saw O'Neill and instantly took off. He leaped down three steps and sprinted down the alley, away from the cops.

O'Neill ran after him, shouting over his shoulder to call it in. Ward grabbed his radio.

'This is 571. Officer in pursuit. Requesting immediate back-up. Suspect is five ten, shaved head and black coat. Heading up Henry Street in the direction of St Anne's.'

Ward then took off after them, cursing. 'More bloody running.'

O'Neill was already 100 yards away before Ward got going. Walczak had made it to the end of the lane and crossed Talbot Street, turning right down a narrow alley. A thought suddenly came into O'Neill's head – this guy could run all day. He'd read a book about some British SAS guys who had been caught behind enemy lines in Iraq. They just put their heads down and ran across the whole country, trying to get away.

O'Neill pumped his arms, oblivious to the burning in his chest. At the end of the lane he turned right and his feet slid out from under him. Leather shoes on greasy cobbles.

'Bastard!'

His right leg hit the ground hard. O'Neill saw Walczak turn a corner 20 yards away. He scrambled up and took off. Back-up was on the way. All he had to do was stay on top of him. They turned down Exchange Street, Academy Street. O'Neill was gaining on the doorman. The latter's heavy coat wasn't helping his cause. By the bottom of the lane they were only a few feet apart.

The bouncer slowed to turn the corner and O'Neill dived. He managed to get Walczak round his legs and both men hit the ground. The doorman was strong and turned, punching the cop in the head. O'Neill had hold of a foot and clamped his arms around it.

Walczak stood up, unfazed by the peeler's hold on him. He leaned down and punched O'Neill in the face. The detective clung on. Walczak punched him again, trying to make him release his grip. He then leaned back, lifting a boot and bringing it down hard on O'Neill's head. He lifted it and did the same again.

O'Neill tried to squeeze tighter, bracing himself against the blows. Ward, he thought, where the fuck are you?

He tried to tuck himself round Walczak's leg as a way of shielding himself. He just needed to hang on. The boot came down again. O'Neill felt his grip slacken. And again, the boot. He swooned. Lightheaded. The boot, again. A wave swept over O'Neill. His hands went limp. He felt the leg lift up and out of his grasp. His arms clutched at thin air. It was the last thing O'Neill was aware of before the lights went out.

THIRTY-SIX

O'Neill woke up. He was warm and surrounded by bright light. He felt as if he was floating.

He could only open his left eye, and blinked several times trying to get the room into focus. He was in a hospital bed. A room on his own. A dull ache throbbed on his right side. He tried to move his arm and felt a searing pain shoot through his shoulder and up his neck, causing him to grimace.

After a few seconds he looked down and saw a sling holding his arm. His left hand had a needle in it and there was a drip going into the back of his hand. He was plugged into a heart monitor, the digital graph rolling left to right, showing his vitals.

I'm not dead then, he thought.

Ward sat beside the bed. O'Neill tried to speak but his throat was dry and his voice croaked. Ward stood up and poured some water into a cup. He leaned over, holding it to the detective's mouth. The water soothed on its way down his throat.

'I thought for a second this might be heaven,' O'Neill said. 'Until I saw your ugly mug.'

'I wouldn't count on either of us getting there,' Ward replied.

O'Neill smiled and a stab of pain hit along the side of his jaw. He spoke again, more quietly than before.

'How long have I been asleep?'

'A day.'

'Walczak?'

'We got him.'

O'Neill felt himself relax.

'I got there just as you blacked out.'

'I was beginning to think you'd stopped for a fag or something.'

Ward laughed softly. 'You and your frigging running.'

He sat down again, pulling his chair closer to the bed.

'He's some piece of work, that Walczak. He's Polish. Ex-Special Forces. You should have seen him in the interview room. He laughed at the idea of jail. "Fucking police. You think I give a fuck about you and your prison?" After that he stone-walled us. Just sat there. Arms folded.'

O'Neill lay on the bed, wishing he'd been there, just to be in the room, to be asking the questions, even if Walczak didn't answer a single one. They had the footprint. They had the DNA. They had the passports.

'Who was he working with?'

'He's not going to give anyone up. He'll do his time. He didn't even blink at the prospect of life. Oh, and the nightclub – Mint? You're not going to believe who owns that building.'

O'Neill guessed. 'You're not serious?'

'Yeah. That's right. Spender's got that whole block. We can't tell how involved he is. He might just be a man with a big building. I don't think so. But that's as far as we can go with him for the time being.'

'What about the black book he found – his son's? The one with all the phone numbers?'

302

'Who knows what he did with it? Maybe he burned it.'

O'Neill tried to adjust himself in the bed, wincing as a fresh stab of pain hit his shoulder. He breathed in through his teeth.

'What about Burke and his brother?'

'They were definitely up to something. Possibly to do with Laganview. Burke's phone record shows they talked eight times the weekend the kid was killed. We don't have anything tying them directly to the body though.'

Despite the pain and the cloud of medication, O'Neill could feel the weight starting to lift from him. Sure, there were loose ends. There always were. They'd got someone though. It was a victory. It meant something.

'So what's my diagnosis then?' O'Neill asked.

'Dislocated shoulder. Fractured skull. You took a few digs to the head so you're not as pretty as you once were. Doctor says it's nothing a bit of time won't fix.'

'You'll need to apologize to Wilson. I don't think I'm going to make my Review Board at this rate.'

'I wouldn't worry about that,' Ward said. 'Walczak's in bracelets. Laganview's over. You're going to be keeping your stripes. I'll tell you better than that – there's a permanent Sergeant's post coming up in March and your name's already been pencilled in.'

O'Neill lifted his eyebrows, raising three fingers on his left hand, thinking about tapping his shoulder. He winced halfway through the movement and brought his hand back down.

'Detective Sergeant O'Neill,' Ward said. 'Yeah. I always thought it suited you.'

O'Neill gave a faint smile. The light in the room was beginning to sting his eyes. He put his head back and closed them.

He heard the door open and someone else walk in. A nurse, possibly the doctor.

He looked up to see Sam Jennings standing at the door, a look of worry on her face. Jennings looked at the DI. She knew who Ward was, but she was new to Musgrave Street, and in uniform. She wouldn't be on his radar.

Ward stood up, raising his eyebrows at O'Neill. 'I've got some paperwork needs doing. I'll leave you both to it.'

As he turned to walk out of the room, Sam stood back.

'Jennings,' Ward said, passing the WPC.

'Sir,' she replied, hiding a tinge of embarrassment. She stepped forward to the bed and put her hand against O'Neill's face.

'You should see the state of the other guy,' O'Neill said.

'I did. Funnily enough, there wasn't a mark on him.'

'Yeah. So they keep telling me.'

Molloy felt as if he was back at school, sitting in the headmaster's office, about to get the caning of his life.

It was eleven in the morning and The George hadn't opened. He sat in a booth along the back wall. Gerry McCann was on a bar stool smoking, a deep frown across his forehead. He hadn't spoken since walking in, and had ignored Molloy. Three dirty pint glasses sat on the bar next to him – leftovers from the previous night. Molloy could hear McCann breathing, each exhale angrier than the one before. He looked as if he was trying to suck the life out of his cigarette.

304

Molloy didn't speak. This was a 'wait till you're spoken to' moment. Most definitely. There were no lights on in The George and the grey winter sky filtered through the window at the far end of the bar. McCann was fuming, surrounded by smoke. He looked as if he wanted to hurt someone.

'Where's Joe Lynch?' He spoke without looking at Molloy.

'Eh, we've had people watching the house, walking round town, in and out—'

McCann repeated the question, slowly with emphasis.

'Where – *the fuck* – is Joe Lynch?'

'We don't know.'

A pint glass flew through the air, smashing above Molloy's head and showering him in glass.

In Cultra, Karen Spender stood on the patio looking down the lawn and out over Belfast Lough. She was smoking again. Two days ago she had bought her first packet in eight years. It was the phone call to Manchester that did it.

She'd hired a private investigator. Wanted him to find Phillip. He had quoted her his daily rate, plus expenses. Who cared how much it cost? She needed to know – even if it was as bad as she imagined. Every time the phone went, she jumped three feet in the air. At least that's what it felt like. She had got into the habit of cutting people short. She couldn't talk to them. Not now.

She hadn't told Zara. Hadn't told William either. This was for her.

William Spender saw the smoke drift past his office window. She was at it again. That frigging detective and his questions.

Spender was going over the profit projections for Laganview. They were back on schedule with the build. They'd pulled in more labour. These Eastern Europeans were grafters, all right. Would work their fingers to the bone and never complain. They'd sold six more apartments in the last week, four of them on the back of chatting to people at the awards dinner. No matter what anyone said, there was money to be made in this town.

Out the back Karen Spender took a last drag of her cigarette. She stubbed it out on an ashtray on the patio table. The rain had made a small puddle in the glass bowl, mixing with the ash and old fag ends. She shivered, rubbing her hands up and down her arms before turning back inside.

Michael Burke opened the doors at the back of the white Transit. It had taken him two hours to get to Dublin, plus another hour trying to find the place. He was at a building site for a new hotel on the south side. It was going to be a high-end gig, catering for pop stars and businessmen. The kind of place where people didn't blink at 500 euros a night and would boast about having stayed there.

Paddy Hewson was in his early thirties. He wore a suit, tucked into a pair of brown construction boots. He was the principal engineer or architect or something. He looked at the three large drums of copper. They were fifteen hundred quid a pop from any wholesaler. It had been a walk in the park getting them out of Laganview. Spender knew about it. He was taking 50 per cent and then claiming the whole lot back again on insurance. Six grand a week. This was a test run and they planned to go for more, next time around. The site had a hundred grand's worth of copper on it. Tony had knocked the cameras out the week before and they had used his keys to get in on the Saturday night. The kid getting killed was unlucky, but it meant no one else at Laganview had noticed the copper was missing.

The man rubbed his chin, shaking his head. He had a Dublin accent, all smarm and honey, like he couldn't do enough for you. Burke had heard it all before. These guys would put a knife in your back if they thought it would make them a few quid.

'I dunno now. We could go five hundred euros.'

'Each?' Burke asked, incredulously.

'No. For the lot of them.'

Burke sighed, shaking his head.

'Take it or leave it,' the man said, all nonchalance.

He would take it, of course. There wasn't a lot of choice in the matter.

Lynch stood in the bedroom of his house in the Markets. They would have had neighbours watching the place so he had left it a few days before sneaking along the rear entry. It was after 10 p.m. and he'd left the lights off as he stuffed his clothes into a sports bag. It was the same worn Adidas bag that he had used when he first walked out of the Maze. He reached under the bed and pulled out a brown envelope. It contained the five hundred pounds McCann had given him. He took a hundred and left the rest sitting on the bed. He would call Marie-Therese, tell her he was sorry, that he'd left something for her and the wee one.

He sat down on the bed and lit a cigarette. This was it, he thought. He'd burned all his bridges. There'd be no coming back this time. Lynch lifted the cigarette to his mouth ...

A fist hammered urgently on the door downstairs. Lynch turned his head, instinctively reaching for the Browning at the small of his back. He got up and peered round the door of the bedroom and down the stairs. More hammering.

The noise was light. A woman's hand.

'Joe!' It was Marie-Therese. She was crying, hysterical. 'It's our Ciara. She's not breathing.'

Lynch took the stairs two at a time. When he opened the door, Marie-Therese was halfway across the street, running home. He took off after her, catching up just as she ran through the front door into her place. He burst into the living room, simultaneously speaking and looking round for the baby.

'Call an ambulan—'

Molloy sat on the sofa, bouncing little Ciara up and down on his knee. In his right hand he held a handgun. Little Ciara cooed and yelped, completely unaware of the story unfolding around her.

Marie-Therese stood at the edge of the room, crying.

'I'm sorry, Joe. They made me do it. They were going to hurt her.'

Molloy smiled, looking up, the gun trained on Lynch. 'Birds, Joe. What can you do, eh?'

Marie-Therese stepped forward and lifted the child from him.

'Afraid this is it, Joe. You picked a side. Only it turns out your team lost.'

'So what?' Lynch said. 'You're going to do me here? In front of the wee one?'

'No. Outside.'

Molloy nodded to the door that led through to the kitchen and the back of the house. Lynch imagined himself being discovered by the peelers, lying in the wet entry, discarded next to rubbish bags and old newspapers. He thought about going for the Browning but Molloy would have a bullet in him before he even got it out of his belt.

Lynch walked through the kitchen and out into the cold night air. The door on the far side of the yard was already open. Molloy followed at a safe distance. Lynch slowed his pace slightly, allowing the other man to get closer. As he reached the door to the entry he kicked backwards and lunged at Molloy. A shot went off. Lynch kept struggling. He hadn't been hit. Lynch was on the other man, managing to get hold of the hand with the gun. He smashed it against the wall of the yard and Molloy dropped it. Lynch punched him in the face and Molloy wobbled. Lynch grabbed a handful of hair and struck Molloy's head against the wall. Once. Twice. At the third time of asking, Molloy's legs went out from under him and he fell to the ground.

Lynch ran out of the yard and off down the entry. It was dark in the alley, the moon obscured behind a ceiling of thick cloud. Lynch could just make out the River Lagan as it flowed by at the bottom of the entry. When he was 20 yards from the end, a figure stepped out of the dark. Lynch slid to a halt. The figure raised its arm, pointing a gun at him. McCann stepped forward and shook his head.

'It's like I told you, Joe. You just can't get the staff these days. If you want something done properly ...'

A pair of gunshots punctuated McCann's words.

Lynch flew back off his feet. He didn't feel his head strike the concrete. The wind had been blown out of him. His chest heaved as he tried to suck in air. A warm wetness began to seep through his jacket. He tried to reach for the Browning but couldn't make his arms work.

McCann walked forward and stood over him. He pointed the gun at Lynch's forehead and pulled the trigger. '... you have to do it yourself.'

Marty looked up and down Damascus Street. It was all clear. He ducked in past the hedge and rang the doorbell of number 9. A guy in his early twenties answered full of fake friendliness.

'Marty, big lad. What about you? Come on in.'

In the front room three students sat like zombies on a sofa, staring at a large television. A bong, full of brown water, sat next to the coffee-table.

'How's business these days?' the guy asked as he followed Marty into the room.

'All right.'

They each bought a quarter and a couple of pills. Seventy quid's worth. One of the stoners looked up as the notes changed hands.

'Don't go spending it all in the one shop now.' He sniggered a stoned laugh at his own joke.

Marty thought about smacking him in the head. They could do all four of these wankers. I mean, what the fuck did he know? He held himself back, thinking about something he'd seen on a billboard – *the customer was always right*. He wasn't though. No. The customer was a cunt.

'See yous around,' Marty said, making his way to the door.

Back on Jerusalem Street he unzipped his tracksuit and pulled out the book he'd stolen from the flat.

'Dopey bastards.'

It was a present for Petesy. Help him on his way. He'd started doing it the week before and had five books piled up at home already. This one was by some Chinese guy.

Sun Tzu. *The Art of War*.

'Fuck,' he said to himself. 'I might have a go at this one myself.'

Marty checked up and down Damascus Street. It was all good. He zipped up his top and turned his collar up. He pulled his cap down and rolled on. There were calls to be made.

ACKNOWLEDGEMENTS

There are several people I would like to thank: Peter Straus at RCW for his belief and support. All the team at Constable & Robinson, but particularly James Gurbutt for his insightful editorial suggestions, Sam Evans, Jo Stansall and Angela Martin. I would also like to thank my former colleagues at the University of Glasgow for their encouragement, especially Gerry Carruthers, Kirsteen McCue and Rhona Brown. The support of my family has been consistent throughout the writing of this book and I cannot thank them enough.